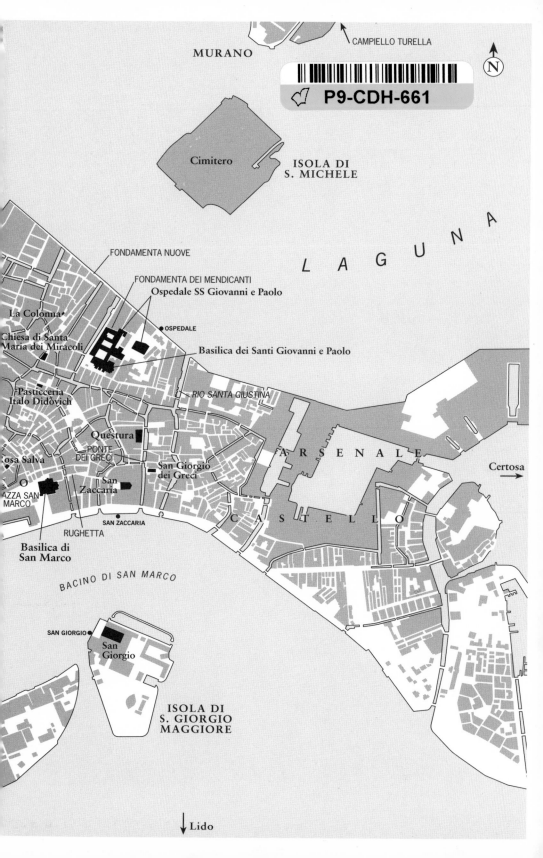

Give unto Others

Also by Donna Leon

Death at La Fenice
Death in a Strange Country
Dressed for Death
Death and Judgment
Acqua Alta
Quietly in Their Sleep
A Noble Radiance
Fatal Remedies
Friends in High Places
A Sea of Troubles
Willful Behavior
Uniform Justice
Doctored Evidence
Blood from a Stone
Through a Glass, Darkly
Suffer the Little Children
The Girl of His Dreams
About Face
A Question of Belief
Drawing Conclusions
Handel's Bestiary
Beastly Things
Venetian Curiosities
The Jewels of Paradise
The Golden Egg
My Venice and Other Essays
By its Cover
Gondola
Falling in Love
The Waters of Eternal Youth
Earthly Remains
The Temptation of Forgiveness
Unto Us a Son Is Given
Trace Elements
Transient Desires

Donna Leon

Give unto Others

Atlantic Monthly Press
New York

Originally published in Great Britain in 2022
by Hutchinson Heinemann.

Published simultaneously in Canada
Printed in the United States of America

First Grove Atlantic hardcover edition: March 2022

Typeset in 12/16.45 pt Palatino LT Std
by Integra Software Services Pvt. Ltd, Pondicherry

Library of Congress Cataloging-in-Publication data is available for this title.

ISBN 978-0-8021-5940-3
eISBN 978-0-8021-5941-0

Atlantic Monthly Press
an imprint of Grove Atlantic
154 West 14th Street
New York, NY 10011

Distributed by Publishers Group West

groveatlantic.com

22 23 24 25   10 9 8 7 6 5 4 3 2 1

For Heike Bischoff-Ferrari

Blessed are they that considereth the poor and needy:
the Lord will deliver them in time of trouble,
the Lord preserve them and comfort them.

Handel, 'Foundling Hospital Anthem'
HWV 268

1

Brunetti had tossed *Il Gazzettino* into the waste-paper bin before leaving the Questura, but still he took the subject of one of the lead articles home with him. As he settled on the sofa with Cicero's *Against Verres* and its denunciation of a corrupt official, Brunetti's thoughts were frequently diverted to the cascade of money opened by the *pandemia* that had, until recently, so ravaged the country.

Not even the deaths of more than 125,000 people had put an end to greed – not that Brunetti had thought for a moment that it would – nor had it dulled the ability of organized crime to get its snout in the virtually unguarded trough. Money had rained down and countless companies had requested compensation from agencies whose task it was to bestow the largesse of a frightened Europe. He'd cringed at the sight of some of the names he'd read, both in the governmental agencies overseeing the disbursement of funds, as well as among the directors of some of the companies receiving them. No doubt he and his colleagues in the Guardia di Finanza would become more familiar with those names as time passed.

Many companies had been rescued, many loans had been granted, and Brunetti knew that much good would be done and many who faced ruin would be saved. He was persuaded, however, that a fair share of the money would evaporate as it was passed on, just as he was sure many companies were being hastily created in order to do nothing else but fail and be bailed out.

Brunetti did not understand economics very well, but he was always alert to the ways people found to cheat and steal and was convinced that the financial devastation caused by the virus would encourage precisely those crimes. He was familiar with the techniques of pickpockets and muggers, who first created a disturbance that would upset and distract their victims, then struck them at their most unbalanced moment to take what they wanted. Although nature had created this other disturbance, enterprising criminals had soon seen a way to profit from the shock and confusion of their victims.

Il Gazzettino had reported that commercial property was currently passing from hand to hand with great frequency. This might seem an encouraging sign in a world of shattered business possibilities, perhaps even evidence of the renewal of the local economy, were it not for the concurrent reports in the national press about the present liquidity problems of the various mafias: they didn't know what to do with all the money that was flooding in and needed to be laundered and reintroduced into the banking system. Why not a prime piece of commercial real estate in Venice? Surely, the old patterns would be restored, the tourists would return, even the cruise ships would bob back to the surface again, although Brunetti, who viewed them as floating coffins, realized that was an improper phrase to use.

He pulled free of these thoughts, telling himself that it was far too soon to engage in this sort of grim speculation. There was always the chance that this universal brush with mortality would have some positive effect upon the way people looked at the world or ordered their priorities.

A noise in the hallway interrupted his thoughts, and he glanced up to watch Chiara disappearing down the corridor towards her room and her hermetic world of social media. Love and fear for his children fell upon him, followed by a surge of hope for a good future for them, despite the damaged world in which they would live out their lives.

Not liking his mood, he went down to Paola's study and, since the door was open, went in. She was at her computer, glasses slipped down to the middle of her nose, intent on the screen. Without glancing up, she said, 'I'm glad you're home.'

'Why?' he asked, going over and kissing the top of her head, ignoring the screen.

She tapped out a few more words, removed her glasses, and looked up at him. He noticed that it took her eyes a moment to refocus on the longer distance.

'Because you're strong enough to keep me from climbing over the railing on the terrace and jumping,' she said in the calm voice one used when giving directions to people on the street.

Brunetti went over and sat on the sofa, kicked off his shoes, and set his feet on the table. Her desk had no papers or books on it, only an empty cup and saucer for her coffee.

'If this is university business, I can go down to the bedroom and get my gun.'

'For me?'

'Not at all,' he said. 'For the person you're writing about.' Then, before she could speak, and to cover all possibilities, he added, 'Or the person you're writing to.'

'You're right the second time,' she said.

'Who is it?'

'That idiot, Severin.'

At first the name meant nothing to him, but then Brunetti remembered a dinner he had attended, under threat from Paola, about five months ago, where they had shared a table with her colleague in the Faculty of English Literature, Claudio Severin, and his quite pleasant wife, whose name Brunetti could not remember.

'His wife's not at the university, is she?' Brunetti asked, remembering at least that much about her.

'No. She's a lawyer.'

'Nice when people have real jobs,' Brunetti remarked, and smiled broadly at Paola, hoping she'd laugh.

She did not, nor did she smile. That meant the matter was serious.

Brunetti started to ask what Severin had done to trouble her so, but he decided not to begin their conversation that way. Far more neutral to ask, 'What are you telling him?'

'That I disagree with his assessment of one of the doctoral candidates.'

'Who is?'

'Anna Maria Orlando. From Bari, I think. Pretty. Writes very well.' Was this, he wondered, going to be a case of prejudice against women from the South who dared to be intelligent?

'And?' he asked.

'And Severin's lost his head for her. She's taken all of his classes, asked him to be her dissertation director. And now he's told me he's suggesting the university choose her as a research assistant.'

'Am I supposed to stand up and slap both hands over my mouth because this is the first time I've ever heard of such a thing?' Brunetti asked. Then, thinking of the ruin he had seen older men make of their lives because of younger women, he lost the impulse to make light of what Paola said, changed register, and asked, 'And your mail?'

'I'm writing to him informally, not as a member of the committee that handles these appointments, and telling him that it is unlikely Signorina Orlando will meet the requirements the department has established.'

'Which are?' Brunetti asked, wiggling his toes as a display of interest.

'Extraordinary performance in class,' Paola said, holding up her thumb. She shot out her index finger and added, 'The support and approval of her previous professors.' Her middle finger jumped out to illustrate the last requirement. 'And at least two articles published in journals of high regard in the student's field of specialization.'

'Which is?' Brunetti asked.

After a moment's hesitation, Paola answered, 'The Silver Fork School.'

This distracted him from his toes sufficiently to enquire, 'The what?'

'Silver Fork School,' she said, adding, 'I think I've explained this to you before.'

Brunetti gave her a blank look, then confessed, 'I don't remember.' After a pause that he hoped – in vain – Paola would fill, he asked, 'What is it?'

'English novels in the nineteenth century packed full of long accounts of what was the right, or the wrong, way to behave in social situations.' When he said nothing in response, she added, 'They were very popular.'

'You've read them?' he asked, never quite sure what she'd been up to at Oxford during those years she'd studied there.

'One.'

'Do you remember the title?' he asked. Paola remembered everything.

She closed her eyes and summoned up memory. Her eyes opened and she said, *Contarini Fleming.'*

Brunetti sat silently until he could bring himself to say, 'Tell me.'

'It's rather complicated,' she replied. 'The hero's mother dies in childbirth, he grows up in Scandinavia, falls in love with a married woman, who rejects him. In despair, he goes to Venice, where he falls in love with his cousin. Who does not reject him, and then she too dies in childbirth.' She stopped there and looked off into the middle distance, a look Brunetti called her 'gestation face', one she wore while formulating a theory.

As if posing a rhetorical question with which to begin a class discussion, she asked, 'Isn't it interesting, the way women in Victorian novels so often died either in childbirth or from tuberculosis?'

Reluctant to be forced to answer her question, Brunetti asked, 'And this was a popular book?'

'Yes. Very.'

'And the author? What became of him?' Brunetti asked, sure he would have come to a bad end from having read this stuff as well as written it.

'He became prime minister of England,' Paola answered.

There ensued a silence of not inconsiderable length, ended by Brunetti's question, 'If I might return to our original subject, how old is Signorina Orlando?' He estimated Severin to be in his late fifties.

'Twenty-one or -two, I'd guess.'

'Oh my, oh my, oh my,' Brunetti said. 'Trouble on the horizon.' Then he added, trying to please Paola with his use of one of her English phrases, 'Tears before bedtime.'

'I suspect bedtime has come and gone, my dear,' she said and bent her head over the screen.

Not in the least deterred by her sarcasm, Brunetti returned to their original subject and asked, 'What are you telling him?'

'I'm sending him a copy of her record and the comments made by her various professors.'

'Is that permitted?'

She looked up, startled. 'Of course. They're part of the official documentation that accompanies a student from year to year.'

'And professors openly write what they think about students?' Brunetti asked, suddenly realizing how beautiful was the idea of academic freedom. Ah, if only ...

'Of course not,' Paola answered, then stopped abruptly and took her hands away from the keyboard. 'That is, they write in code, and everyone understands the code.'

'Ah,' Brunetti sighed, pleased to learn that academics were just like the police when asked to evaluate their colleagues: writing everything with an eye on the possible repercussions of saying anything negative or critical. 'Filled with enthusiasm' for 'rash'; 'admired for his seriousness' for 'tedious'; 'interested in her colleagues' opinions' for 'incapable of making a decision'; 'displays great intuitive understanding' for 'appears unfamiliar with the penal code'.

Brunetti smiled and nodded, now freed from the illusion that somewhere there existed a work situation in which people's performances were rated dispassionately and honestly.

He stopped moving his toes and said, 'What I don't understand is why you're bothering to write to him at all.'

'I've told you before, Guido: he was good to me when I started teaching.' She turned to glance at him but immediately looked back at the screen, almost as though she were embarrassed by what she'd just said.

Brunetti, who recalled this now, did no more than nod. He never knew if Paola's sense of unending indebtedness to anyone who had ever been kind to her was a virtue or a weakness. Nor, in fact, could he remember why he thought it a weakness.

'So what are you telling him?'

Eyes on the screen, she answered, 'That it might be wise to take a look at the exact requirements for the position that the university has put online and ask himself if Signorina Orlando meets all of them.'

'That seems modest enough,' Brunetti said.

'It is,' Paola agreed, then added, 'I mention in particular the requirement for two publications in well-regarded journals.'

Brunetti was a brave man, a curious man, and so he asked, 'What publications are well regarded?'

Paola closed her eyes and consulted her memory, opened them, and said, 'There's *Victorian Literature and Culture* and *Journal of Victorian Culture.*' Seeing that her husband registered these titles with no surprise, she added, 'And, of course, there are many more.'

'They sound like those magazines strange, pale people try to sell you in the street.'

'We're in Venice, Guido,' she said and returned to her computer.

Accepting defeat, Brunetti got up and went to the kitchen to see if there was anything to nibble on to sustain him until dinner time.

2

As Brunetti walked to the Questura the following morning, the sun warmed his face as he crossed the Rialto Bridge. He paused at the top and studied the façades that wandered down towards the university and disappeared to the left.

At the bottom of the bridge, he decided to walk and turned to the left, not stopping until he came to Didovich, where he paused for a coffee and read the headlines on the newspaper of the man standing next to him. He chose to walk along the side of the Miracoli, then straight on down towards SS. Giovanni e Paolo, where he opened his senses to the knockout punches of the façades of the Basilica and the Ospedale. He lingered in the *campo*, wishing there were some way to see it as he had seen it the first time. But then the thought came to him that he had probably been three years old when that happened, and he had noticed nothing beyond the lions on the Ospedale and Colleoni's horse.

To stop and gaze at beauty had not been possible in the recent past, when he and all those who still had to go to their places of work did so with great caution, choosing the most direct route, avoiding the vaporetto if they could, walking through rain and any sort of inclement weather, dodging out of the way of people passing by, attentive to those who did not wear a mask. Now, in a calmer time, Brunetti could return to the past in this tiny way at least and choose to do something for pleasure and not from fear. In the long span of life, it was precious little, but to Brunetti it was no less precious for that.

Pendolini, the guard at the door, still wore a mask all of the time. Many of those who worked inside had pretty much given up the habit, but Pendolini had not. Brunetti had no idea if the others thought they were invulnerable because they were police officers or if they had made some other calculation of the odds before deciding not to wear one. He had spoken to his brother, Sergio, who worked at the Ospedale Civile, who said he always wore a mask at work but not otherwise, adding that Brunetti, vaccinated twice, had little need unless he was enclosed in a small room with a person who might be at risk.

'There's a woman who wants to see you, Commissario. She's been here for some time,' the officer said from behind his mask. He pointed across the enormous entryway, where Brunetti saw the left side of a woman sitting on the long bench where visitors were told to wait. Her other half was blocked from sight by the man who stood in front of her, apparently engaged in conversation. Behind them hung a photo of the Fountain of Trevi, whose presence there had always puzzled Brunetti.

'What's her name?'

'She didn't tell me, sir. She said she knows you.'

'Who's that with her?' Brunetti asked.

'Looks like Lieutenant Scarpa to me,' the officer said. 'He must have come downstairs after I sent her over there to wait.'

When the man standing in front of the woman, alerted by her glance towards the entrance, stepped to the right and turned to the door, Brunetti saw that it was indeed Lieutenant Scarpa, the assistant – although others thought it closer to the truth to call him the henchman – of Vice-Questore Giuseppe Patta, Brunetti's direct superior.

Seeing Brunetti, the Lieutenant smiled at him, bent his head and said something to the woman, then turned slowly from her and started walking towards the staircase. Although Brunetti now had a clear line of sight to the woman, his eyes remained fixed on the Lieutenant as he climbed the stairs and disappeared on the first landing.

Returning his gaze to the woman, whose face was partly obscured by a mask, Brunetti did not at first recognize her from this distance. Slender, hair cut short so well as to look anything but boyish and so filled with traces of blonde as to seem anything but grey.

Her eyes, too, had followed Scarpa climbing the steps. When he was gone, she looked towards the entrance and finally saw Brunetti. She raised her left hand to wave in his direction, quickly back and forth, like the ticking of a metronome. The sight struck some atavistic chord in Brunetti's memory – not one he was particularly happy to find there – and by that old habit she revealed herself to be Elisabetta Foscarini. Her family had lived in a much larger apartment above the Brunettis when they lived in Castello, decades ago. Brunetti's father had been given a small ground-floor apartment by an old army companion in return for his acting as general handyman. He cleaned the steps, carried out the garbage, saw to small chores for other people in the building and the neighbourhood, even ran errands for some of them. In Castello, few secrets existed, so it was common knowledge that the family was poor, the father strange, and that they lived there for free.

Brunetti turned and asked Pendolini for a mask. Surprised, the officer took a step back into his office and quickly emerged with one for his superior. Brunetti thanked him, slipped the elastic loops behind his ears and started towards Elisabetta.

He had been in middle school when they moved into the apartment. Elisabetta, an only child, five or six years older than he, was enrolled at the Morosini, even then considered to be the best school in the city.

After less than a year in the apartment, Brunetti's father could no longer endure the charity of his friend, and the family had moved to an even smaller apartment, an even grimmer ground-floor place near Santa Marta where he and his brother Sergio had shared a bedroom and his father's behaviour had become so strange that he, an ex-soldier, had been sent to a military hospital and kept there for long enough to have become almost mute and thus less likely to say peculiar things. When he was released, Brunetti recalled, his father had become more affectionate towards his sons and wife, turning his feelings into gestures and embraces that were easier for him to make – and for them to interpret – than words.

He watched Elisabetta get easily to her feet and start towards him. As she had in the distant past, she stood plumb-line straight as she walked, her pace long. How well she looked, and how kind the years had been to her. She stopped when he did, a metre between them. The smile was evident in her eyes. 'Ah, Guido, how very nice to see you,' she said, speaking Italian and not Veneziano. Her family had never spoken the dialect of the lower orders, he recalled.

'You look so well,' she continued. 'It's been ... ' she paused and closed her eyes, '... ages since your family left Castello. But at least we've been able to say hello on the street.' Her eyes smiled again and she added, 'Very Venetian, isn't it?'

Brunetti smiled and nodded, recalling the many times they had greeted one another over the years. He had watched a few men come and go from her company, then watched one remain for some years. Then the two of them had added a baby who had turned into a little girl, and then a teenager.

He had watched Elisabetta's hair change colour and style a number of times, and soon after she'd started to cut it short, he had watched the hair of the man who still walked with her now begin to turn white, something she apparently prohibited her own from doing. Occasionally, Brunetti and Elisabetta would stop and summon up old times, but only the good memories. Once, the white-haired man had been with her and had come along for a coffee. He proved to be Bruno del Balzo, a successful businessman well known in the city. He owned factories abroad making machine parts, clothing, and shoes, as well as supermarkets in Marghera and Mestre and a boutique food emporium near Campo Santo Stefano that catered to foreigners and the growing numbers of vegetarians and vegans in the city.

Some years before – more than ten – Brunetti had stopped seeing them around San Marco and had assumed they'd moved to another part of the city. Then, three or four years ago, just as he was leaving Rosa Salva in Campo SS. Giovanni e Paolo, he had looked to his left and recognized the white-haired man opening the door to the last *palazzo* in the row.

'Well, well, well,' Elisabetta said, not bothering with any of the nonsense gestures adults now used as substitutes for a handshake or a kiss. Memory, Brunetti knew, played many tricks, but he realized that he felt little delight in seeing her again, not because she belonged to – and thus reminded him of – the roughest part of his life, but because he remembered that once, when she was entering the building and had clearly seen Brunetti's mother approaching, she had not paused to hold the door open for her. She was a young woman, born of a respectable family; she had many friends; her family was thought to be wealthy; and yet this failure of common politeness had shocked the young Brunetti and put a dent in his previous admiration for Elisabetta.

Before he could say how happy he was to see her, she said, glancing around the enormous entrance hall as though it were Brunetti's own, 'We followed your career, my mother and I.' She was still as tall as he and could look him in the eye. There were a few wrinkles, a few patches of dark, aged skin, but great beauty abided in her face. 'For some reason, my mother felt very proud of your success,' she told him. 'She was so very fond of you.'

'Really?' he asked, pleased that her mother had remembered him.

All the time they were going through the almost ritual behaviour of people meeting after some time, Brunetti kept asking himself why she was there. Surely, she had not dropped in for a chat about old times nor to reminisce about how different Castello had been all those years ago.

She looked around and asked, 'Is there some place we could talk, Guido?'

He nodded, thinking that she'd called him by his first name twice, which suggested that whatever she wanted was important. He was curious to learn what that could be.

Brunetti gestured towards the staircase the Lieutenant had taken. 'There's my office. That is, if you don't mind walking up two floors.'

'Good heavens, that's nothing,' Elisabetta said. 'We're on the fourth. And there's no lift.'

Brunetti thought of the building her husband had entered and wondered what the view would be. Surely, from the fourth floor they would be able to see the mountains. Nodding, he asked, 'Shall we go up, then?'

He did not offer her his arm, remembering that many people, now, didn't like to be touched. No more kissing friends on the street, no more embracing, no more casually touching the arm of a stranger to get their attention and tell them they'd dropped something or were meant to use a different door to enter a building. Without even a clap of thunder, icy formality had been imposed upon them all, and Brunetti realized how much he missed the soft, caressing humanity of the past.

As they climbed the stairs, she asked him about his family, wife, children with what sounded like sincere interest. He told her that his wife was still teaching at the university and his son was studying there, his daughter planning to enrol in two years. In his turn, deliberately slowing their pace, Brunetti asked her about the little girl he'd watched grow up, avoiding mention of her husband.

She paused at the bottom of the second flight but finally said, 'She's not a little girl any more. She's more than thirty.' Brunetti noticed that her summary was as brief as his had been.

At the top of the stairs, he paused on the landing for a moment to let her catch her breath – an unnecessary courtesy, he quickly realized. Suddenly from behind them he heard footsteps and turned back to see Claudia Griffoni coming up the stairs. Seeing someone with him, she smiled and raised a hand but continued up the steps.

'Claudia,' Brunetti called.

She stopped, turned, and came back to join them.

'I'd like you to meet an old friend of mine.' He stepped back a bit, saying, 'Elisabetta Foscarini.'

Griffoni smiled and extended her hand, a gesture that seemed to surprise Elisabetta. She smiled and shook her head, and Griffoni said, 'Oh, I'm sorry. Really. I still forget.'

Her hand remaining at her side, Elisabetta said, *'Piacere.'*

'The pleasure is mine, Signora.'

Hoping to ease them all past this awkward moment, Brunetti told Griffoni, 'We lived in the same building when we were teenagers.'

Griffoni looked at the other woman, as if wanting to make her complicit, and said, 'I had no idea il Commissario had ever been a teenager.'

Elisabetta gave a very indelicate snort and then allowed herself to laugh out loud. She grinned quickly towards Brunetti and then back at Griffoni.

Before Brunetti could say anything, Griffoni nodded to them both and proceeded up towards her office.

Inside his office, Brunetti opened the window to allow some air into the room. When he stepped back from it, he almost bumped into her and backed away quickly, saying, 'Sorry.' He asked if he could hang up her coat, and she slipped it off and gave it to him. He had admired the cut; now his hands had a chance to appreciate the cloth.

He hung it in his cupboard and walked over to adjust one of the chairs in front of his desk. He had toyed for a moment with the idea of retreating behind his desk, but instead placed the second chair facing her, although at some distance. He removed his mask; encouraged by the gesture, she slipped hers off and fitted it into a plastic ziplock bag she carried in her purse.

Sitting opposite her, her face now fully revealed, Brunetti saw more clearly how her beauty had endured. She was thinner than he remembered her being, and time had been busy with the flesh around her eyes and under her chin. Her glance was no different from the one he recalled: dark-eyed, insistent, steady, with no sign of the latent flirtatiousness often conveyed by attractive women.

Had he been at least partly in love with her? Brunetti wondered. In some way, probably, but the times had been different, and a boy of his class would not have dared to aspire to a girl of hers. Perhaps with no more than a glance she had made the rules clear, or perhaps the incident with the door had put paid to his admiration.

Her voice brought him back to the present, where they sat at the same level on facing chairs. 'What nice people you work with,' she said by way of opening. When he said nothing, she asked, 'You aren't busy, are you?' She spoke with a deference that made him uncomfortable.

'I've got plenty of time: there's almost no crime these days.'

'Well, that's a good thing, isn't it?' she said absently, not bothering to ask him why crime was scarce, in fact, seeming uninterested in his remark. 'I don't want to keep you from anything.' She sounded almost hopeful that their meeting would have to be brief, a common wish among people who came to see him at the Questura.

Without thinking, she reached out a hand, perhaps to touch his arm, but pulled it back before contact could be made. She lowered it and then her eyes. Neither of them spoke.

Suddenly he recalled a late afternoon – he might have been thirteen – when he was interrupted while doing his homework at the kitchen table, the only flat surface large enough to write on. Someone tapped at the door to the apartment; he had to answer it because his mother was out, cleaning the landlord's home, as she did twice a week.

He set his homework aside and went to the door to see who it was, and found Elisabetta's mother there holding a large pot.

She was a tall, painfully thin and not very pretty woman, hair thinning and pulled back into the same tiny bun his own grandmother had worn. One would never have supposed that she was the wife of a wealthy notary, that is, unless one were Venetian and knew the background of her marriage. In that case, they would have known that she was the only child of Notaio Alberto Cesti, one of the most successful notaries in the city, and would also have heard that his assistant, Leonardo Foscarini, had fallen in love with her – it was said – at his first sight of her father's client list and the fees they paid him each year.

Elisabetta's mother greeted the young Brunetti and said she had come down to ask a favour: could she leave the pot? He glanced at it, saw how large it was, and offered to take it from her.

'Thank you, Guido,' she said. 'It's hot, so I'll just put it on the stove.' She moved around him and crossed the kitchen in three steps to place the pot on one of the burners, waving her hands to cool them after holding on to the handles for so long. The aroma escaped the lid, and the Brunettis' kitchen was filled with the odour of herbs and tomatoes and onion.

He thought to offer her something, but there was nothing to offer except water, and he was embarrassed by that. 'What shall I tell my mother?' the young Brunetti asked.

'She gave me her recipe for *pasta e fagioli*, and I tried it out today.' Elisabetta's mother broke off to laugh – Brunetti, who had never heard her laugh, found it a beautiful sound. She rubbed her hands down the front of her apron – Brunetti seldom saw her, or his mother, not wearing one – and said, sounding somehow awkward, 'I didn't pay attention and must have put in too many beans and too much pasta, because I ended up with a giant pot of it.'

This was not the first time Signora Foscarini had brought down evidence of her culinary incompetence, always imploring whoever answered the door to save her the embarrassment of having to serve 'such a mess', or 'a complete failure', or 'twice what the recipe said' to her family. Luckily, the Brunettis were fond of her and willing to save her from the shame of having prepared too much food or having made an error so grave as to force her to prepare the meal again.

She pointed towards the stove, where the pot now sat. 'I kept having to add water, but it kept growing, so I had to put it into two pots.' Pointing towards the evidence, she said, 'That's not even half of it. We'll never eat it all, so I'd like your mother to ask all of you to help finish it.'

Brunetti had not been raised in a world where food was given away, especially in large quantities, but he knew then that Elisabetta's mother was a good woman. Only later was he to understand how careful she had been to make it sound like the truth, so he thanked her, again wishing there were something he could offer her, even an apple.

She went to the door and opened it. 'I hope you like it,' she said and smiled. 'I'm afraid we're all going to be eating it until the end of the week.'

When she was gone, Brunetti walked over to the stove and removed the lid, which was still hot. The aroma embraced him fully: beans, tomatoes and onion, rosemary and thyme. And on top, small wheels of carrot outnumbered by similar circles of sausage, more than he had ever seen.

Brunetti was overcome by a sense of safety: if he could have a quarter of what was in that pot, he would have enough to eat. Now, decades later, he did not remember if they ate the pasta that night, nor how much of it he ate. He remembered only that sweeping rush of certainty that he would be safe from hunger, at least for that evening.

Suddenly, without reason or plan, Brunetti said, warmth in his voice for the first time since he met her downstairs, 'It's very good to see you again, Elisabetta.' The lingering memory of her mother's kindness led him to add, 'We were very lucky to live near your family.'

He saw her astonishment. She looked down at her hands, entwined in her lap, then up at Brunetti. 'My mother always said you were a good boy, Guido.'

Brunetti felt himself blush. To move away from this, he asked, not finding a more evasive way to say it, 'Is she still alive?'

Elisabetta shook her head. 'No. She died some years ago.'

'I'm sorry,' Brunetti said, meaning it. 'She was very kind to my mother.' As he said this, another memory broke loose and started drifting towards his consciousness.

'Oh, she was kind to everyone,' Elisabetta said, as though the compliment embarrassed her. That was it, Brunetti thought, something about kindness and her mother or his mother.

'She gave my mother someone to talk to,' Brunetti added.

'Yes,' Elisabetta said, nodding. 'My mother told me how attentive she was with you and Sergio.' Brunetti managed to hide his surprise that, after all these years, she remembered his brother's name.

Brunetti paused for a moment, but the only thing he could say was, 'I didn't understand anything then, not how lonely she was, or how sad, but I knew it always made her feel good, sometimes for days, when they could be together and talk.'

Elisabetta's astonishment was visible. 'Are you talking about my mother?' she asked, one tone short of indignation.

Her voice dislodged the memory and he heard his mother, kindest and most patient of women, saying, 'I think Elisabetta's mother realizes how little of her kindness Elisabetta has.' He could still see her pause while ironing one of his father's shirts and add, 'But it doesn't seem to bother Elisabetta.'

The memory still filling his mind, Brunetti struggled to find an adequate answer to Elisabetta's question and finally blurted out, 'No, not at all. I barely knew her. I was talking about my own mother, Elisabetta. Please believe me.'

Elisabetta closed her eyes and pressed her lips together, incapable of speech. She started to say something, stopped, opened her mouth again, then her eyes, and finally said, 'I'm sorry, Guido,' quickly adding, 'I misunderstood.' Then, speaking slowly, as though trying to understand a new idea, she added, 'I suppose women need to talk more than men do. It helps us if we can talk about how people treat us, and what we think of others, and what makes us happy, or sad.'

'While men are busy talking about money and power?' Brunetti asked, trying to make it sound like a joke.

'Exactly,' Elisabetta said, ignoring the joke or, he suspected, pretending to miss it.

Silence fell between them until he leaned towards her and placed his hand on the arm of her chair. 'Why did you come to see me, Elisabetta?'

Her hands tightened. She tried to push herself into the chair, but she was as far back as she could go and could do no more than make the chair creak. She looked at him, turned, and looked out the window.

Brunetti watched her take a few deep breaths. She wiped her hand across the side of her face nearest Brunetti. Finally, looking at him directly, she said, 'It's about Flora, my daughter,' and stopped.

She looked towards the window, perhaps waiting for the words to come. Brunetti knew that, in situations like this, it was best to maintain a rock-like silence and simply wait the person out.

After she'd had enough time, she raised her eyes to his and said, 'Her husband said something to her that frightened her.'

3

Brunetti had trained himself, over the years, to display little emotion in response to the statements given to him by witnesses, victims, or suspects. He had listened to people confess to murder while keeping his face from displaying anything except interest; he had listened with an expression of nothing stronger than concerned attention as victims sobbed out accounts of violence, assault, and rape; his face had remained placid when murderers told him that the surveillance video of the victim's house must be wrong.

In this case, his habit restrained the impulse to reach out and take Elisabetta's hand to comfort or help in this moment of exposure to the abyss that always encircled a parent: harm to a child.

Brunetti knew nothing about the person Elisabetta had become, nothing of her marriage, nor of her daughter. What sort of daughter would Elisabetta raise: did she resemble her mother or her father? Were there grandchildren? As he sat, just as silent as she, Brunetti decided that the best way was to treat her as he would any unknown woman who came in and told him the same thing.

Rather than wait for her to speak, Brunetti said, 'If I'm going to understand this, Elisabetta, I need more information. It might be unpleasant for you to talk about certain things, personal things, but there's no other way for me, for the police, to be able to help you.'

She lurched forward and said, voice higher than it had been, 'That's what I don't want, Guido. You know what a small city this is, how people gossip and repeat rumours, even about people they don't know.' Her voice had changed, and she sounded on the brink of anger or even something stronger.

How well he knew this. The only way to keep a secret was to tell no one, but few people were capable of this. She raised her chin. Speaking very clearly and so slowly it was almost as though she were asking him to memorize her words, she said, 'Guido, in all those years, my mother never repeated anything – not one thing – that your mother told her.' When he didn't say anything in response, she added, 'And I never repeated anything your mother said when I was there with them.' Had this been a stranger speaking to him, he would have heard a threat; instead, he interpreted it as a sign of her seriousness.

Was she expecting the same from him? He doubted that anything his mother had told Elisabetta had concerned even the possibility of wrongdoing, but if she was worried enough about what her son-in-law had said to come and talk to a policeman, then crime must surely be an option.

Crime was alien to people of her parents' generation, as it had been to his own parents. His father was an honest, honourable man whose mind had been affected by years in a prisoner-of-war camp but whose central core of decency had not been touched. At times he raved, but those were only words. Besides, the passage of years had washed away the importance of whatever secrets Brunetti's or Elisabetta's parents might have had, eliminated the possibility of scandal. He drank? She drank? The kids shoplifted? He had a lover? She did? No one cared any more about this sort of thing. Social changes would have put most blackmailers out of business. Her mother had been good to his; little else mattered to Brunetti.

As though she'd taken his failure to respond as reluctance to enter into some sort of pact, she opened her mouth. She only had time to say, 'But I told you I don't want—' before Brunetti interrupted her.

'All right, Elisabetta,' he said, still under the effect of memory. 'It's private, between you and me. No police.' Did everyone distrust the police? he wondered. Were people able to put their trust only in family or friends? And even then, he knew, it was done with some reservation.

He considered the work that might lie ahead – family trouble was always terrible – and added: 'I'd like to ask Commissario Griffoni to help.'

Her response was clear in her eyes; to prevent it reaching her mouth, he cut her off and said, 'You can trust her, Elisabetta. As much as you can trust me.'

Elisabetta considered this for a long time before she nodded.

He pulled his phone from his pocket and pressed Griffoni's number.

'*Sì?*' she answered at the first ring.

'I'd like you to come and listen to what my friend has to say.'

'Two minutes,' Griffoni said and broke the connection.

'She's coming,' Brunetti said, at a loss for what to talk about until Griffoni arrived. He did not want to introduce the subject of her daughter: that would come soon enough.

'Your mother, was she clear in her mind until the end?' he asked, knowing it was invasive and cruel to do so. Because his own mother had died years before her body did, Brunetti was unable to decide which sort of death was worse, and for whom. In all these years, although he had asked many people who had lost a parent, he had never had an answer that would decide the case for him.

Her voice was hard to hear as she said, 'It was a long illness, but she was with us until she died.'

They were spared further discussion by Griffoni's three short knocks and then her entrance.

She smiled at Elisabetta, walked over to the window and brought back the third chair, placing it to create a triangle, and sat. She was entirely relaxed, and Brunetti could see how Griffoni's calm transferred itself to the other woman.

He decided to explain to Griffoni the agreement in which she had become involved, however involuntarily. 'Signora Foscarini has come to speak to me as an old friend, not as a policeman,' he began, then paused to let Griffoni ask about this if she pleased.

She did. 'Does that mean we're doing this privately and it isn't recorded as an official case?' Griffoni's voice, as she asked about breaking the rules – if not the law – was entirely relaxed and normal. So was her assumption that she was bound as tightly as he by whatever agreement he had made with his friend.

'Yes,' Brunetti told her.

She had a notebook in her hand, and she held it up. 'May I take notes?'

'Yes,' Brunetti said, then paused and glanced towards Elisabetta.

Elisabetta continued to study Griffoni, then said, as though to test the limits of her power, 'But only in your notebook; nothing goes into a computer.' She glanced sideways to see Brunetti nodding in agreement.

Griffoni smiled at the other woman and said, 'Of course, Signora,' opened the notebook, and pulled a pen out of her pocket.

Brunetti turned to Elisabetta. 'You told me your son-in-law said something to your daughter that frightened her.' Elisabetta nodded but did not speak.

Griffoni held up her pen and said, 'Could I ask you to give me their names, Signora, as well as their ages, and tell me how long they've known one another and how long they've been married?' She held up the notebook, as though it were a living thing that had somehow managed to ask these questions itself.

This was a technique Brunetti often used and recommended: get the witness talking about something familiar to them, ask them simple questions to which there are simple answers – numbers are helpful. The momentum built up by this often led the speaker to continue answering when the questions became more detailed and, sometimes, compromising.

'Flora del Balzo, she's thirty-one. Her husband is Enrico Fenzo; he's two years older. No children.' She stopped, then added, 'Not yet.'

'And how long have they known one another?' Griffoni asked, glancing up from her notebook and smiling as though she were about to listen to the happy love story of Elisabetta's daughter.

'About six years. They've been married for three.'

Griffoni wrote this down. Head still lowered, she paused to ask, in quite a conversational way, 'Would you say it's a happy marriage, Signora?'

Elisabetta glanced quickly at Brunetti, surprised by the question. Griffoni kept her eyes on the pages of her notebook, and Brunetti tried to look interested but not intrusive.

'I suppose so,' Elisabetta said finally. 'At least until about two months ago. Flora told me then that Enrico had changed.'

'In what way?' Brunetti broke in to ask.

'Flora said that he seemed nervous and was always thinking about something else. She never said anything about it until I invited her and Enrico to come for dinner.' Her voice ran down and she stopped, putting the fingers of her right hand to her lips.

After a long time, Griffoni asked, 'What happened, Signora?'

'Flora called me the day of the dinner and said they couldn't come. Well, she could, but she didn't want to come without Enrico, because he had to work that night.'

Holding her pen suspended above the page, Griffoni asked, 'What sort of work does your son-in-law do?'

'He's an accountant.'

Brunetti had no idea when accountants did their work, but he let her remark pass without question, not wanting to interfere with the rhythm of question and answer Griffoni had established.

Nodding as if it made sense that accountants worked at night, Griffoni asked, 'And who does he work for, if I might ask?' She looked up and gave a warm smile, the sort that Brunetti had seen, in the past, defrost the most reluctant witnesses.

'For himself, I suppose you'd say,' the older woman answered, then began to explain. 'He's a *ragioniere*, just a normal account- ant. He has a number of private clients: people with small businesses who don't earn enough to make them need a *commer- cialista*. He has an office over by Il Giustinian and works there by himself.'

'Has he always worked that way?' Brunetti asked, thinking it was time for him to begin to participate but still too early to ask more serious questions.

'No. After he graduated and received his accreditation, he worked for Caritas, and after that for an accounting firm in Noale, but then he decided to start his own business.'

Brunetti and Griffoni exchanged glances, and at her almost invisible nod, Brunetti asked, 'Do you know who any of his cli- ents are?'

Elisabetta stopped to consider the question and then said, 'Just at the beginning, right after he set up his office, he worked on a project for Bruno, and he was so pleased with his work that he recommended Enrico to a number of his friends.'

The expression on Griffoni's face made her failure to understand clear, and Elisabetta said, 'That's my husband, Bruno del Balzo.'

'And his other clients? Do you know anything about them?'

'No, not really. He's talked about two restaurants and an optician.' She opened her purse, hunted around inside for a moment, then pulled out a dark brown glasses case: Brunetti recognized the optician's name. She turned her head aside as she tried to remember more of her son-in-law's clients and finally shook her head.

Because he thought it true, not because he wanted to flatter Elisabetta's son-in-law, Brunetti said, 'Given the times, he's probably wise to work for a wide variety of clients. Even in the strictest lockdown, some things are bound to be open.' My God, he wondered, does this disease infect every thought we have now?

'But you don't remember their names?' Griffoni asked. Elisabetta gave every evidence of trying to recall them, and finally said, 'One of the restaurants is owned by Ottavio Pini.' After giving that name, Elisabetta said, 'I could ask Flora. She might know.'

Brunetti had gone to middle school with Pini and occasionally ate in his restaurant: Pini could be counted on not to say anything to Fenzo if Brunetti called him to ask about his accountant. This might not be true of all of Fenzo's clients, so Brunetti said, 'No, best not to, Elisabetta.' By the change in her face, he saw that she was both puzzled and relieved, so he left it and let silence surround them.

After waiting for Elisabetta to speak and then realizing that she would not, he asked, 'Did he study here, Elisabetta?'

She seemed to welcome the question. 'Yes. Soon after he finished school, he met Flora at a dinner with friends.' That said,
her voice took on a warmer tone and she added, 'She called me
the day after she met him.' Then, as if she'd seen the road of
sloppy sentimentalism opening up before her, she added, 'Flora
isn't a person who confides much.'

Griffoni and Brunetti glanced at one another, a motion
Elisabetta did not see because she'd turned her attention to the
window. 'There's one thing—' she began and stopped suddenly.

'What is it, Elisabetta?' Brunetti asked.

'Well, his is a very ... simple family. His mother never worked –
there were four children – and his father worked at COIN until
it closed, selling shoes, I believe.' She raised her open hands to
the height of her bosom and let them fall back to her lap, saying,
'They come from a different ...' She stopped, either not finding
or feeling reluctant to use the word 'class', but Brunetti realized
what she meant.

'Like me and Paola,' he said neutrally, assuming she would
know that he had married above his station and hoping that she
would somehow understand it could be done successfully. He
held her gaze and said, 'It can work, Elisabetta.'

She let some time pass before she said, 'It might have. Until
now. I know my daughter.'

'Until?' Griffoni asked, eyes on her notebook.

That stopped Elisabetta. Her lips separated, but she did not
speak, and Brunetti was sure she would say no more. He shot
a glance towards Griffoni, who did not raise her head. She set
her pen inside the open notebook and folded her hands on top
of it.

Nothing stirred in the room. Elisabetta's breathing was audible to the other two.

After some time, Brunetti drew in a quiet breath of air and
tried to think of a way to tell Elisabetta that there was little he

and Griffoni could do. Opposite him, Griffoni stiffened and shot him a fierce glance, managing to furrow her brow in a clear order that he be silent.

A long time passed, and then some more. Then Elisabetta sighed deeply, and said, 'I'm afraid he's doing something bad.'

4

As though she and Elisabetta were singing a *recitativo*, Griffoni picked up the lyrics without dropping a note. 'Bad in what way, Signora?' she asked, and turned a page of her notebook so quietly as to suggest she wanted nothing to distract her from Elisabetta's remarks.

Elisabetta raised a closed fist and unleashed a finger with each example she provided. 'He doesn't talk to her about his work any more. He won't answer Flora's questions: if she asks what's wrong, he tells her nothing's wrong and to stop nagging him.' She started to say something else, lowered her hand and pressed her lips together. But silence failed her. 'It might be a woman.' Saying this seemed to exhaust her and she fell silent.

'Why do you say that?' Griffoni asked.

'What else could it be?'

Brunetti interrupted here to ask, 'You said this started about two months ago?'

'That's when Flora told me about it, but she's always been shy, never wants to talk about herself or about Enrico.' Elisabetta stopped, as though surprised to hear herself mentioning her son-in-law's name. She pressed both hands flat on her thighs and gave her attention to her fingernails. After some time, she said, 'When his phone rings, sometimes he goes to another room to answer it.'

'It happens,' was the only thing Brunetti could think of to say. Hearing Brunetti's response, she put her hand to her mouth. 'But Flora's my baby,' she said, almost choking on the last word.' She took a few deep breaths and resumed in a more sober voice, 'I can't press her about it; I have to wait until she tells me more.' Her hand went to her mouth, as if to stop those traitorous words. She lowered her hand and pressed her open palms together, then hid them between her thighs. She looked at them so long that Brunetti feared she had finished.

'What did she tell you, Elisabetta?' he asked.

Elisabetta shrugged, raised her hands to the height of her shoulders, then let them fall back to her lap, suggesting complete helplessness.

Griffoni leaned forward to bring herself closer to the other woman and asked, voice low, as though worried about being overheard by someone else who might be in the room, 'Has anything happened that your daughter thought strange?'

The older woman's chin shot up and she stared across at Griffoni. 'Who told—' she began, but stopped herself from completing the sentence, no doubt because she realized how absurd it was to think that someone had already spoken to Griffoni. She started to her feet, moving very slowly, pushing herself up on the arms of the chair. Ignoring them, she walked over to the window and turned sideways in semi-defiance.

Brunetti and Griffoni exchanged glances but said nothing. His hands were in his lap, and he raised one finger slowly and pointed towards Griffoni.

Griffoni let a long time pass, then finally said, 'Signora, I don't know your daughter, or you, or your son-in-law, but I've often seen it happen that some small incident is enough to make a person understand a larger problem. A word, a gesture, perhaps a remark made by some other person: it comes from nowhere, but suddenly it makes things clear. It's like fitting a piece into a puzzle: you see half an eye, and all of a sudden you realize someone's hidden behind the tree.'

Both of them saw Elisabetta's reaction: her face grew rigid. She remained like that for a few seconds, then slowly turned away and looked out of the window, reminding Brunetti of the many times people had taken that same position while speaking to him: distant from him, higher, and near an exit, even if it was only a window. Perhaps the combination of those three opportunities for escape somehow freed them to say what they needed to say.

As if speaking to whatever she saw from the window, she said: 'Flora came to visit last week. She seemed distracted or nervous about something, but I pretended not to notice, and we went into the kitchen for a coffee, the way we always do.'

She stopped speaking, as though trying to retreat into the harmony of that scene, then turned back to face them and continued. 'We sat down at the table, Flora kept putting sugar into her coffee – three spoons, four. She was looking at what she was doing, but she didn't see it.

'I reached over and took the spoon from her and gave her my coffee: I hadn't put sugar in it yet. It's how Flora drinks it. She didn't notice what she'd done to the other cup, and she drank mine.' Elisabetta waved her hand in the air.

'It took her a while, but she finally told me she'd confronted Enrico with the way he'd been acting. All he'd say was that he was having trouble at work and didn't want to talk about it.'

Brunetti suddenly found himself listening to Elisabetta's story in a different way, his suspicions alert to other possibilities in what they were being told. Elisabetta's story had begun to sound like a problem for Social Services or – suggested the cynicism that always lurked in a corner of his mind – a soap opera. What was the next plot development? Flora asks who called, and Enrico bursts into tears and tells her he's in love and wants a divorce? Wasn't it time Elisabetta started to cry?

The wish was father to the deed, and he watched Elisabetta wipe her face with the back of her hand. Griffoni looked at him and let her eyebrows give a minimal shrug.

Brunetti opened the fingers of one hand and placed them on top of his watch. Griffoni nodded.

Elisabetta looked over at Brunetti. 'I'm not being hysterical, Guido,' she said in a flat voice, and then continued in the same tone. 'Flora told me she snapped then, lost her temper completely, and told him she didn't believe him, that he was making it up to disguise what he was doing.

'She said he pushed himself away from the table; he knocked his chair over when he did. He got up and leaned over, then grabbed her shoulders and pulled her face close to his. She doesn't remember exactly what he said or did, she was so shocked. He said something about how dangerous it would be for them if other people learned what was happening.' Brunetti heard the echo of Elisabetta's own shock as she recounted this.

It was obvious to Brunetti that she was not finished but had to search for the right words. Finally she said, in a voice so soft it could have been a child's, 'He didn't say another word to her or explain or excuse himself for what he did to her. He walked out of the house and didn't come home until after midnight.'

Silence filled the room until Brunetti finally said, 'So you came here.'

She walked back to the chair where she had been sitting and resumed her place. She nodded a few times and finished with her eyes looking at the floor. 'I thought about it for days: you're the only person I know who might be able …' she began, but failed to finish the sentence.

Brunetti glanced at Griffoni, who remained silent, still writing in her notebook.

Before Brunetti could think of what to say, Griffoni stopped writing and looked across at the other woman to ask, 'Did you tell us exactly what your daughter said, Signora?'

'Excuse me?'

Not looking at her notebook, Griffoni said, 'Something about danger.' She looked down at the page then and read out, '"How dangerous it would be for them if other people learned what was happening."'

She looked at Elisabetta, who, although surprised to hear her own words repeated back to her, nodded and said, 'More or less.'

Griffoni gave a small smile and went on, 'Could you try to remember talking to your daughter and tell us if that was exactly what she said?'

Elisabetta thought about this for a moment. She tilted her chin a bit to the side and closed her eyes. Brunetti noticed that she pulled her fingers into tight fists and tapped them gently on her thighs. Her lips moved, as though she were speaking to herself. Her eyes opened and she said, 'I can't remember exactly what she told me, but I'm sure she told me he said it would be "dangerous" if people found out what was happening.'

Calmly, almost casually, Griffoni asked, 'For both of them?'

'Yes,' Elisabetta answered without hesitation.

'Without telling her what it was about?'

Elisabetta nodded.

'Thank you,' Griffoni said, smiling across at her. In a much warmer voice, she went on, 'It must have been terrible for your daughter.' Then, as if the thought had just come to her, she asked, 'Was there any trouble between them before?'

Elisabetta considered this for a moment and then gave a forceful, 'No. Never.' She nodded in self-affirmation. 'I'd know. I would have sensed it.' She brushed idly at the sleeve of her jacket, removing an invisible speck, and crossed her hands in her lap. Then, almost apologetically, she added, 'If he hadn't said it was dangerous, I wouldn't have come here, believe me.'

Brunetti waited for her to say more, and when she did not he asked, keeping all signs of impatience from his voice, 'What is it you'd like us to do, Elisabetta?'

She glanced at him, obviously embarrassed. 'I don't know, Guido. I told my husband, and he said it's none of our business, that a man and his wife have to work things out between themselves.'

Before either Griffoni or Brunetti could ask, she added, 'He said Enrico has a demanding job, and she has to understand that.' She looked at Brunetti and raised her eyebrows while pressing her lips together in an expression that made it clear that opposition to her husband was not easy.

Griffoni looked at the other woman and asked, 'Is his practice busy enough to support them?'

'I think so, yes. My husband says his friends think he's very good. They've always got on well together, Bruno and Enrico.' Then, voice suddenly serious, Elisabetta added, 'My husband was *un imprenditore.*' She paused to let that sink in, then went on. 'He's retired now. But he keeps busy. He owned a number of businesses here and had interests abroad.'

Griffoni's eyes lit up in visible admiration.

'You said your husband and son-in-law got on very well?' Brunetti said, making it a question.

This caused Elisabetta to stop and consider, but finally she said, 'Yes and no.'

'What didn't they agree about?' Griffoni asked, then added deferentially, 'If I might ask.'

'The usual things,' Elisabetta said after a moment's reflection.

Smiling, Griffoni interrupted to ask, 'Could you give me an example, Signora?'

'Bruno doesn't think Flora should continue now that she has a husband.'

'Continue what?' Brunetti asked, recalling that she'd been married for three years and was already in her thirties, so she must have some sort of career.

'Working,' she said, then explained: 'She's a veterinarian. She has a clinic on Murano.'

'Good for her,' Griffoni broke in to say.

Elisabetta turned quickly, and Brunetti saw her study Griffoni as though she'd only just now noticed her. Her glance was not clement.

Allowing his impatience to show, Brunetti said, 'Elisabetta, you told us your son-in-law worked for your husband at the beginning of his career. Do you remember how long they worked together?' When she didn't answer, he repeated, 'Do you?'

Griffoni sat motionless, perhaps puzzled by the coolness of Brunetti's question, phrased in the familiar '*tu*'.

'A few months,' Elisabetta finally answered. 'And it was only on a single project. Once that was finished, Enrico went back to his other clients.'

When he spoke again, Brunetti's voice had lost its edge and returned to a more pleasant register. 'Well, it was probably a good experience to be able to dedicate himself to one client for a time.'

Griffoni responded to the need to bolster the normalcy of the situation and said, using the voice she reserved for the speaking of meaningless generalities, 'Better not to lock yourself into one job early in your career,' then quickly changed the subject. 'I've always thought it would be a wonderful job, being a veterinarian.'

'You like animals?' Elisabetta asked.

'Yes, we grew up with them: two dogs and three cats.'

'How was that possible in an apartment?' Elisabetta asked with real interest.

'Oh, we lived on a farm, about twenty kilometres from the nearest city.' Griffoni's voice grew warm with the syrup of childhood memory. 'It was paradise.'

Brunetti knew little about Griffoni's past, but he did know she'd grown up in the Spagnoli neighbourhood of Naples, hardly a farm and certainly not paradise.

'Elisabetta,' he said, calling her back from the bucolic idyll Griffoni had tried to create, 'could you tell us what it was your son-in-law and husband worked on together?'

She turned her attention to Brunetti, the mood broken. When it was obvious that Brunetti was going to wait for an answer, she said, 'It was a charitable foundation Bruno had been thinking about for a long time. Once he stopped working, he had the freedom to dedicate himself to it.'

Charity was not a virtue Brunetti was much accustomed to finding in businessmen, but he put on an eager face and waited for more.

'Coincidentally,' Elisabetta continued, 'the company Enrico had worked for in Noale had set up two similar foundations, so he was familiar with the forms and rules.'

'What was the organization involved with?' Brunetti broke in to ask.

'Healthcare.'

That didn't provide Brunetti with much information so he asked, 'Could you tell me a bit more, Elisabetta?'

He saw her face relax at the question, probably because it saved her from having to continue revealing family information, although she still sat nervously straight in her chair.

'While he was still working, and this was years ago,' she began, 'Bruno contributed to a charity a friend of his was setting up in Brazil. But his friend died, and the charity was so badly managed by his heirs that it was dissolved.' She paused to consider this, then said, 'It was terribly complicated because of the different laws between the two countries. Or at least that's what Bruno told me.

'So when he retired and decided to try to do some good in the world, he asked our parish priest for suggestions. Don Marco put Bruno in contact with a priest who'd been his classmate in the seminary and was now a missionary in Belize, working as chaplain in a small clinic.' She looked up and smiled, as though she were somehow responsible for this. 'Bruno got in touch with this priest, and things began there.'

Then, in a more serious voice, she went on: 'I think Bruno always kept in mind what had happened to his friend's project. That's why, in the planning, he asked Enrico to see that the charity was set up correctly so that it would do what it was meant to do.'

She stopped speaking for a moment, and Griffoni asked with eager curiosity, 'What was that, Signora?'

Elisabetta smiled and said proudly, 'Bruno wanted to build a hospital.'

She paused and looked from one to the other, as though she wanted to know if she should continue. Interpreting their smiles as assent, she went on. 'They created the charity so they could expand the existing clinic and turn it into a proper hospital, but when they began, Enrico and Bruno almost went mad with all the red tape and permissions and certifications from the government there and the medical authorities. Even the local bishop wanted to be sure that the offer was legitimate.' She paused, considering what she had just said, and added, 'Strangely, all of the red tape came from the other side. The Italian part – if I remember correctly what they said at the time – was relatively easy.'

Seeing that they were following her closely, Elisabetta added, 'It took months to get things worked out over there, and for the building to begin.' She paused and then added, 'But, to give them credit, once they began, it went very quickly.'

'Is that when your son-in-law left?' Brunetti asked.

Elisabetta stopped for a moment, as though assessing what she could tell them. 'He stayed until the permits were granted, and the work could begin.' She paused and considered what she'd just said and then added, 'You've got to understand that Enrico wasn't being paid. From the beginning, he'd refused to accept a salary for working on a charity project, even though his own business was still small. So when it turned out that the whole process was going to be more complex than either of them had foreseen, he and Bruno agreed that he'd leave when the permits were granted, and he'd return to his other clients.'

Then, with an innocence that surprised and pleased Brunetti, Elisabetta said, 'Bruno asked Enrico what he could give him for all the help he'd provided.' She looked back and forth between them, like a child about to do a magic trick, and said, 'Enrico told Bruno to decide on a sum and give that to the foundation as the first contribution.'

She must have sensed something in their silence, for some of the wonder disappeared and she said, 'That's how it started.'

It was Griffoni who reacted first. She set down her pen on her open notebook and said softly, 'You must be very proud of him, Signora. Of both of them.' Hearing her and seeing the sincerity of her smile, Brunetti was certain she had gone to Catholic schools: it was only there that children mastered the alchemical formula of untruth and hypocrisy that was sure to persuade even the most sceptical listener.

Passing to deceit without a pause, Griffoni asked, voice still subdued by the presence of so much goodness, 'Is your husband able to run the finances by himself now?'

After a moment's reflection, Elisabetta said, 'Not completely. He told me that Enrico, before he left, set up a computer system to handle the donations that come by bank transfer, and Bruno feels comfortable doing that by himself now.' She lowered her head in what seemed to Brunetti an old-fashioned gesture of female helplessness and said, 'I'm afraid I don't really understand how it works, especially now that they do everything online.' She raised her head and smiled. 'They've had to create a website.'

'Has it grown that much?' Griffoni asked with undisguised admiration.

'Oh, yes,' Elisabetta answered. 'Luckily, Bruno hired a very competent secretary who comes in two days a week to take care of the correspondence and found a volunteer, a girl who comes in for an hour or so every morning. She has to open the post and record everything: the coins taped to pieces of cardboard, the unused stamps, and the small bills people send them. Once a week, she takes the money people send in cash to the bank.' She looked to see that they were both following. 'They all work in another apartment we own in the building. Only two rooms, but there's enough working space for them.'

Still recovering from the idea that there existed people who sent money through the post, Brunetti asked, 'Anyone else?'

Elisabetta hesitated for some time but then gave a definite, 'No,' only to correct herself immediately and say, 'There's a woman who takes care of publicity, but I've never met her.' As if to explain that, she added, 'She lives in Mestre and works mostly from home.'

Brunetti could think of nothing further to ask her. The charity hardly seemed pertinent to the problem she had brought to them. Worse, he could no longer ignore his sensation that everything Elisabetta had said and everything they had asked her had somehow been askew from the beginning. Elisabetta, he thought, showed little real interest in her husband's charity and was concerned mostly with her daughter's situation.

When people were stressed, Brunetti knew, they often said things that they knew were not true or were wild exaggerations of the truth. Elisabetta's description of her son-in-law's behaviour had sounded a bit like this.

Elisabetta responded to his silence by saying, 'It's strange, Guido, but talking to you about this makes me all of a sudden hear how vague it all is, and that I'm probably overreacting.' She bowed her head and appeared to close her eyes. 'But there's no one else I can talk to.'

She looked up, a small smile on her lips. 'Maybe Bruno's right, and it's something Flora and Enrico have to work out between them.'

Brunetti could find no suitable response to this, so he nodded to Griffoni and got to his feet.

5

Griffoni stood a moment later and thanked Signora Foscarini for coming to talk to them, without mentioning any action that might result from her having been to the Questura. Brunetti moved to stand beside Elisabetta and accompanied her to the door of his office, then decided to continue to the exit with her. While they walked down, he tried to think of something he could say to make her believe that old friendships created obligations and she had done the right thing in coming to talk to him.

'I'll ask around,' was the best he could find to say, as if that minimal promise would both suffice and somehow satisfy them both.

She paused on the last landing and, turning towards him, shook her head a few times. Sounding exasperated, she said, 'It's hard to understand him.'

Brunetti, who had started down the last flight of steps, believing that Elisabetta had said all she had to say, paused with one foot raised, then turned to look back at her. 'I don't understand what you mean, Elisabetta.'

Leaving one hand on the railing to anchor herself, Elisabetta turned a bit towards him. 'I'm a married woman with an adult child, Guido. But I don't know anything about people or how they are today.' He saw the tears in her eyes, heard the misery in her voice. 'I've lived longer than you have, and I don't know anything.'

Brunetti turned back and walked up to stand beside her. He waited until she took her hand from the railing. 'Come on, Elisabetta. *Forza. Coraggio*,' he said, making a joke of his command that she be strong and courageous. His words, however, seemed to pass into her spirit and revive her. She used her sleeve to wipe her eyes, then stepped back from him, saying, 'Thank you, Guido. This has been on my mind for days. I think it got the better of me.'

Brunetti started down the stairs again, thinking to lead her back to the bench where she had been sitting when he came in. As they approached it, she slowed her pace and stopped. In a steady voice, she said, 'I think I'll go home, Guido. I'm not used to this sort of thing, you know?' Here she smiled, giving Brunetti a fleeting glance of the young woman who had lived above them in Castello.

He paused and asked for her phone number, entered it in his phone, then followed her to the door and watched her leave. She did not pause to look back, simply went outside, turned right, and disappeared, leaving him with the sight of the bridge and part of the now empty *campo* on the other side of the canal.

He walked back to the steps and up to Griffoni's minuscule office, certain that she would have returned there. He hadn't been up to her mini office for some time and was relieved to see that the door was open, a sure sign that she was there. The door opened inwards, its arc so inconvenient that Griffoni often sat with part of her chair projecting into the corridor and only shut the door when leaving in the afternoon, when she had to stack her chair on her desk to succeed in doing so.

Given the fact that she had only to lean back in her chair to see who was approaching, the formality of knocking had disappeared. Brunetti stopped in the corridor and asked, 'What did you think of what she said?'

'Signora Foscarini?'

'Yes.'

She stood and slid her chair to the right, allowing him to squeeze past her and take the second chair placed against the back wall.

Griffoni sat down and urged her chair back under her desk. She spent a moment preparing an answer and finally said, 'I think she's been lucky in life.'

'I beg your pardon.'

'You heard what she said: she has a daughter and a son-in-law who seem to be leading decent, respectable lives; her husband had a good career and continues to work for the good of others, and no one's ever going to fire him.' She paused to allow Brunetti to respond, but he chose to remain silent.

'So at the first sign of trouble in paradise, she panics and comes to see you. As if there were some way you could figure things out and fix them.' Griffoni spoke with dispassion.

When he understood that she was finished, Brunetti said, 'That's rather an unsympathetic way to view it, don't you think, Claudia?'

She gave a broad smile and said, 'It's a very unsympathetic way to view it, I agree, but I'm afraid I see it that way.' Before Brunetti could object, she continued, 'That young married people argue seems normal to me, Guido.' Before he could comment, she added, 'And I say that because it's true, not because I come from the hot-blooded South ... '

She stopped, and into the silence she left him, Brunetti said, 'I agree it's normal. It's the volume at which people do it that differs.'

Griffoni considered this, then asked, 'Don't you think your friend is overreacting?'

She opened her notebook and began to look through the pages. After some time, she stopped, pointed down at her notes, and read, '"Grabbed her shoulders and pulled her face close to his."' Looking up, she added in a slow, thoughtful voice, 'Hearing that would upset any mother, I think.'

Although she stopped, it was clear to Brunetti that she had not finished. She ran her hand across the surface of her desk, swept something invisible over the edge, and looked at him. 'But what if he'd done that to kiss her? It's the sort of thing we see in films all the time.'

'But she told us he delivered some sort of warning to her. And frightened her. Don't you believe what she told us?'

'Remember, we've got the story not from the person it happened to but from someone who heard it from her.'

Brunetti knew her well enough to know she was building up to something, so he didn't speak.

'So it's sort of second-hand, isn't it?' she asked calmly.

He thought about it for some time, aware that Griffoni was doing no more than suggest a way to undramatize the story or to view the drama differently. We grab people in an effort to protect them, don't we? We over-respond to any suggestion that those we love might be at risk. Viewing it through the lens Griffoni held up for him, Brunetti realized that Elisabetta's reaction had been extreme. But mothers' reactions often were, he told himself.

Remembering that he had promised to do what he could, Brunetti returned to the subject at hand and suggested, 'It might be his work that's troubling him.' After a short pause, he added, 'And we could take a look at the project he did for his father-in-law.'

He looked at his watch and, seeing the time, said, 'I have to be in Treviso all afternoon, so perhaps we could talk about this tomorrow?'

'Good idea,' Griffoni said. She raised her hand and, in a speculative manner, rubbed her fingers along her lower lip. 'I've always thought the people who want to help save the world are probably the worst people to be in charge of a charity.'

'Otherworldliness?' Brunetti ventured.

'Something like that,' she said. 'It's a weakness in their character.'

'Why do you say that?' Brunetti blurted out in surprise.

She got to her feet and tucked her chair under her desk, missing Brunetti's arm by a few centimetres. She took the handle of the door and swung it halfway towards her. She waited for Brunetti to walk in front of her and out into the corridor, then closed the door and pulled a key from her pocket.

Her back to him so that he could not see her expression, she turned the key and said, 'Because I'm Neapolitan.'

Brunetti turned and led the way to the staircase.

6

The next morning, Brunetti arrived at the Questura as he usually did, a bit past nine. The guard at the door told him that Commissario Griffoni had gotten there about twenty minutes before and said she'd be in her office.

He stopped by his to drop *Il Gazzettino* on his desk and check his emails, then went up to Griffoni's office. He found the door open, and when he looked in, had to admit that the room semed strangely smaller.

Griffoni glanced up and moved her chair closer to the table to let him go behind her to the guest's chair. When he was seated, she asked, smiling, 'Where were we?'

'What about having a look at his private life? It's just as likely the problem could be there.'

'The infamous "Other Woman"?' she asked in a trembling voice.

'Always high on the list,' he agreed easily. Then, before this conversation went any further, he said, because he thought he had to say it, 'Before we continue with this, I think we should consider whether we really want to take it on.'

'Because it might not be worth the trouble?'

'No,' he said instantly. 'I mean doing it because a friend of mine asked me to, not because it's a criminal matter. Or gives any sign that it might be one.'

Griffoni got to her feet and walked over to stand below the afterthought of a window: so small and so unreachably high as to lead anyone who saw it to suspect that the builders had simply punched a hole in the wall to allow themselves some fresh air while they finished working on the attic of the original building and then decided it was less trouble to turn it into a window than to close it up. She stuck her hands into the pockets of her jeans, leaned her head back until she put her equilibrium in jeopardy, and stared at the distant clouds.

She watched them for what seemed to Brunetti a long time – she seemed so intent that she might even have been listening to them – removed her hands, and went back to her chair. She crossed her legs and waited a bit before speaking, then did so as though to herself. 'She's an old friend. We use police contacts and powers to help her with a personal problem, and we find nothing.' Brunetti took heart from her unconscious use of the plural. 'So, to a person who chooses to interpret our actions in a certain way, we will have wasted, squandered, abused ...' She paused here on an uprising note, and Brunetti was struck by the melodrama of her timing. '... police time and authority,' she said, completing the sentence.

She kept her eyes on his, attentive to his response.

'Lieutenant Scarpa, I presume?' Brunetti asked in English.

She held up a hand and said, 'And not only he, though he'd surely be first among equals.' Brunetti gave her the grin she deserved, and she continued. 'If, after his brief conversation with the Signora, Scarpa learned that we were investigating the family of a successful businessman who is also the head of a charity, one of what I suspect are the very few non-profit organizations remaining in the city, on the hearsay evidence of a childhood friend of yours – or, for that matter, of mine ... or Vianello's ... or Pucetti's – it could lead to a lot of trouble.'

She pursed her lips, a gesture most women made at some risk, but not she. 'You have a longer history with the dynamics here, Guido, so you're better able to think of a way to go ahead with this while avoiding trouble.'

'When Lieutenant Scarpa's name is used in a conversation, it's almost impossible to avoid the word "trouble",' Brunetti replied. Was it Paola's affection for Oscar Wilde's plays that always made him speak of Scarpa as though he were a minor figure in one of them and not the grey nemesis of the Questura?

'Vianello might be able to help,' he suggested.

'Often the case,' Griffoni answered.

Deciding this meant she was as willing as he to continue, Brunetti said he'd go downstairs and have a word with the Ispettore.

Downstairs, in the officers' room, he saw Vianello at his desk near the far wall, a newspaper lying on its surface, his head a good distance from the page; it was the first time Brunetti had noticed this. As he drew nearer, Brunetti noted the distinctive orange and blue masthead of *Il Gazzettino*.

He stopped beside Vianello, who glanced up and said, pointing to the front page, 'I suppose you've seen this?'

Brunetti looked down and saw the article he'd already read. 'Those boys?' he asked.

Indeed, the photos of four young men – boys, really – smiled up at him, as they had from the tops of the piles of newspapers on every *edicola* he had passed on the way to work. The four of them, classmates at the university, had been returning to Venice at three in the morning after an illegal house party in Padova, when the driver, because of what the newspapers always referred to as '*Un colpo di sonno*' – 'a sudden attack of sleepiness' – had, at a speed estimated to have been 160 kilometres an hour, driven into a plane tree at the side of the road.

The observation of the medical examiner had been precise and, ignoring all mention of *colpo* or *sonno*, had determined that the cause of death had, in all cases, been blunt force trauma, multiple and fatal.

Not mentioned in *Il Gazzettino*, but made clear in the police report both Brunetti and Vianello had read, were the details that none of the young men had been wearing seatbelts and that blood analysis had registered a stupefying level of amphetamine in the blood of the driver and evidence of the same, though in lesser quantities, in the blood of the other three.

'Why did they let him drive?' Vianello asked in a haunted voice.

Echoing the dispassion of the medical report, Brunetti said, 'Because they were young and tired and drugged, and he probably insisted on driving.' This was usually the case.

'So just like that,' Vianello said, folding the paper in half and pulling a file of papers over the top of the front page, eliminating the photos, but leaving the headline to scream its way across the top of the article.

'It's Padova's problem,' Vianello said finally, although both of them were aware that Venice would become involved sooner or later.

By mutual agreement, they turned away from the subject of drugs. They both had teenage children who were not, to the best of their knowledge, interested in them, but was that not what every parent thought until they thought something else?

Brunetti pulled over a chair and sat at the side of Vianello's desk. Remembering why he'd come down, he asked, 'Do you know anything about a businessman named Bruno del Balzo?'

Vianello looked away, and his lips moved as he repeated the name softly. 'I've heard it, but I don't remember where, or why,' he said. The Ispettore furrowed his brow and raised his chin. He stared across the room at another officer bent over a computer and two other uniformed men standing in front of a window, deep in conversation. 'Why do you ask?'

'I spoke to his wife yesterday. She's someone I knew years ago,' Brunetti told him. 'I met them together only once, for a coffee. I've heard his name mentioned over the years, but not for any reason I remember. You know how it is.' Then he finally got to the point. 'It seems their son-in-law is acting strangely.'

'Guido,' Vianello said easily and with a smile, 'if everyone who was acting strangely were reported to us ...' The Ispettore stopped himself there, leaving Brunetti to finish the thought as he chose. When he did not, Vianello said, 'Why are you asking about his father-in-law?'

'I'm not sure I know,' Brunetti admitted.

'Who is he, this son-in-law?'

'Enrico Fenzo. He's a *ragioniere*. Has his own office. She's worried for her daughter.' Brunetti struggled to find a way to make any of this clear to Vianello. 'The woman who spoke to me, his mother-in-law, is an ex-neighbour of mine,' he told him, almost embarrassed by how quintessentially Venetian the explanation was. Or typical of any small town, anywhere. People left traces of memory on others as they passed through life: their friends from school, the family doctor, the priest of the parish church, the first person they kissed, or married. Everyone was witness to the behaviour of others and grew up watching them behave well or badly, spend their time in good or bad company, succeed or fail at school or work or love. Long before computer chips could collect someone's personal data, their neighbours did. The difference was that neighbours and friends knew the reasons for the divorce, the unfinished degree, the move to a smaller apartment, the lost job, while the chips could provide only the written records. Chips read the documents; friends try to read the heart.

'Sounds ridiculous, doesn't it?' Brunetti asked. 'I've seen her a dozen or so times over the years, although we never did much more than say hello and ask about the other's family. But as soon as she told me she hoped I could help her, I didn't have a choice, or felt I didn't.'

'Why?' Vianello asked.

Feeling not a little bit foolish, Brunetti said, 'Because her mother was good to mine.'

Vianello's face lit up with understanding and he said instantly, 'I hope you aren't waiting for a better reason.'

That was all the encouragement Brunetti needed. 'I told her I'd look into it,' he said, trying to make it sound as non-committal to Vianello as he'd tried to make it to Elisabetta.

Brunetti repeated what Elisabetta had told him: her daughter Flora's marriage had been happy until her husband began bringing something dark back to their home from work. Or perhaps, he paused to add, from something or somewhere else. Or someone.

Brunetti said nothing that could suggest an opinion or suspicion, merely repeated with almost stenographic accuracy what Elisabetta had told him about Enrico's early work setting up his father-in-law's charity before leaving to attend to his own growing practice. When he got to the part about Enrico's putting his hands on Flora and repeated what he'd said, Vianello interrupted to ask, 'Who's he afraid of?'

'I have no idea,' Brunetti said. 'Apparently neither does his wife, nor his mother-in-law.'

'But he believes he and his wife will be in danger if they talk about it?'

'It would seem so,' Brunetti answered.

Vianello asked, 'Does he know she's told her mother?' Then, before Brunetti could answer, the Ispettore went on, 'Worse, will he learn that her mother told the police?'

'I don't know,' Brunetti hedged.

Vianello dismissed that with a wave of his hand, saying, 'You've told Griffoni and you've told me, so now three of us know about it, as well as her mother.' Vianello slid the newspaper back and removed the file from on top of it, giving both of them another chance to see the four faces smiling at them from wherever death had taken them. The Ispettore tapped his finger just below the line of photos and said, 'Once that many people know about something, it's only a short time before we'll see a story about it here.'

Brunetti had to admit that his friend was right, if only in theory. 'That's why I want to find a light-handed way to ask about him,' he said.

Vianello slid the newspaper aside and said, 'Tell me again who they are, and I'll have a look at what I can find.'

'His name is Enrico Fenzo, and his wife is Flora del Balzo. He's an accountant and she's a veterinarian. Her parents are Elisabetta Foscarini and Bruno de Balzo; they live in Campo San Giovanni e Paolo.' Vianello wrote their names and addresses in his notebook.

If he viewed curiosity about Elisabetta Foscarini's son-in-law as an infection, Brunetti could see it had already begun to spread. Questions from the police were often the first germs, and from there the infection spread exponentially to those who were questioned, then to the relatives and friends they told about it, who then mentioned it to people they knew. Sooner or later, it would pass to a person who was peculiarly at risk from the disease. Some were struck down; others paid legal doctors to find a cure.

Vianello broke into Brunetti's reverie by asking, 'Do you have any idea of what the trouble might be?'

'None.'

Vianello sat quietly, nodding repeatedly, as though having a conversation with himself, then broke it off to ask, 'This isn't official, is it?'

'It's just a favour for a friend. We shouldn't have to spend a lot of time on it,' Brunetti said, only then realizing how casually he had assumed that Vianello would want to help. 'I'd like to find out what's bothering or frightening him, then tell his mother-in-law, and let them work it out themselves.'

'Sounds easy.'

'Oh, stop it, Lorenzo,' Brunetti said. 'I don't much want to do this, and before you point it out to me, yes, I know I'm willing to involve other people: you and Claudia.'

'And probably Signorina Elettra,' Vianello said amiably.

Brunetti put his elbow on the desk and cradled his forehead in his hand. 'It's already out of control, isn't it?'

Instead of answering, Vianello smiled and rubbed his feet on the floor under his desk, as though he were preparing to charge across the arena. 'It's better than sitting here and brooding about what might have been done to stop those kids from being killed,' he said, nodding his chin at the newspaper.

Brunetti smiled and shook his head. 'All right, Lorenzo. Let's do it this way: I'll try to find out anything there is to find out about Fenzo's clients, and you – but not with Signorina Elettra – see what you can find out about him.'

7

Uncertain about what to say next, Brunetti made a humming noise, the sort old people make when they want to keep their place in a conversation but don't know how to do it.

Vianello waited. Brunetti stopped making the noise and asked, 'All right?'

Vianello picked up a pencil and began to draw small triangles in the lower margin of *Il Gazzettino*. Each one grew minimally smaller, all of them connected by the same baseline. When he reached the right side of the page, he set the pencil down and, making no attempt to disguise his lack of interest, asked, 'Do we include this charity he helped set up?'

Brunetti nodded.

Vianello pushed back in his chair and said, 'There must be information online about how to set one up. And a central office where charitable institutions are registered once they're approved by whatever office sees to that. And their financial records have got to be stored somewhere, at the national level, or by province.' He took up the pencil again and began to fill in the empty spaces of the triangles, being very careful to remain within the lines.

Eyes on the paper, Vianello went on, 'You know what it is to try to do something simple …' His hand stopped moving as he searched for the proper words. 'Install or cancel a landline, or get the gas hooked up in a new apartment.' That said, Vianello returned to the remaining triangles.

Brunetti waited, although he knew where this was going.

'I'm trying,' Vianello said, 'to suggest how difficult it must be to set up a non-profit organization and to do it online, especially one that operates in a different country.' He looked at Brunetti and gave a shake of his head. 'Think of the work and the expense of it.'

Brunetti was about to comment but decided not to, aware of how little computer credibility he had.

Vianello smiled and returned to his triangles. 'Before you begin, let me have a look online: the information has to be some-where.' In a much warmer voice, he said, 'Let me do it, Guido. It'll be easier.'

Helpless before the kindness with which Vianello stated this truth, Brunetti could only nod.

Vianello filled in the last triangle, set the pencil down, and got to his feet. He bent over his desk, supporting himself with his splayed palms.

'I don't know how the parents will bear it,' Vianello said, as if in answer to a question. 'They weren't even twenty yet, not one of them.'

Brunetti found no words. One of the officers on the other side of the room slapped the man next to him on the shoulder and laughed: both noises seemed inordinately loud to Brunetti. He walked around behind Vianello, paused long enough to place his hand fleetingly on his friend's arm, and went back to his office.

Inside, he called down to the office at the entrance.

'*Sì*, Commissario?' Pendolini answered.

'Is Pucetti on duty today?'

'He's on the morning shift, Dottore. He got here at eight.'

'Would you see if you can find him and ask him to come up to my office?'

'Of course,' Pendolini said and replaced the phone.

Habit took Brunetti to the window, which he left open for a few minutes while he went back to his desk and turned on his computer. He was about to take his place in front of it, when some papers on his desk fluttered into the air and started chasing one another to the ground.

Brunetti hurried to close the window, came back, and went down on one knee to start picking up the papers. 'Signore?' he heard from the door.

Glancing up, he saw Pucetti in full uniform, pistol in place, missing only his hat. 'Come in, Pucetti, and have a seat,' Brunetti said, picking up the last papers and slapping them back on his desk. He pushed himself to his feet with one hand and went behind the desk and sat. He noted that it was only then that Pucetti allowed himself to walk over to the chair in front of Brunetti's desk and sit.

Not wanting to spend more time on something he already regretted agreeing to do, Brunetti said, 'I've a favour to ask you, Pucetti.'

'Yes, sir?' Pucetti asked, his curiosity audible.

'It's something that has nothing to do with any of the cases we're investigating now.'

'That's fine, sir. I'm happy for anything that's different from the usual routine.'

'I'm not sure how different this will be,' Brunetti said. 'Except that you'll be out of uniform.'

'Does that mean it's personal, sir?' Pucetti could not keep the eagerness from his voice, though his face remained calm.

Brunetti smiled. This would not be the first time he'd enlisted Pucetti in something that was not an ... official investigation. Surely, 'personal' would do as a description. 'Well, it is related to the Questura,' he said. 'I had a conversation with someone who fears that a person she knows might be in danger; I told her I'd try to find out if there is any reason she should be troubled.'

'I see,' Pucetti said softly. 'What is it you'd like me to do?' Somehow, a notebook and pen had appeared in his hands.

'I'm interested in two people: Enrico Fenzo, an accountant, and Flora del Balzo, a veterinarian who works on Murano. I'd like you to get an idea of what their neighbours think of them. I'm interested to know if either of them has been behaving strangely. Worried, preoccupied: that sort of thing.'

'Nothing more specific than that, Commissario?' When Brunetti did not answer, Pucetti added, 'It might help me ask the right questions.'

Brunetti smiled and answered, 'I'm not sure there *are* any right questions, Pucetti.' In the face of Pucetti's continuing silence, he added, 'Think of it as a fishing expedition. I don't know what fish you're looking for, so I can't tell you what bait to use.'

Pucetti looked up, surprised, and smiled. 'When would you like me to begin, Commissario?'

'Why not this afternoon? You can leave a few hours early: tell Pendolini I've sent you on a special assignment, and he's to check you out at the normal time.'

'Isn't that against the rules, sir?' Pucetti asked nervously.

Brunetti smiled again. 'It's against the rules of the Questura, yes. But Pendolini is someone who makes his own rules.'

It was Pucetti who smiled then, and opened his mouth to speak, but closed it and sat up straight in his chair.

'You were going to say?' Brunetti asked pleasantly.

He watched Pucetti's face while the young man thought about how to answer. Tell the truth and presume too much? Say nothing and give the appearance of thick-headed obedience?

'Like Signorina Elettra?' Pucetti asked.

Brunetti smiled before he thought he had best not do so. 'You think she makes her own rules?' he asked.

'Yes, sir,' the young officer answered instantly.

'Do you approve?'

'It's not for me to approve or not, sir,' was Pucetti's self-effacing response, after which he added, 'The fact that we profit from what she does makes it difficult to decide, at least for me.'

Brunetti did not want to get himself involved, at least not with a person so much younger than himself, in a discussion of whether the end justified the means. His opinion of that, he knew, had changed in the last few years, and he had grown more suspicious of the desire to expand the limits of the permissible. Few people ever admitted to selfish aims; most were persuaded that they acted from noble motives, no matter how foul their behaviour, how base their goal.

'I see,' Brunetti said. He pulled some papers towards himself, glanced at them and then back at the young officer, and added, 'I don't think there's a law – even a rule – that forbids a police officer who is not wearing his uniform from stopping in a bar and starting a conversation with the people there.'

Not allowing space even for a comma after what his superior had just said, Pucetti finished the sentence: 'Nor from going into a tobacco shop to charge up his Carta Venezia and asking – in Veneziano – if his friend Enrico Fenzo still lives in the neighbourhood.'

'Indeed,' Brunetti said.

Pucetti got to his feet smiling, wished the Commissario a good day, and left, leaving Brunetti to wonder if anyone he trusted at the Questura was still capable of obeying the rules.

It was less than an hour before Vianello returned, knocking and entering without being told to do so. He had some sheets of paper in his hand and eagerness writ large on his face.

Not bothering to speak, Brunetti raised his hand and waved Vianello over to the desk, where he kept hold of the papers and sat facing Brunetti.

'Tell me,' Brunetti said, not looking at the papers.

'I found the rules for creating an ONLUS,' Vianello began. When Brunetti started to speak, Vianello raised a hand, palm towards Brunetti, as though he were a traffic warden commanding him to STOP.

'I thought it would be complicated, the way things always are. Especially for an organization that would be giving money away and not making a profit.'

'Which means not paying taxes,' Brunetti said.

Vianello ignored the comment and said, '*Organizzazione Non Lucrativa di Utilità Sociale.* I never knew what the letters stood for,' he admitted. '"Non Profit-Making and of Social Usefulness".' He shook his head, as at the sound of a remark he didn't understand. 'It's like something from the sixties.' He gave Brunetti a long look and asked, 'When's the last time you heard anyone talking about "social usefulness" as though they believed in it?'

Brunetti smiled. 'I hear it often from my children.'

That stopped Vianello, but only for a moment. 'So do I, but do you ever hear it from adults?' he asked, sweeping the possibility out of the conversation, perhaps out of the room.

Brunetti disturbed the dust by saying, 'Some. Yes.'

That caused Vianello to pause and reflect, then, apparently deciding to ignore Brunetti's comment, he returned to the topic at hand. 'It's easy to set one up. Anyone can do it in min—' he began, but after hearing the first syllable of 'minutes', he veered around the word and changed it to, 'minimal time.'

'That means?'

'Well, I didn't actually go through the process,' Vianello said, and looked up to smile. 'But I did read all of the instructions, and then I called a friend who works in the Ufficio delle Entrate in Udine and asked him if what I was reading was the truth.'

'And he said?'

'He said it was perfectly true. It's been made very easy to set up an organization like this, be given tax-free status, and then off you go to save the world.'

'Or your small part of it?'

Vianello nodded and said, 'If you prefer.'

Although his friend hardly needed to be prodded, Brunetti asked, 'What else did you learn?'

This summoned the papers from Vianello's lap. He took his glasses from his pocket and put them on, managing to avoid glancing at Brunetti as he did so. He looked at the top two pages and slid them in turn towards Brunetti, saying, 'These are the forms necessary for opening an ONLUS. Form one – only one page – requires details of the age and residence of the person wanting to open the ONLUS. Form two – also only one page – the name and details of the purpose and function of the ONLUS, and, again, of the person who is opening it.'

Brunetti glanced down and saw the standard government forms with spaces left blank for information. 'Pages three and four,' Vianello went on, shoving two more pages across the desk, 'are the instructions for the preceding two pages.' These, Brunetti saw as they came sliding to a stop in front of him, looked at first like computer code, although the letters became comprehensible when he put on his reading glasses. Brunetti paused, returned his attention to the first page of the instructions, and realized that, even though the individual phrases were comprehensible, the paragraphs were not. Government forms, indeed.

'And this is the last of it – five more pages – the forms that can be used to self-declare in place of having a notary fill them out on your behalf. It seems simple enough: explain what the organization will do, who the founding members are, and how the money will be raised.'

'That's all you have to do?' Brunetti asked, pointing towards the few papers Vianello held.

'It would seem so,' Vianello said and put the papers back in order. 'I've read through all of these pages, and it looks to me as if anyone who is the least familiar with bureaucratic language would easily be able to understand and complete the forms.'

Brunetti said, 'I assumed you'd need a lawyer or a notary to start one, or at least have one on the board.' He shook his head in wonderment. 'Anything else?'

'I found its name,' Vianello said and smiled.

'Which is?'

'Belize nel Cuore.'

Brunetti put his right hand over his eyes and sat quietly for a moment. Finally he removed his hand and said, in a voice so moderate it surprised even himself, 'I suppose that's what you have to do: make people put Belize in their hearts.'

'Excuse me?' a confused Vianello asked.

'Marketing,' Brunetti said, using a word now as omnilingual as 'taxi' or 'pyjama'.

'But it's a charity,' Vianello said.

'Even more necessary, then,' Brunetti answered.

Vianello said nothing for a long time and then surprised Brunetti by saying, 'Four Paws Rescue, Happy Paws Shelter, Best-Friend Refuge.'

'What are those?'

'I just made them up. Names for dog shelters. If the places that save dogs can have names like that, then why not those that save people? They give the same suggestion of happiness and virtue.' Then, after a reflective pause, he added, 'Or maybe it's just a declaration of the truth. You have to have strong feelings about people to be motivated to try to save them.'

8

Brunetti pushed himself back in his chair and crossed his legs. 'Tell me more about Belize nel Cuore,' he asked, pronouncing the name as though it were a perfectly normal phrase.

Vianello pulled out his notebook and paged through it. Brunetti saw him raise a finger to his mouth, preparing to lick it, then abruptly stop his hand halfway and return it to the upper right-hand corner and continue to flip through the pages one by one.

He stopped and bent the pages back, bracing the notebook on his thighs. 'Its legal seat is here: it was constituted three years ago, by Bruno del Balzo. The other members of the board are Luigino Guidone and Matteo Fullin.' He looked at Brunetti and asked, 'You know either of them?'

'Not Guidone,' Brunetti answered immediately. 'But I've met Fullin.' He tried to remember when or where, but the scene refused to come into focus and remained just out of his sight. He shrugged and said, 'Maybe it will come to me.'

Neither man spoke for a long time, until Brunetti, assuming that the papers on his desk were copies for him, pulled them towards him. 'Thanks, Lorenzo.' He looked at the top page with a certain lack of interest and said, 'I've asked Pucetti to go over to Fenzo's neighbourhood and ask a question or two.'

Smiling, Vianello said, 'He's very good at that sort of thing. Has a face and a manner you'd trust.' Then, changing to a heavier voice, he added, 'Never know he's a cop.' At Brunetti's smile, the Ispettore continued, 'What's he going to be, an old school friend from the days when they both played soccer?'

Brunetti's smile grew as he answered. 'Pucetti will give himself an identity that the person he's talking to is likely to approve of.'

'Little old ladies wouldn't be safe around him,' Vianello volunteered in tribute to Pucetti's skill as a liar.

'The ladies or their pensions?'

'Their pensions. He'd have them in five minutes, to send to schoolchildren in Calabria or for the people in Irpinia.'

The name of the second place surprised Brunetti, as if a ghost from the events of forty years before had walked into the room. How can we joke about things like this? Brunetti wondered. Are we so debased that the disappearance of billions from the relief money meant for earthquake victims is no longer a crime, nor even a scandal, but some sort of grotesque metonym for business as usual?

Brunetti looked at his friend, sure that he was thinking the same, their memories captured by those grim events. His mind flailed about for a way to free them both from yet another grim tale.

Vianello was there first, and most likely for the same reason. 'Do we have a sell-by date on this favour you're doing?'

'Meaning?' Brunetti asked and realized immediately how provocative his response must have sounded.

Vianello made no attempt to disguise his impatience. 'How long do we ask questions about these people before we pack it in and admit we can't find anything, and you tell your friend she has to take care of her own problems?'

Well, he had a point, didn't he? The city had larger problems, yet Brunetti was trying to use the police to salve a friend's uncertainties.

'Let's give it a couple of days?' Brunetti said, turning it into a question.

It took Vianello some time to decide. 'All right. But if something else unquestionably criminal happens, we switch our attention to that.'

'All right,' Brunetti agreed and decided it was time to go home for lunch.

The meal, a risotto with radicchio di Treviso he'd been requesting for days, both delighted and satisfied him. Paola placed a large platter of cheese on the table after it, explaining that she'd been delayed after her morning class and had only had time to get this on the way home. The lingering effect of the risotto made forgiveness easy for them all, especially when one of the cheeses was a hunk of Gorgonzola, wrapped in an icing of mascarpone.

Brunetti left Paola and Raffi to do the dishes – his turn that week – and went into the living room to read for a while before going back to work. That week's *Espresso* carried an article about the 'anniversary' of the earthquake, perhaps explaining why Vianello had made reference to it. Brunetti noticed that the magazine had put the word within quotation marks. His reading was interrupted by Chiara's arrival.

'*Papà*, can I ask you something?'

'Um?' he asked, glancing up from the photos, their horror unchanged even after four decades.

'What do you think the greatest Greek play is?'

'Huh?' he asked, having thought she'd ask for an advance on her allowance. 'Greatest Greek play?'

'Yes.'

He thought a bit and finally answered, 'That's a bit like asking what your favourite thing to eat is. Today, I'd choose *risotto alla trevigiana*, but if you were to ask me in June, I'd make a different choice.'

She came over and flopped down beside him. He set the magazine face down on the table in front of him and put his arm around her shoulders.

'I thought you were going to hit me up for ten euros,' he said, following that with a wary, 'That'd probably be a lot easier.'

'Than choosing a play?'

'Than limiting it to one,' he said. He moved his arm up to the back of the sofa and turned towards her. 'How come you're asking?' he enquired, though it had to be for her Greek class.

'The prof's asked us all to name our favourite play, then he'll choose a scene from the one most of us name – whichever one it is – and we'll look closely at that one scene.'

'In Greek?'

'Of course,' she said, then asked, 'Didn't you read them in Greek when you were in school?'

'Just one. I think the professor thought any more than that would have been too difficult for us.' After a moment, he smiled and said, 'And he was right: they're hard going. I've tried since then to read them in Greek, but I never really feel the power.'

She smiled and put her hand to his cheek. 'But you know enough to know the power is there, don't you?'

Brunetti said, almost embarrassed to confess, 'If you read them carefully, even in Italian, you really can't escape feeling some of the power. It comes through.'

'You really mean that, don't you, *Papi*?' It was the name she called him during their most serious conversations, and he joyed in the sound of it.

'Yes, I do.'

'So what's your favourite play?'

'Can I cheat and have three?'

'For the price of one?' she asked.

He laughed, as he was sure she intended him to. 'If you'll allow, then I'd say the *Oresteia.*' He had reread the plays only a year before and had been overwhelmed by the modernity of their concerns: the roles and rights of women, the source and purpose of justice, how to punish crime.

'And which scene do you think is most important?'

Not because he suspected she wanted him to give her an answer so she could pass it on to her teacher but because she really wanted to know, Brunetti said, 'There are too many, *stella mia.* There's Clytemnestra's opening speech when she welcomes Agamemnon home; her back and forth with him, when he shows his vanity and his ridiculous pride; even her sparring with the chorus, or when she talks to Cassandra. Every time she opens her mouth, she's in charge of things.' He stopped for a moment, then confessed to his only daughter: 'I've always loved Clytemnestra, and each time I read the play, I love her a little more.'

'Love?' Chiara asked.

Caught up short by the speed with which her question came, he paused and thought for a while, then said in a softer voice, 'Maybe it's not love, but admiration and respect and sympathy.' He put his hands behind his head and locked his fingers together, staring across the room and across the rooftops. 'No, it's not love, not really. There's somehow too much of her: she's too big, too untamed.' A gull flew up and landed on the railing of the terrace, and for a minute he feared it was Clytemnestra come to listen to what he had to say about her.

'And I'd always be afraid of her, I suppose,' Brunetti finally confessed.

'Why?' Chiara asked in a rapt voice.

'Because she's so much stronger than I am.'

*

Returning to the Questura, Brunetti was trapped: for two days, he'd been avoiding a favour asked of him by a friend, a commissario in Mestre. He had asked Brunetti to read a copy of the original arrest report filed by two of his officers who had later been accused of having beaten the suspect for trying to sell drugs near a middle school. The request was informal: Commissario Tamiello had sent the copy by courier, but his name was not on the package. Clearly, then, he was requesting Brunetti's opinion of the report and whether Brunetti thought charges against the pusher should be pursued.

The first thing Brunetti noticed was the absence of the official Questura stamp, always put on reports upon submission, bearing time and date, arresting officers, crime, and the name of the accused. All of this absent, Brunetti had only the report to read, which began, *Because he looked like a North African, we decided to check to see if he was there to sell drugs,* and got no better in its two brief pages. No further reason was given to explain why the officers chose to stop and question, then search, the accused, nor was there a witness to verify how close the pusher had been to the school. The fact that he was discovered to be carrying more than a hundred capsules that proved to contain amphetamines, LSD and methadone, as well as thirteen plastic vials containing cocaine and heroin, was rendered useless as evidence, Brunetti realized, by and from the opening sentence.

He lowered his forehead to his desk and moved it from side to side, as if it were a blotter and he was wiping up the ink used on the report. Rather than put his opinion in writing, Brunetti looked through his phone contacts and dialled Tamiello's *telefonino* number. Tamiello answered with his name.

'*Ciao*, Pietro,' Brunetti said in a cheery voice. 'I thought I'd give you a call and see how you are.'

'Ah, *ciao*, Luciano,' Tamiello answered, leading Brunetti to wonder who might be interested in Tamiello's phone calls, and why. 'How are you?' his colleague asked.

There followed an exchange of meaningless pleasantries and then Tamiello asked, 'Did you watch that film on Netflix I told you about?'

Making his voice as disgruntled as he could, Brunetti said, 'Yeah, I watched it, but I didn't like it very much.' Then, as though the thought had just come to him, Brunetti explained, 'Maybe it was the opening scene that ruined it for me: really clumsy, I thought.' After a short pause, he added, 'Sort of gave the whole story away.'

'Ah,' Tamiello said, drawing the sound out. 'That's what I thought, too. But I did find some of the later scenes interesting.'

'Useless, Pietro. I've watched other films like that, and none of them has ever been any good at all after an opening scene like that. Frankly, it ruined the film for me.' He allowed a moment of reflection to pass, waiting for a response from his colleague and trying to think of a way to continue phrasing his opinion in the language of Cinecittà.

Into Tamiello's continuing silence, Brunetti said, 'Lousy script-writer, I'd say.' He was careful to use the sort of voice that made it clear he had no more patience for the subject. 'I wouldn't tell any of my friends to watch it.'

'Oh, well, we can't always like the same things, I suppose,' the other commissario said with embarrassed joviality. 'But I hope you'll still try to watch any films I recommend?'

'A suggestion from you, Pietro, is an order,' Brunetti said with a laugh, then said goodbye and put down the phone.

After he hung up, Brunetti couldn't help but think about what was going on in Mestre. The withdrawal of lockdowns and curfews and the return to something approaching normal life had – as Brunetti had feared – opened the dam and allowed drugs to start flooding back into the city.

Always attuned to changes in the mood of the market, drug dealers had quickly realized the advantageous commercial consequences of a year of continual stress. When the numbers of infections increased, so had the need to find drug-induced solace in what seemed like the Valley of the Shadow of Death. When the numbers decreased, what better way to celebrate the possible return to life than with a little of this or a lot of that? Even now, with things calmed down, the stress, it seemed to Brunetti, had not disappeared, nor had the desire to seek the comfort of narcotics.

Brunetti had been born before drug use had become widespread in Italy and thus his taste for pleasure did not include them. His immunization resulted not only from the year of his birth but from his family's relative poverty. He'd passed through his youth not being able to afford drugs and had reached adulthood without having formed an interest in them. He'd spent part of his professional life seeing their effect on people's lives and now lived with the fear that his knowledge and his own antipathy towards drugs might not suffice to shield his children from their allure.

To distract himself from brooding, Brunetti decided to begin doing the fair share he had promised Vianello and have a look at Fenzo's clients. Although he and Ottavio Pini hadn't spoken for at least a year, he still had his number and dialled it.

When Pini answered, saying hello and asking Brunetti how he was and where he'd been, Brunetti said, '*Ciao*, Ottavio, here in the city, protecting you and all good citizens.'

Pini laughed, probably never having been called a good citizen before, and said, 'Good to hear your voice, Guido,' sounding as though he meant it. 'What can I do for you?'

'Couldn't I be calling just to find out how you are?' Brunetti was careful to make himself sound like an offended teenager.

'Yes. And I could be the President of the Republic.' Pini let a few beats pass and added, 'But I'm not.'

Brunetti decided not to spend time sparring with Pini, something they'd both enjoyed in the past. Jokes were harder to make, now. 'All right, and I really don't want to waste your time with—'

'The restaurant's been closed for two weeks,' Pini interrupted, 'so I've got lots of time to waste.'

'I didn't know that, Ottavio.' These were strange times, and many people still did not feel comfortable eating in a restaurant among strangers. But time had passed, and things were better, and surely there were enough tourists in the city to keep most restaurants open. It made no sense that one as good as Ottavio's would be closed.

Pini was an old friend and so Brunetti could ask, 'What happened?'

'The usual mess,' he answered, but then paused and corrected himself. 'It's a mess, but it's not usual.'

'What is it?'

Pini let a long time pass before he said, 'You know the restaurant?'

Brunetti grunted.

'I've got twenty-one tables inside and five out on the pavement. It took me years to get permission for the *plateatico*, but having the outside tables adds at least a third to what I make every day during the summer and even now, when people still want to eat outside.' Pini stopped and then said, sounding weary, 'You don't want to listen to this, Guido.'

'Pretend I do. Tell me anyway.'

'You know there's another restaurant on the other side of the *campo*?' Pini asked.

'The one next to the mask store?' asked Brunetti.

'Sweet Jesus, everything in this city is next to a mask store,' Pini said with some disgust.

Brunetti spared them both any comment.

'Anyway, the owner – he's just been there a year – applied for a permit for a *plateatico*, and because of the size of the *campo*, he was refused permission to put more tables outside. So one day, when I was still open, he called the *vigili urbani*, and when they responded, he pulled one of those folding rulers from his jacket pocket and measured how much space I was using for mine.' Brunetti heard Pini's voice growing tighter and faster.

'The back legs of the chairs at two tables were ten centimetres into the public space, and one table was half in the public space.' Pini took a few deep breaths and, after gaining control of his voice, continued. 'He had one of his waiters come over and take photos of him measuring, and he asked the *vigili* for their names.' Before Brunetti could comment, Pini said, 'They were in uniform, so their names were on their jackets anyway.' He stopped.

'What happened?'

'A week later, I got a letter from the Commune saying that there had been a complaint against me for "abuse of public space", and a case file had been opened, and until such time as the complaint was investigated and resolved, I was to close the restaurant.'

'You aren't joking, are you, Ottavio?' Brunetti asked.

'I wish.'

'What can you do?'

'Find a better lawyer,' Pini said bitterly, but quickly added: 'Forget I said that: mine's done everything he can, called in favours, no luck.' Pini paused, and when he continued, he sounded calmer. 'Apparently, there were a lot of complaints when the city changed the rules and allowed people to expand any *plateatico* by fifty per cent. A lot of people had the doors to their homes blocked by tables. So now, when there are few tourists and no real need for the outside spaces, they make a big show about how concerned they are about residents' rights ...' Here, Pini stopped to give a loud laugh. 'And that means they'll fine you for five centimetres and close you down for ten.' Suddenly the anger drained out of his voice and he said, 'No one knows what's going to happen, so no decisions are being made.'

'And you're closed?'

'And I'm closed,' Pini said with uncharacteristic resignation.

Before Brunetti could speak, Pini continued, 'This will pass, Guido. No one's sick, so it's just money.' Brunetti asked himself when he'd ever heard anyone in the city say something like that; the strange thing was that Pini sounded like he meant it.

'What is it you'd like to know, Guido?' he asked, sounding as though he'd be glad to talk about anything but his problem with the restaurant.

'It's about your *ragioniere*.'

'Enrico?' Pini asked, unable to hide his surprise. Then he asked, 'You still a policeman, Guido?'

'Yes. Why?'

'Because it is impossible that a policeman could ask me about Enrico. He could ask about a client, my barber, my wife, but not about Enrico.'

'You trust him that much?'

'More than I trust my clients or my wife. Maybe not as much as I trust my barber.'

'How long has Fenzo worked for you?'

'You should really ask how long I've worked for him.'

'Meaning?'

'Meaning that it is only by the grace of God that I am not in the hands of the Guardia di Finanza, being tortured in their cellars – even though there aren't any cellars – to tell them where

I've put the money I stole from the government in the years before Enrico started to work for me.'

'Bad?'

'Hopeless. I hired a cousin.' Pini's voice deepened and he said, 'My wife told me not to. My wife told me not to. My wife told me not to. But I did.'

'And?'

'And he cheated the state and he cheated me, and I'm sure he cheats every one of his clients.'

'How'd you find out?'

'I had a call from a friend in the Guardia di Finanza, who told me that they had their eye on my *commercialista*, and it might be wise for me to think about making a change.' He paused and then said, with real affection, 'We were thrown out of catechism class together when we were twelve.'

Presumably, Brunetti assumed, this meant the man in the Guardia, not his *commercialista*. Before Brunetti could ask, Pini said, 'My friend told me to call Enrico, so I did.'

'And?'

'And he's probably saved my business. He showed me some of the stuff the other accountant was doing; I think about it sometimes and it still frightens me.'

'Frightens?'

'I'm responsible for whatever documents he sent them.' Then, in case Brunetti hadn't understood, he added, 'Legally responsible.'

Brunetti let some time pass before he repeated his question. 'How long has he worked for you?'

'Almost three years.' This time, it was Pini who let time pass before he spoke again. 'Why are you interested in him?'

'His name's come up in relation to another person, and we wondered about him.'

'I hope I've convinced you,' Pini said.

'Even more than that, Ottavio. Thanks, and good luck with the *plateatico*.'

Pini could do no more than sigh; Brunetti said goodbye and hung up.

9

Brunetti walked to the window and looked across the canal into the garden of the villa on the other side. The autumn had been unseasonably dry, and the vines that had taken up residence on the canal side of the brick wall surrounding the property extended themselves in parched desperation towards the water. Brunetti was struck by the resemblance between the vines, exposed to the sun almost all day, every day, and *The Raft of the Medusa*. The human limbs in the foreground of the painting, like the vines on the wall, fell weakly towards the water, while the figures behind stretched towards a glimpse of what might be a boat, a speck of land, or yet another swiftly arriving wave, bent on their destruction.

How much worse the vines looked than the men on the raft, even though the accounts of the incident that inspired the painting spoke of dehydration and starvation. Each time he'd seen the painting, Brunetti had looked, but looked in vain, for signs of dehydration or starvation, only to detect, instead, a triangle of well-muscled torsos, arms, and legs rising up in a frenzy of pennant-waving. But artists, he had long since concluded, were rather like politicians in their interest in the tasteful appearance of truth rather than in the truth itself.

While these thoughts were running through his mind, they stumbled against a faint flash of memory of the name 'Fullin'. He lowered himself into his chair and stared at the doors of the *armadio* where he stuffed boots, umbrellas, and coats, hoping that the memory would be easier to open than the door to the wardrobe. He knew it was some years since he'd heard the name, perhaps at a dinner, perhaps at a meeting of some sort. Other people had been present, men and women both, and there had been a particularly robust Montepulciano.

The memory of the wine brought back the dinner, and that returned Brunetti to the scene and the woman sitting on his left, a woman with an unlikely job. What was it? Guns? Judo? He stared at the doors of the wardrobe and waited, as it were, for the woman to appear. He knew that if he just waited and stared at the doors ...

Fencing. That was it. She was a fencing coach at an American university, one of the good ones, but he could no longer remember which. She'd come to Venice – this reminded him that the dinner had been at his parents-in-law's home – to visit her family and pay her respects to her old maestro, a man now in his eighties who still taught fencing over near Sant'Alvise.

He recalled what she'd said of him. 'First we shook his hand and said, *"Buon pomeriggio, Maestro,"* and then we went and stood and waited for him to tell us what to do, whom to partner with for practice.'

He remembered the way her voice had changed when she spoke of her maestro, the reverence she paid him with every word. 'No talking. If we did, he gave a glance, and the boy, or girl, never spoke out of turn again. In fact, I remember two boys who started to cry when he gave them that look.' She picked up her glass then and held it for a long time. 'It was wonderful, what he could do, how he taught us. He never raised his voice, he seldom smiled. He was ...' She sipped at her wine, set the glass down, and looked at Brunetti. 'He was fierce.'

Smiling then, Brunetti had asked, 'And are you?'

She laughed outright and smiled to answer the question. 'Yes. My students are terrified of me.' She spoke in such a pleasant, warm voice that Brunetti found it hard to believe her.

'I'm savage with them, believe me. No one talks in my class, and no one ever criticizes another student, even from another school. Respect, respect, respect. If they don't have that, I don't want them in my class.'

Suddenly, an elderly, broad-shouldered man on the opposite side of the table who had said almost nothing at all during the dinner and displayed no interest in the people near him, save for a small woman who was clearly his wife, got to his feet. Brunetti was amazed at how long it took him to do it: not because he was in any way infirm but because there was so much of him to stand. He was almost two metres tall, Brunetti estimated, and stood straight to attention. Deeply tanned, with a broad forehead and a full head of white hair, he seemed even larger than he was. He reached down and picked up his knife and fork and, quite casually, as though he were in the habit of doing so, slipped them into the pockets of his jacket. In a low voice, audible in the silence that had fallen among those who had seen what he did, he spoke to the woman on his left. 'I want to go home, Antonia.'

The woman, white-haired and drawn, got to her feet: she stopped rising well before her head reached his shoulder. She put a hand on his arm.

'Of course, Matteo. It's very late and we shouldn't overstay our welcome, should we?'

The man shook his head and continued doing so until she reached up and put her hand on his cheek. 'Let's get our coats now, shall we?'

Before he could start to nod, she stepped back from the table and, hand now resting on his forearm, led him towards the door. Contessa Falier, Brunetti's mother-in-law, was already at the door, her face lit with a warm smile. Il Conte was speaking to a servant whose head was lowered to allow him to hear il Conte's orders.

When the servant nodded and walked away, il Conte approached the other three and took the man's hand in both of his, saying, 'My boat's just outside, Matteo: it'll take you home.' With a soft smile, he said, 'You're in sole command,' and lifted his right hand in a languid salute, the sort an officer would give to one who outranked him, but barely.

'Let me walk down with you.' Before either the man or his wife could object, la Contessa turned to the other woman, saying, 'Come along, Antonia. Let's find your coats. I think the weather's changing, and you'll be glad you wore them.'

Oh, how very English it was. No matter what happened, no matter how fraught a situation might appear, there was nothing like the weather to smooth things out. Commenting on the sudden drop in temperature, la Contessa led the small group from the room, and the conversation spent a minute or two pulling itself together and beginning again.

Later, when they were leaving, and Brunetti and Paola stood next to her parents at the door to the stairs, Brunetti said, 'You were both very kind to your friend.'

Paola's parents exchanged glances and la Contessa said, 'Ah, Matteo Fullin. His wife, Antonia, was one of the first people I met when I moved to Venice, and she was very kind to me. We've known them forever.' For a moment, Brunetti thought that was all she was going to say, but then she went on.

'Orazio and I try to invite them with people who've known them for as long as we have, so no one will say anything that will upset Matteo.' Then, smiling, she added, 'Antonia will send someone with the silverware tomorrow.' She pressed her lips together and grew serious. 'It's not the first time.'

Paola touched her mother's arm, saying, 'You told me about it when he was first diagnosed, but I had no idea he'd got so bad. I saw them on the street a few months ago, and he seemed ...'

Paola's voice trailed away, and Brunetti watched her replay the scene of their meeting. 'He didn't speak at all,' she said, obviously surprised not to have found this strange at the time. 'Antonia did all the talking.' Paola paused and made a helpless motion with her right hand. 'I had no idea,' she repeated, then, sounding almost resentful, 'Antonia didn't say anything about what was happening.'

La Contessa started to speak, paused, but must have decided to continue. 'That's because there's nothing to say, darling.'

She stood on tiptoe then to kiss her daughter and waited for Brunetti to bend down to kiss her goodnight. At the time, Brunetti had been struck by the fact that Paola had said nothing further while they walked home. He remembered, too, that la Contessa had been right: it had got much colder, and they were glad they'd worn their coats.

The doors to the wardrobe in his office remained closed, but the memory of Fullin's behaviour opened Brunetti's mind to possibility. He knew that certain forms of dementia were described as 'galloping', while others were more sedate in their devastation of memory, dignity, reason. They differed in terms of speed, but both were aimed at the same inexorable nothingness.

Fullin, he recalled, had been diagnosed not so long ago. But, from his experience with his mother, Brunetti knew that diagnosis took a long time to catch up with symptoms. 'Oh, I just can't remember anything any more.' 'Who was that woman who spoke to us in the supermarket?' 'I can't find my shoes.' 'Oh, did I leave the water running?'

In his mother's case, the symptoms had been snaking around in their lives for years before either he or his brother Sergio took serious notice of them. Wilful ignorance, protective stupidity, loving blindness. But then he'd been seconded to Livorno for two weeks, and when he returned to Venice, he'd noticed the mess in her kitchen, the food stains on her clothing, and her sullen answers to his questions.

He pulled away from his thoughts and started to dial Signorina Elettra's number but hesitated when he realized it would be more opportune to go and speak to her. On the way downstairs, he thought of the avenues that might lead to the discovery of medical information about Matteo Fullin, but beyond the medical files at the Ospedale Civile – if he was a patient there – he could think of nothing.

She was at her desk, gazing attentively at its surface. At first glance, it seemed to be empty of everything save her computer, which was shoved to the back. The door was ajar, and so as not to startle her, he tapped a few times.

She looked up, smiled, and returned her gaze slowly to the surface of her desk. Brunetti approached, curious now, and as he drew closer he saw a small black object, about half the size of a stick of chewing gum, though thicker, lying on the dark wood.

Before he could say anything, she held up her right hand, then moved it towards her face and held her index figure upright in front of her mouth. He stopped and opened both palms in a visual question.

Signorina Elettra pointed her finger at the object, then poked it repeatedly at the space under her desk. Seeing that she had his complete attention, she pointed again at the black object, then to her mouth, which she moved in an exaggerated demonstration of speaking, before pointing again at the object.

Brunetti nodded and raised his hands helplessly in the air to ask her what she was going to do.

She picked up the object and held it with two fingers. She rolled her chair back very quietly and slipped her head and shoulders under the desk. Brunetti froze, not wanting to make a sound, or to hear one.

A few seconds later, she emerged, smiling, and said, 'Oh, Commissario Brunetti, I'm afraid I didn't hear you come in. I was trying to move my computer a bit to the left. Would you help me with it?'

'Of course, Signorina,' Brunetti said with the patently artificial delivery of the voice-overs in foreign films, every emotion raised by at least thirty per cent in an attempt to sound authentic.

Brunetti picked up the computer and moved it in her direction as she said, 'A bit to the left.' And then, 'Just a bit to the right, if you would.' And finally, 'That's perfect. Thank you so much.'

In a voice that emoted polite interest, she asked, 'Is there some way I can be of help, Commissario?'

'Yes,' he said, trying to think of something to tell her. Seeing that Patta's door was open, a sure sign that the Vice-Questore was not there, he asked, 'Would it be possible for me to have a word with the Vice-Questore?'

'Oh, I'm so sorry. He called earlier and said he wouldn't be in until late in the afternoon. He mentioned an appointment with the Prefetto.' She allowed some time to pass, as would be normal in a conversation like the one they were imitating, and then asked, 'Shall I tell him you'd like to speak to him?'

'No, that's not necessary,' Brunetti said. He reached into her waste-paper basket and pulled out an envelope. 'He mentioned that his tailor had closed his shop and asked if I could give him the name and number of my father-in-law's.'

He rustled the scrap of paper, held it flat on her desk, and wrote, *Help?*

Reading the message upside down, she smiled but said nothing.

Brunetti pulled the paper back and wrote, *Matteo Fullin – medical information – Alzheimer's?* Then he added, *For me.*

He slid the paper right across to her, and then, speaking clearly for the invisible listener to her conversations, said, 'Here's the name and number. He can use my father-in-law's name if he asks for a reference.'

After reading the message, she said primly, 'Thank you, Commissario. I'll see to this.'

'Oh, one moment,' Brunetti said and pulled the paper back towards him. 'Let me add his *telefonino* number, just in case.' He bent over the paper and added, *Other information, too.*

Signorina Elettra put a manicured finger on the paper, slid it back, turned it again and read the addition.

'Ah, yes,' she said, 'that's often more important and sometimes hard to find if you don't know the person and his friends.' Adopting an energetic tone, she said, 'I'll put this on the Vice-Questore's desk now, Signore.' She got to her feet and made a lot of noise pushing back her chair.

Leaving the paper on her desk, she started towards the door to Patta's office, and Brunetti returned to his. The first thing he did when he got there was pull back his chair and get down on his hands and knees at the back of his desk. He stuck his head inside the opening between the two rows of drawers and took a careful look at the wooden panels. Still not satisfied, he got back on his chair and pulled out each drawer, emptying their contents on his desk and stacking them on the floor beside him. He examined all of the drawers both inside and outside, then ran his hands along the wooden slats that held them in place.

There was nothing, certainly not anything that resembled the device he'd seen on Signorina Elettra's desk. He reinserted the drawers, crossed his legs, and sat back in his chair. The view from his window included a swatch of sky, and he stared at that, seeking an explanation.

Patta would not hesitate an instant, Brunetti was certain, to put some sort of surveillance device in his office, but the Vice-Questore would never dare to do the same to Signorina Elettra. Brunetti's superior had spent his years in Venice doing two things: lamenting his absence from Palermo, 'the most beautiful city in the world', and flattering, charming, and misleading his superiors into believing him to be an astute police officer and an inspiring leader of the men and women who worked for him.

In fact, Patta neither inspired nor led, but he had had the good fortune to find a secretary soon after taking over the position of Vice-Questore and the good sense to recognize her abilities. It would be an exaggeration to say that Signorina Elettra ran things; it would also be insulting to her, for it would suggest that she had somehow made her power evident. This was not the case, any more than the behaviour of the alpha meerkat is obvious when a cobra has to be chased away.

Patta thus excluded as the person who planted the device, Brunetti slid him from the category of perpetrator to that of victim and reconsidered possibilities. Access was far easier to obtain to Signorina Elettra's office than to Patta's, so anyone wanting to know what Patta was doing in his professional capacity would place it in his gatekeeper's desk.

Unless, of course, she was the intended target, which would suggest that the person who had placed it under her desk was curious to learn the extent of her influence upon Patta's official behaviour and decisions. Or, more interestingly, that the person was curious about the extent to which her skills were being used in pursuit of information to which she did not have legal access.

Brunetti uncrossed and recrossed his legs and returned his attention to the patch of sky visible from the window. To discover her methods would be to discover that she was committing, and recommitting, criminal actions. But there was no danger to her here, for the discovery of her illegal methods would have to be done by illegal methods. Thus – if Signorina Elettra was the target – the person was interested in her discoveries for some reason other than to stop her from achieving them.

Brunetti was struck by a sudden desire for a coffee, but he resisted it and vowed to sit there until he had a plausible explanation.

Why else would this person want to know to whom she spoke, and what she said to them? It is child's play to tap a phone: anyone who could have managed to plant the device could more easily have done the other instead. But much of Signorina Elettra's illegal searching was done in response to conversations she had in her office, conversations she had with him.

At no time during this thought process did Brunetti consider the possibility that her computer had somehow been hacked. Hackers could enter the Pentagon and stroll through its records. They could get into the financial records of the European Union and the World Bank or, for all Brunetti knew, into the Vatican's files about the criminal behaviour of its prelates.

But not into the computer that sat on Signorina Elettra's desk.

'Perhaps they're after me,' Brunetti said out loud, pleased with himself for having concluded his analysis. He got to his feet and went down to the bar on the corner for a coffee.

10

Brunetti was not much troubled by the discovery of the device planted in Signorina Elettra's office. He understood how deeply the impulse towards suspicion slept in the marrow of every Italian's bones. Did there not exist a word for it? *'Dietrologia'*: the study of what *really* lay behind any event. He was inclined to view the listening device as yet another manifestation of this desire to discover the Real Truth.

The news reports, the official explanation of any event, had only to be spoken or published for listeners and readers to begin speculating about what had *really* happened and what it *really* meant. Why had it proven so difficult/easy to apprehend the killer? Why were no/six autopsies performed on the victim? Why was no/so much money found in her accounts? Why had his briefcase/body never been found? Wasn't it his cousin/ brother who used to be the Minister of Education?

Brunetti suspected that this inability to trust was the ineluctable consequence of centuries of firm, unconsidered, and unquestioned religious faith, the sort that prevailed in Italy well into the last century. Until it didn't any more.

People who used to believe in God and the Pope and the Immaculate Conception – although Brunetti had never met a person who knew what that was – realized they didn't really believe any of it any more but had nothing else to believe in. God had proved very difficult to replace. There was the wealth brought by the economic boom, but subsequent events had proven that wealth was not eternal; there were new political parties, but everyone knew they were recycled and hardly new; there was 'wellness'/Pilates/yoga/a sprinkling of new cults, but they seemed to give little in return for all the time and money a person invested in them. God had filled so much space with so little effort.

He tried to think of who would be sufficiently curious about Signorina Elettra's conversations to risk placing that device beneath her desk: they would have to have entered and left her empty office at least twice. Most communication was by phone or, where documents had to be read, by email. Few people had the habit of consulting Signorina Elettra in her office. Seeking a historical parallel, Brunetti recalled that, in former times, few people had stopped in for a chat with the Sibyl.

Brunetti, who depended upon her talents, had always spoken to Signorina Elettra directly about those things he requested her to do that were – he fought his reluctance to use the correct word, but, aware that he was speaking to himself, decided to risk it – illegal. Over the years, her skills had increased in sophistication and breadth; her circle of contacts and colleagues had broadened and now included people who worked in various offices, libraries, state ministries, and archives. Brunetti had never learned the true names of any of them, although he had come to know and appreciate what they were capable of doing and had a few of whom he was particularly fond.

First among them was an ex-Monsignore – in honour of the rank he once held – defrocked and dismissed from the Vatican some years before, cast out without either explanation or permission to return to his office. Signorina Elettra, usually discreet about her sources, told Brunetti only that this prohibition had in no way discomfited the ex-Monsignore, who wore upon his chest a wooden crucifix made for him by an artisan in Trastevere, his memory stick always secreted in its hollow left crosspiece, the opening mechanism the nail driven through the right hand of the crucified Jesus.

Brunetti pulled his thoughts together and, ever more uncertain of the wisdom of doing a favour for a person who was not a friend and who had never really been one, decided that he would speak to one more person about Fenzo and, if nothing screamed at him, he'd call Elisabetta – or see her – and tell her that he could find nothing that confirmed her suspicions about her son-in-law.

He thought about the people who had been mentioned to him, drew a sheet of paper towards him and began to write their names at random places on the page. Elisabetta in the top-right corner, her husband in the bottom left. Her daughter, her son-in-law. Pini, the two board members, Fullin and Guidone. The optician in Barbaria delle Tole had turned out to be a dead end: the shop now sold masks. He studied the names on the page, trying to think of a way to draw a line connecting any two of them in an interesting way.

The only straight lines Brunetti could think of were those that led from Bruno del Balzo to Fullin and to Guidone. He found no landline listed for Luigino Guidone, nor was he listed in the file the police had of *telefonino* numbers.

Checking national files, Brunetti discovered that Guidone had never been arrested, nor owned or signed a contract to rent a house. He had attended no university and had not done military service.

Brunetti pulled out his phone and punched in his mother-in-law's number. La Contessa responded with, 'How sweet it is of you to call, Guido. How can I help you?'

Removing all surprise from his voice, Brunetti said, 'By not assuming I'd call you only to ask a favour.'

'Have you and Paola decided to get a divorce, then, and you're calling to let me be the first to know?'

He laughed out loud and said, 'Caught.'

'Tell me,' she said.

'I'd like you to introduce me to a friend of yours.'

His remark was followed by a long pause.

'May I stop by on my way home and explain?' he asked. 'It's complicated.'

'Of course,' she said, and then, 'Would you like to stay for dinner?'

'Thank you, Donatella, but we're already invited for dinner, and your daughter would ask for a divorce if I called her at this short notice to announce I'd accepted another invitation.'

This time la Contessa laughed and then asked, 'Would four-thirty be convenient? I have another appointment in the afternoon.'

'I'll see you then,' Brunetti said and hung up the phone.

He was on time. La Contessa, wearing a thick grey woollen sweater, black trousers, and a single strand of pearls, stood at the door to the room everyone referred to as 'La Sala dei Giochi', although it was more than a century since it had been used as a room for gambling. Il Conte's great-great-great-grandfather was said to have been addicted to gambling, as was, legend has it, every nobleman in the city. Jewels, bags of gold, even *palazzi* were won or lost on the turn of a card or the roll of the dice. Every noble family has its story to explain their vanished wealth: improvidence and stupidity are never among them.

The Falier family, instead, boasted of their ancestor's triumph at a game of Trappola, played, it was always explained, in this very room. Until the end of the game, the Sala dei Giochi, along with the rest of the building, had belonged to the last heir of the now extinct Pisani family. With the tabulation of the score, however, its ownership had passed to the head of the Falier family, owners of large expanses of land north of the city and a substantially smaller *palazzo* that was not on the Grand Canal.

Three months later, Giambattista Falier had moved his family into the larger *palazzo*, which was on the Grand Canal, having persuaded il Conte Pisani to accept the smaller building as consolation for having lost his family home. This offer had entered the spoken mythology of the city and was often pulled out to show the largesse of the families whose names were inscribed in the *Golden Book*, as well as the grace with which they sometimes consoled bad fortune.

La Contessa was in the small room she used for reading and seeing close friends. She'd had her hair cut since the last time Brunetti had seen her: it was now short as a boy's and startling in its whiteness. She went to meet him at the door and walked with him back to her chair, as if she feared he'd lose his way. Brunetti went automatically to the chair he always used when visiting her and was glad to see the tray holding a silver coffee pot and two small cups and saucers.

She took her usual place, sitting bolt upright, although there were two cushions leaning against the back of the chair. When Brunetti was seated, she poured them each a coffee and slid the sugar towards him.

He drank his coffee quickly and replaced his cup just as she took the first sip of hers. When she set the cup down, she said, 'Who is it you'd like to meet?'

Brunetti had never so much as considered not telling her the truth. He spent his career giving half-truths, dissimulating and misleading people, and as a kind of prophylaxis had vowed to himself years ago that he would never lie to anyone in his family.

'Your friend Antonia.'

'Matteo's wife?'

In response to her expression, Brunetti said, 'I'm interested in something her husband might be involved in.'

Her face changed, and her age surfaced for a moment, especially near her mouth, where the lines deepened. 'I don't think Matteo has ... much interest in anything any more, Guido.'

Brunetti nodded and said, 'I assumed that. I saw him here, at dinner, some time ago, and he seemed not in control of his ...'

'Mind?' she asked.

'No, not exactly. It was more that he seemed unable to control his impulses.' He thought it might help to say more, although it was nothing he liked talking about. 'I saw it in my mother: it took us some time before we learned how to distract her.' He let that register before adding, 'But as time passed, it became impossible to stop her. Once she got an idea in her head—'

'I never met her,' la Contessa interrupted to say, not mentioning that Brunetti's parents had arrived late at their son's wedding, sat in the back row, and then disappeared after the ceremony. 'From everything you've told me about her, I think we would have liked one another.'

La Contessa often surprised Brunetti, and so it was now. He spent some time searching for a diplomatic response and finally said, 'I'm not sure she would have been capable of liking you, Donatella.'

This time it was la Contessa who was surprised, and all expression left her face. 'I beg your pardon.'

'No, it's not what you're thinking. It's just that she was afraid of all this,' he said, waving a hand at the books, the paintings, the carpet beneath the low table.

'We wouldn't have had to meet here,' la Contessa said, sounding poignantly defensive.

He smiled to calm her and said, 'I'm not sure there exists a world where she would have been comfortable meeting you, Donatella.' Then, before she could be hurt again by what he said, he added, 'Although I suspect, if you'd been from the same ... background, you would have liked one another. You both have the same impulse to kindness.'

Her look was steady and long, and then she said, 'Tell me more about this business Matteo's involved in.' Then in what was perhaps an excess of correctness, she added, 'Or was involved in.'

Brunetti pushed himself back in his chair and crossed his legs. 'Three years ago, he became a member of the board of a charitable institution located in Belize. But registered and run from here.'

La Contessa nodded slowly to acknowledge having understood this, although her face suggested that the information puzzled her.

'The other member of the board is someone about whom I can find nothing and whose name I'd never heard: Luigino Guidone.'

She shook her head to show she didn't recognize the name. 'Don't you have the professional means to do this?' she asked.

'I do,' Brunetti said.

'Then why aren't you asking Signorina Elettra to do it?' la Contessa asked.

'Because what she finds for me is usually factual information: numbers, hidden ownership of companies and properties, criminal records. The institution exists, and I know who's in charge, and I know that Signor Fullin signed the papers establishing—' He stopped abruptly at the sight of her raised hand.

'Vice-Admiral Fullin. Guido,' she said, almost reprovingly. 'Weren't you told that when you were introduced to him?'

Brunetti thought back to the dinner and recalled that he had been delayed and had slipped into his place just as dinner was starting, leaving him no time but to give his surname and hear those of the people he didn't know, the Fullins among them.

'No, only his surname,' he said.

'Matteo's an old friend of the family,' she said, then quickly added, 'This one, the Faliers, not mine in Florence.'

'And the connection?'

'After the war, Orazio and he were in the same *liceo* for two years, but then Matteo transferred to the Naval Academy and spent his life in the Navy. By the time he retired, he was a vice-admiral, as I said, and still in charge of something called the San Marco Brigade. Divers and raiders, I think, and he was as tough as any one of them.' She paused a moment and said, 'You should have seen him thirty years ago: he could have put me on your back and tossed the two of us across the room.'

Brunetti entertained this idea for a moment and then asked, 'You mean he was violent?'

She laughed and said, '*Santo cielo*, Guido. Just the opposite. Antonia once said she never heard him raise his voice.' Again, before Brunetti could get there, la Contessa said, 'Of course, at work he was different.' A small smile appeared on her face; she leaned closer to Brunetti and said, 'Rather like you, dear.'

Brunetti waited until this remark had floated out of the room and then asked, 'When did he retire?'

'Oh,' she said and paused to remember. 'At least fifteen years ago. They were living in Rome, but they'd always kept the place here, so they came home.' After a moment, she added, in a much softer voice, 'Better they did.'

Then, in a brisk voice, she said, 'Why do you want to talk to her, Guido?'

He saw no reason not to tell her. 'I want to ask his wife if she thinks he was still able to understand what he was signing. Only someone very close to him can tell me that.' Not mentioning that Signorina Elettra was looking for Fullin's medical files did not count as lying, Brunetti told himself.

'And you want to use my friendship with his wife?'

Brunetti failed to disguise his shock. 'It's hardly betrayal, Donatella. In fact, it might be the opposite.'

'What does that mean?' she asked.

'If he was unable to understand what he was signing, then he's not responsible for how well the association is being run.' Vianello had shown him the contract establishing Belize nel Cuore, so he knew that board members were not legally liable for the activities of a non-profit organization, regardless of their mental state when they signed the papers. But Venice was a city where reputation had an inordinate importance, if not to a man whose mind was failing, then surely to his wife and family.

'That's what I want to find out,' he concluded.

'Why?' she asked.

Brunetti raised both hands in a sign of surrender. 'I have no real idea. I've only just heard about the organization.' He paused here to give her the chance to ask questions, but she said nothing. He noticed, however, that she had leaned back against the cushions behind her.

'When I learned that one of the board members was a man I'd met a year ago and whose condition then struck me as being ... serious, I thought I'd find out more about him.'

She smiled and asked, 'Is this how your mind works, Guido?'

'To be suspicious when things might be other than they appear?'

'You could call it that,' she said, still smiling.

He gave her question some thought and finally admitted, 'I suppose it does work like that.'

A peaceful silence fell between them. Brunetti turned a bit to his left and studied a portrait he had always admired of a woman said to be a female ancestor of Paola and the one thought to be responsible for his wife's blonde hair. There was a portrait in the dining room of yet another ancestor, this one with Paola's nose. How strange it had always been for him, to walk through the *palazzo* seeing bits and pieces of his wife.

'And if Matteo wasn't fully competent when he signed that contract, what will you do?' When Brunetti hesitated to answer, la Contessa added, 'I need to give Antonia a reason you want to talk to them.'

'I want to find out if someone asked him to sign a document he couldn't understand,' Brunetti said.

'So that's the person you'd then be interested in?'

Brunetti nodded.

'And then?'

'Then I'd try to find out why he asked the Vice-Admiral to join the board.' Brunetti let what seemed to him a long time pass and then said, quite without emotion but with belief, 'You don't do things like that to helpless people.'

'I see,' la Contessa answered, pushed herself away from the pillows and got to her feet. Brunetti started to stand, but she held up a hand to stop him. 'No, Guido. Stay here. I'm just going into the next room to phone Antonia.'

She put her hand on the back of his chair, as though to steady herself, and left the room.

11

Brunetti had nothing to read with him, not even *Il Gazzettino*, so he stood and walked over to the portrait of Paola's purported ancestor. He wasn't sure, but it probably was Venetian, as he'd always been told: he saw that in the straight cut of the woman's bodice, and the single-strand woven gold necklace, and there was, of course, the blondish hair. Brunetti had been told in school that Venetian women spent hours during the summer applying lemon juice to their hair and sitting in the sun, waiting for it to turn blonde, but he had always found it hard to believe.

Didn't they have houses to run, even the wealthy ones? And where did they get all the lemons? He walked closer to the portrait and took out his reading glasses, the better to study it. How did women take care of their hair during the glory years of the Serenissima? Even to wash it would be a chore, what with the water that had to be carried to wherever they washed it, to make no mention of heating the water, for surely they did not, during most of the year, dare to come in contact with cold water. Even today, people panicked at the thought of exposure to cold, or wind, or any combination of the two.

How many times, when trains still had windows instead of air conditioning, had he been told to close the window to avoid *'una corrente d'aria'*, a draught of air being as potentially lethal as a loaded weapon left with a child.

His speculations were cut short by the return of la Contessa, who smiled when he turned towards her, giving Brunetti hope that her friend Antonia had agreed to speak with him. 'She asked when we would like to come, and I suggested tomorrow afternoon, about four.' Then, for the sake of politeness, she added, 'Is that convenient for you, Guido?'

'Yes, it is. Of course. Thank you for arranging it.' Then, not certain how to phrase it, Brunetti said, 'Do you think she felt obliged to ask you to come as well?'

'No, not obliged. I think it's because she doesn't know you very well.' She paused, considering, and added, 'One thing, Guido: she wanted to know if any of the men in your family had been in the war.'

'What?'

'I don't know why, but she said that if you have any medals one of them might have been given, you should wear them on the lapel of your jacket. She told me that her husband sometimes responds favourably to seeing them.'

'But that's ...' Brunetti began, but stopped himself in time and altered the word to '... strange.'

'No stranger than other things about him now, Guido,' she said, making no attempt to hide her sadness.

'Could it be to disguise that I'm a policeman?' he asked, trying to lighten the mood.

After some time, la Contessa answered, 'Probably not. People of her class tend to trust the authorities that keep them in power and the workers who keep them safe.'

'Have you been reading the letters of Rosa Luxemburg again, Donatella?' Brunetti asked in a normal voice.

She laughed her bright laugh, a sound he delighted in hearing because to be thought clever or amusing by this woman was, to Brunetti, a jewel of great price.

'No, dear. Not recently. Besides, they're very serious and filled with lofty thoughts about the inner contradictions of capitalism, and I'm too old to enjoy reading things like that.' She gave him a level glance, as though she were testing how far she could go – the same look he had sometimes been given by her daughter – and added, 'And too rich.'

This time it was Brunetti who laughed.

The next day, he met la Contessa in front of Palazzo Albrizzi, not far from his home, at five minutes to four. She saw the medal pinned to the lapel of his jacket, nodded in approval, and asked, 'What was it for?'

'Bravery, I think. My father never said. He thought it was all a sham.'

She touched his arm with a mittened hand and said, 'Many of us did.' Then she poked the thumb of the other hand on the doorbell marked 'Fullin'. A man's voice pronounced an interrogative '*Sì?*' and she responded, 'Falier.'

The door snapped open and Brunetti pushed against the thick wood panels to allow them into the enormous entry hall. The edges of the white and orange paving tiles had been nibbled by centuries of *acqua alta* but nonetheless shone in what light there was. The thick cloth *felze* that had once rested on top of the gondola of the last Contessa Albrizzi stood against the left wall, the family crest incised into the glass window still identifiable.

La Contessa stopped and stared up at an enormous metal and glass lantern suspended from a ceiling beam. 'Orazio maintains that's the lantern from the galleon of Angelo Emo, the last admiral of the Republic. Do you know if that's true?'

'It's what I've always been told,' Brunetti answered.

She smiled. 'In Venice, they're believed to be the same thing, aren't they?' When Brunetti laughed, la Contessa led the way to the lift – or what served as one – and they stepped in. La Contessa pushed the button for the third floor; they looked at one another in shared speculation.

'It's taken me faithfully to see both Antonia and my dearest friend, Emanuela, who lives on the fourth floor.'

Before Brunetti could respond, the small lift gave a sharp jerk, and they felt themselves rise a bit, then stop, then a twinge, and then another lurch. Brunetti thought of nature documentaries of Canadian geese attempting to lift themselves from the water of a pristine lake. Flap, splash, flap, stamp, stamp at the surface of the water, another flap, and then the lift moved slowly and with imperial seriousness to the third floor and stopped.

Brunetti pushed open one of the wooden doors and held it while la Contessa pushed the second and stepped out onto the small landing. Brunetti followed her.

A handsome young man with very fair skin and short brown hair, dressed casually in jeans and a light sweater, opened the door directly in front of the lift. He recognized la Contessa and bowed his head. Without taking her hand, he kissed the air above it, the hand somehow having been unburdened of its mitten so that it now hung, suspended, untouched, in the air between them. He said, '*Buon giorno, Contessa,*' and stepped back; with a graceful wave of his arm, he invited her to pass in front of him. Then he turned back to Brunetti and nodded. 'Girolomo Fullin.' He paused a moment and Brunetti gave his name, but nothing more.

'Please come in, Signore.' He stepped back to allow Brunetti to enter the apartment.

The first thing Brunetti noticed was the temperature. Here, in the entrance, it was very pleasant, very mild; he heard la Contessa sigh with relief. 'Ah, Girolomo, did you make it warm for me?'

The young man smiled and said, 'I remembered from your last visit.' He closed the door to the apartment quietly, as if that would trap more warmth inside.

'When you lent me a sweater?' she asked and laughed at the memory.

'And that was only September,' he said. 'What must it be like for you in the winter?' Brunetti heard real concern in his voice, and commiseration.

La Contessa responded to that as much as to the question itself, and she said, 'Paola decided to stop skiing a few years ago, thank God, and she stored all of her clothing and equipment with us.' Then, dryly, 'Probably waiting for Chiara to grow into it all.' She shook her head a few times, as though she and il Conte lived in a one-bedroom apartment near the train station.

'What will you do with it until then?' the young man asked.

'I'll wear it, my dear. In the winter, I always wear at least two of her sweaters. And that's at home.' She smiled at the thought, or the memory. 'The socks are a dream.'

Brunetti had known this woman for decades, but he had not known the profundity of her hatred of the cold, nor the lengths to which she'd go to protect herself against it.

The young man smiled at this and said, '*Nonna*'s in the small reception room.' In a quiet voice, he added, 'With *Nonno*.' Then, perhaps because la Contessa was an old family friend, he added, 'He's been very quiet these last few days, thank God, and seems like his old self again.'

Taking the liberty granted by long friendship, la Contessa asked, 'Did something happen?'

The young man looked at the floor, almost as though he wished he could call back his last words, but then he met la Contessa's glance and said, 'Last week, an old friend from the Navy, Capitano Pederiva, came to visit; they served together for years during the nineties. *Nonno* recognized the Captain when he came in, spoke a few words. So I thought he was fine and I could leave them alone for a few minutes while I went to get *Nonna.*'

Brunetti watched the young man's face grow tense as he followed his memory. 'I wasn't gone three minutes before I heard a crash and *Nonno* shouting. Not words, just making noises.'

'What happened?' la Contessa asked, her hands suddenly pressed together in fear.

'I don't know. When I got back, *Nonno* was standing in front of the Captain, waving some scraps of paper in the air and making a strange noise, like he was trying to talk but couldn't remember how to do it any more.'

Girolomo paused, but neither la Contessa nor Brunetti spoke. Brunetti remembered that same sound: he'd heard it in his mother's house and then in the clinic where she, and it, lived on for years: a wordless, targetless, primal, rage-given voice.

'Pieces of paper?' la Contessa asked.

'Yes,' Girolomo said distractedly. '*Nonno* threw them on the floor, and I thought they had upset him, so I picked them up and stuffed them in my pocket so he wouldn't see them any more.'

They arrived in front of a door. Girolomo turned to Brunetti and, looking away and then quickly back, said, 'I apologize, Signor Brunetti, but could we two wait out here for a few minutes? My grandmother said she'd like a bit of time alone with la Contessa.' Then, as though this needed explanation, he added, 'They're old friends.'

Brunetti smiled and nodded, then stepped back a few paces so as not to be visible to the people in the room. Girolomo opened the door and let la Contessa pass in front of him. He closed the door softly after her.

There were wooden chairs standing against the wall of the corridor; Girolomo walked to them, pulled one away from the wall and gestured to Brunetti to sit, then turned one to face him and sat down.

With the easy grace of his class, Girolomo said, 'I thank heaven for your mother-in-law every day. I think it's her loyalty that helps my grandmother keep going.'

'I'm sorry for her trouble,' Brunetti said, meaning it.

A long moment passed and then Girolomo said, 'It's very strange.'

'What is?' Brunetti asked, thinking of his mother and knowing that, yes, it was strange.

'There are times when he's almost the way he was.' Brunetti nodded, and Girolomo continued. '*Nonno* has told me – in the past – a lot about his life at sea, and what always struck me was the isolation.' When he saw how attentive Brunetti had become, he said, 'He was a vice-admiral for a few years before he retired, and in the Navy that's sort of like being a god, or a demi-god. No one dares to speak to you unless spoken to first. No one would dare speak of anything personal. Sometimes he was at sea for months.' He leaned forward and put his head in his hands. 'Think of it, months when he really couldn't talk to anyone.'

'What did he do to survive that?'

Girolomo smiled and sat up straight, his back nowhere near that of the chair. 'He read.'

'What?'

'He told me he read books about the sea, chiefly novels. He read in Italian, so he didn't have as many available to him as a reader of English would – he read those in translation.'

'What did he read?'

'All of the writers about the sea: Conrad, Dana, Melville, Forester. He loved the Hornblower books. But the writer he loved most was the one he always referred to as Padreek Obreen,' the young man said and laughed out loud. 'How he loved Padreek Obreen.'

'Who?' Brunetti asked, entirely at sea.

'Patrick O'Brian. He was *Nonno*'s absolute favourite: he wrote about the fleet of Admiral Nelson and the wars with France. There were only seven translated when he started reading them, but he'd read them all many times, and he kept reading the new ones as they were translated, one after another. He always told me that Signor Obreen understood the sea and the wind and the sailors, and what it was to be at sea, and what it was to be an officer, and to do one's duty. And that he understood loyalty and keeping faith.'

'I haven't read the books,' Brunetti confessed, 'but I have heard of him.'

Still smiling, Girolomo went on. 'There was a movie about fifteen years ago: full of the endless sea and sea battles and cannons and men with swords. We have the DVD of it, and *Nonno* watches it at least once a month.' It was evident to Brunetti that the young man was proud of this, even delighted by it.

'And he asks me to read them to him, over and over.'

'Do you?'

'Of course,' Girolomo said, sounding as though he didn't understand the question. 'It makes him happy to hear them.'

'Does he understand them?' Brunetti dared to ask.

Girolomo had to think about this for a while, but finally he said, 'I think he still does, that the magic charms him out of wherever it is he's gone.' He leaned back in the chair, closed his eyes, and rested his head against the high back. 'I think part of him is still here with us.' He turned his head towards Brunetti and opened his eyes. 'Do you think that's possible, that he could go back and forth?'

'Brought back by the magic of Signor Obreen?' Brunetti asked.

'Yes.'

'Of course,' Brunetti said, meaning it. 'Magic is magic, and it works.'

The door to the room down the hall opened, and la Contessa stepped into the corridor. 'You can come in now, gentlemen. We've gossiped enough, I think.'

They got to their feet and Girolomo and Brunetti, far more at ease with one another now, walked back to join la Contessa. Brunetti stopped just outside the room.

'Could I offer you tea, Contessa?' Girolomo asked.

'Oh, how very kind of you to ask, Girolomo. Perhaps when we've finished talking.' She turned to Brunetti, knowing how much he disliked tea, and asked, 'You'll join us, won't you, Guido?'

'Of course.' From the very beginning of his time with Paola, when he was still a street dog, yapping at her heels, Brunetti had been sensitive to the elegance of her family's behaviour, both in action and in speech.

Until he met them, he had never heard people make such frequent use of the subjunctive and the conditional. 'I think it would be better if ...' 'You might enjoy it more if we were to ...' Luckily, ever since childhood, Brunetti had been enchanted by the beauty of Italian and the splendid grammatical clarity of his language. He'd studied it, he'd learned it, but he had not spoken it at home, for there they spoke Veneziano.

Passing time with Paola or with her family was, at the beginning, like a perpetually refilled first glass of champagne. They were Northerners, but Brunetti had never heard anyone other than Southerners use the *passato remoto* and use it correctly. Nor was it the custom in the Brunetti household for men to get to their feet every time a woman entered the room.

Girolomo stepped behind la Contessa and pulled the door fully open to allow the other two to go into the room, then retreated silently, closing the door behind him.

12

Signora Fullin, whom Brunetti saw only now, was thinner than when he had last seen her and looked as though she had not had much sleep since then. She nodded to Brunetti and returned her attention to her husband, who remained as distant and immobile as he had been at the dinner. He could have been on the deck of his ship for all the attention he paid to the people in the room; Brunetti suspected he would be far happier if he were.

The Vice-Admiral's hair was still thick and white, his body still straight and powerful. His face, however, was vacant of expression, and he stared out as though he'd given up all hope of ever being freed from whatever had taken possession of him. He looked up as they came in but seemed not to notice – or to see – them.

La Contessa walked over to pat her friend on the shoulder, although she had left her only a moment before. She said something in a voice so soft that Brunetti could not make out the words. While the women spoke, the Vice-Admiral got easily to his feet, as though la Contessa had just entered the room for the first time. When she had finished speaking with her friend, he took la Contessa's hand and kissed the air above it.

'How lovely to see you again, Matteo. And looking so well.' He nodded but did not reply. Undaunted by this, la Contessa turned and placed her hand on the back of the chair facing her friend Antonia.

Brunetti waited for la Contessa to take her place and then, bowing and introducing himself to the other woman, turned to her husband and repeated his bow, which was answered by a nod of the old man's head and the slow motion of his lips that gradually turned into a smile. Brunetti could think of nothing to say to that austere figure, who seemed to be looking at Brunetti's knees. Brunetti sat, and now the older man's eyes were on his chest.

Brunetti's attention was caught by a dark walnut credenza standing to his right, its surface covered with a flock of silver-framed black-and-white photographs. While the women spoke in soft voices, Brunetti studied the photos. All of them, it seemed, showed men in white military uniforms, even one with what looked like egret feathers on his white helmet. Abyssinia? Brunetti wondered. Some, given the beards and moustaches, must have been from the First World War; others looked like they were from the war in which his father had fought, a war where few wore egret plumes. He looked again at the photo of a man wearing rows of medals, removed his moustache, fleshed out both mouth and nose, and found the face of a younger Matteo Fullin.

His attention was summoned back by la Contessa's voice. 'I'm very grateful you found time to talk to us, Antonia.' She used the familiar 'tu' and spoke with the warmth Brunetti had always heard her use with family and her closest friends.

The other woman smiled and patted the back of la Contessa's right hand. 'I'm not sure I understood everything you told me,

Donatella, but I'm certainly glad to give you any help I can.'
Impulsively, caring more for the love of friendship than the fear
of contagion, she grasped her friend's hand in both of hers and
closed her eyes for a moment, then glanced quickly at her husband, who stared at la Contessa with an easy, affectionate smile
on his lips. He seemed to ignore the two women's conversation,
although his eyes went back and forth between them.

'I'm not so sure I understand myself, Antonia,' la Contessa
said. 'Perhaps my son-in-law could explain it to you more clearly.'

Signora Fullin shifted her attention to Brunetti. 'Donatella
said it concerns my husband.'

Brunetti had been looking at the man, who, although his eyes
went from speaker to speaker, had failed to react. Giving his
attention to Signora Fullin, he said, 'Thank you for speaking to
us, Signora. It's very kind of you, and I'll try to be as quick as
I can.'

Suddenly the Vice-Admiral leaned forward in his chair, one
finger extended. He brought it to rest on the medal Brunetti had
pinned to his chest, a simple copper Greek cross suspended
from a blue ribbon. Brunetti had leaned forward as well, perhaps hoping to make the medal easier for the old man to see, but
the pressure from the Vice-Admiral's single finger moved
Brunetti relentlessly away from him until he was pressed against
the back of his chair.

The old man's face softened and he smiled, first at the cross
and then at Brunetti, who looked back and saw the man the
Vice-Admiral once had been. 'It was my father's,' Brunetti said
in a normal voice. 'He gave it to me.'

Fullin moved his hand back from the medal and this time
pointed his finger towards his own chest, which had somehow
become inflated and seemed broader. His finger continued to
the place where a medal would have been, had he been in uniform. 'Navy,' he said clearly. Then, perhaps as the result of some

inner process or connection, he added, speaking directly to Brunetti, 'Honour.'

Brunetti's eyes followed the Vice-Admiral's finger from his chest back to his lap. When he looked up at the old man's face, the sailor had abandoned ship, leaving behind only wreckage.

As if she had not seen what happened, Signora Fullin asked, 'What is it you'd like to know, Dottore Brunetti?'

Speaking softly but clearly, Brunetti began. 'Some years ago, your husband signed papers that made him a member of the board of a charitable foundation that was established here in the city.' He paused to give her time to respond.

Her face was attentive, but she gave no sign of recognizing what he was talking about.

Brunetti went on. 'The foundation was set up in order to build a hospital in Belize.'

'Belize,' the woman repeated, neutrally. Then she said, 'Isn't that in Africa?' a question that diminished Brunetti's hope of leaving this room with any useful information. He was half ashamed to realize he was almost grateful for this.

'No, Signora, it's in Central America, between Mexico and Guatemala.'

She shook her head. 'I don't remember Matteo ever saying anything about this to me.' She glanced sideways at her husband, and for a moment Brunetti thought she was going to ask that now silent statue of a man if he remembered having signed the document. Instead, she looked back at Brunetti and asked, 'When did you say this happened?'

'I was told it was three years ago, Signora.'

She looked down at her lap, where her hands lay. She glanced at la Contessa, who nodded. Encouraged by this, she said, 'I'll have to ask Girolomo to check Matteo's diaries.' She looked at Brunetti, and said, bleakly, 'He still tried to use one then.' For an instant, Brunetti thought she was going to start crying, but, instead, she turned to her husband and said, 'It's easier now, isn't it, Matteo, not having to go to all the trouble of pretending?' Brunetti wondered whether she was speaking to her husband or to herself.

Looking away from the Vice-Admiral, she said to Brunetti, as if what she'd said needed explanation, 'It's true, Signore. It's better, letting it all go and not pretending that everything is normal.' After a pause, she added, 'Or that anything is.'

She placed her hand on her husband's and held it as she continued. 'Matteo pretended for a long time that things were fine, nothing was wrong. But ... I knew, and our daughter knew. And Girolomo.' As she said her grandson's name, she smiled briefly and Brunetti noticed the fine structure of the bones of her face and the smoothness of her skin.

Addressing la Contessa, she said, 'We wasted so much time, acting like everything was fine.' She looked at her husband, anguish scrawled across her face, and said, 'Some days, once or twice a month, perhaps, it's as though he's come back for a visit. He answers questions, tells me what he'd like for dinner. Or we go for a walk and say hello to people we know. And then ... and then it's all over, sometimes in the middle of a sentence. Just so. He's not there any more.'

She suddenly got to her feet, saying, 'I'll ask Girolomo to have a look.' Smiling, she explained, 'Everything's in the computer, so I wouldn't know how to find it.' She gave herself a small shake and asked Brunetti, 'What month did you say it was?'

'March, Signora.'

'And who asked him to join this organization?'

'Bruno del Balzo,' Brunetti said.

With no warning, Fullin's right foot kicked forward, as if struck by sudden cramp, and gave la Contessa a glancing kick on the shin. She pulled her legs sharply to the left to avoid another blow, but Fullin had pulled his leg back and replanted his foot next to the other.

From above him, his wife said, 'Matteo, Matteo, try to sit still. We have guests now.' Her voice struggled to be kind and loving, but Brunetti heard the stifled panic, and the fear.

Fullin blinked a few times but gave no sign that he understood what she said. His wife bent and kissed him on the top of his head, saying, 'I'll just be a moment, dear.' She walked to the door and left the room. His eyes followed her to the door and remained there.

Brunetti sat as silent as the other man; la Contessa, he noticed, rubbed her fingers lightly back and forth across the grain of the brocade cover of her chair. He realized he was intimidated by the silence of the other man and the sense that, no matter how much he was physically present, he was not always there mentally.

Where did they go? Did they go anywhere? What did they hear or see? His mother? Towards the end – although she was long years getting there – she had screamed abuse when she saw him or Sergio, so he sat motionless now, terrified that this man would begin to scream as well.

He tensed at the sound of footsteps in the hall, and la Contessa looked towards the door, but the footsteps passed and diminished, and they remained alone with the silent man and the aura of stifled anger his kick had let into the room.

Brunetti tried to think of something, anything, to distract himself, but all he could think of was the man who sat opposite him and whether he was going to launch himself against one of them.

The door handle squeaked, propelling Brunetti to his feet. It was Signora Fullin, followed closely by her grandson, who had a sheet of paper in his hand. Signora Fullin looked quickly, nervously around the room, as though fearing that something had happened while she was away and they were trying to hide it from her. Her husband got quickly to his feet, nodded to her, and smiled, then waited until she was seated before sitting down again.

'Girolomo took a look at the entries for March, and on the sixteenth my husband had an appointment with a friend, the man you named. He's made you a copy.'

Looking at Girolomo, Brunetti asked, 'Is there any indication of what the meeting was about?'

Instead of answering, the young man approached Brunetti and handed him the sheet of paper.

Brunetti thanked him and recognized the standard form for the pages of a business diary. Inside the square for 16 March was printed: *Bruno, 13:00. Sign papers. Lunch.*

'It's not very much, but I think it's enough,' Brunetti said to the young man, who gestured that he was welcome to keep the paper. Brunetti folded it and slipped it into his pocket.

'Shall I ask for tea now?' Signora Fullin asked feebly, her reluctance painted over with politeness.

La Contessa got to her feet and moved quickly towards her friend. 'That's very kind of you, Antonia, but I think it would be better if we left. Matteo might like to be alone with you.'

When Brunetti got to his feet, the Vice-Admiral stood as well and offered his hand. Brunetti – rules be damned – took it and realized what the man's strength could do to his hand, but his touch was only firm, even gentle.

'*Piacere*,' the Vice-Admiral said clearly and sat back down.

'*Grazie, Vice-Ammiraglio*,' Brunetti answered.

Unnoticed, the young man had moved closer to his grandfather. He removed the older man's handkerchief from the breast pocket of his suit, wiped at the moisture that had accumulated on his lower lip, and put the handkerchief carefully back in his pocket. He sat in the chair in which Brunetti had sat, facing his grandfather, who reached out and put a proprietary hand on his knee.

Turning to his grandmother, Girolomo said, 'I'll stay with *Nonno* if you'd like to see your guests to the door, *Nonna*.' The young man's ease of manner left Brunetti wondering if a certain kind of social grace was a hereditary trait that passed down through the generations. Or if it came with the possession of silk-covered chairs in the small reception room?

Brunetti walked to the door and held it for the two women. La Contessa took her friend by the arm as they walked towards it. When they had passed through and he'd shut the door, Brunetti spoke from behind them. 'Signora Fullin, I'd like to ask you a painful question.'

Both stopped and turned. It was la Contessa who spoke first. 'Guido, perhaps we've had enough questions for today.'

He could have stopped it there, ended it all, walked la Contessa home and continued to the Questura to call Elisabetta and tell her that he had found nothing in her son-in-law's affairs or acquaintances that seemed strange. Instead, he said, 'It's only one thing, Donatella.'

'One painful thing?' she asked, shifting herself slightly closer to her friend and making her motion obvious.

'Yes, painful,' he confirmed.

Signora Fullin turned to la Contessa and said, 'Thank you, Donatella. But I think I've got beyond the point where words can be painful.' She looked at Brunetti and said, 'What is it you'd like to know, Signor Brunetti?'

'You saw the date on the paper your grandson gave me, didn't you, Signora?'

She nodded.

'Was your husband, three years ago, when he signed the papers, capable of understanding what he was reading or whatever was explained to him about it?'

Her face did not change when he asked her this question. She looked down at her arm, the one la Contessa had taken into her temporary possession, and studied it. With her free hand, she pulled at a white thread sticking through one of the buttonholes on the sleeve of her sweater. She grasped its end and pulled, and the button came loose and fell to the floor.

It was easy for Brunetti to see it on the dark wooden parquet. He stooped and picked it up and put it in her outstretched hand. She thanked him and closed her hand around it.

Then she looked at him and said, 'Perhaps. But perhaps not. We were still pretending then, and he could still make people believe he understood what they said to him and what he was doing. Enough to make them want to pretend along with us. Just in case.' After a long pause, she added, 'I don't know.'

Then, briskly, she asked, 'Is that your only question?'

Brunetti nodded, incapable of speech.

'For what it's worth,' Signora Fullin said, 'Bruno is one of the few old friends who have remained faithful to Matteo and still comes to visit. Most of the others,' she went on, her voice growing tight, 'have stopped.'

Neither Brunetti nor la Contessa said a word, waiting for Signora Fullin to regain her composure.

When she did, she said, 'And he talks to us as he always did, asks Matteo questions about his time in the Navy, asks about Girolomo and how he's doing at university.' Her tone had lightened at this evidence of human decency. 'And I must say Matteo often rises to the occasion and follows the conversation, even talks sometimes.' She smiled and let out a snort of near amusement. 'He even brings along papers and asks my husband to sign them, just as Matteo did in the past.'

'Papers?' Brunetti asked.

'Oh,' Signora Fullin said, raising her hand as if to wave away the possibility. 'It's just blank sheets of paper. But I think it makes

Matteo feel like he's an important person again: signing documents; making decisions.' Her voice broke on the last word but she managed to contain the sob.

She hurried towards the door, opened it, kissed la Contessa on the cheek and smiled at Brunetti.

He surprised himself by bowing over her hand and making a soft kissing noise while his lips were still two centimetres above it.

She closed the door behind them, and the lift respected the moment by behaving itself while it took them to the ground floor.

They did not linger in the small *campo* but turned in the direction of San Silvestro, where la Contessa could get the Number One towards home and Brunetti could easily walk to the Rialto and continue towards the Questura. He slowed his pace to hers, and they walked automatically, neither of them having to hesitate about where to turn or which bridge to take: the unconscious navigation of the average Venetian is surpassed only by that of the albatross.

When they arrived at the *imbarcadero*, Brunetti glanced at the sign and saw that they had four minutes to wait. They stood on the outer platform: there were no other people. 'What are you going to do?' la Contessa asked.

He'd known, as they walked, that this was the question she would ask, but he hadn't prepared an answer. 'I'd almost hoped she'd say that he'd understood what he signed and that an honourable man would never sign something he didn't understand.'

'It's not a question of honour, is it?' she asked.

'Hardly. More of lucidity. People don't become incompetent overnight: they go in and out, lose control and then get it back.'

'So?'

Before he could find an answer, his thoughts were interrupted by a sudden roar as the approaching vaporetto's motor slipped into reverse to slow its approach to the *imbarcadero*.

As surprised as he, la Contessa pulled her travel card from the pocket of her coat and pressed it against the sensor, then walked through the opening gates, which closed behind her. She turned back and started to call something to him, but the sailor slid back the metal gate to let a few people get off, obliterating la Contessa's voice.

'What?' Brunetti called to her. She turned towards him, but the captain gunned the motor and Brunetti heard only that, although he saw her mouth move before she turned towards the boat.

He held up his arm and waved, and she did the same, moving back from the railing. The sailor pulled the gate closed and the vaporetto moved ponderously away from the dock. She stood outside, the wind bouncing her scarf against the side of her face. She grabbed it with one hand and raised the other towards him again. The boat moved into the centre of the canal, and when Brunetti lost sight of her among the other people on deck, he turned and headed towards the bridge.

13

When he got to the Questura, Brunetti went to talk to Signorina Elettra. He glanced in from outside the door to her office and stopped still, amazed at what he saw. His mind flashed to fairy tales about mermaids, giant fish, all manner of sea wonders, for there at the desk he saw something shimmering in the light. She must have heard his intake of breath, for Signorina Elettra looked up suddenly and, seeing him, smiled. She was – well – her jacket was indeed covered from shoulder to waist with countless rows of tiny silver scales.

Brunetti held a finger to his lips while pointing to the lower part of her desk where she had found the listening device. He raised both hands in a questioning gesture.

'Oh, no need to worry any more, Commissario: it's been taken care of.'

It seemed to Brunetti that even her clearest statements cried out for interrogation. 'Does that mean it's gone?' he asked.

'As they say in spy movies, Dottore, "It's been rendered inoperative."'

'What happened?' he asked.

'It all turned out for the best.' She pushed back from her desk and crossed her legs. 'I'd lost touch with my friend Giorgio in the last few months, and I thought this would be a good opportunity to renew our ...' Brunetti watched her select a word from what seemed a very long list. '... collaboration.'

'Giorgio who works for Telecom?' Brunetti enquired, calling to mind some of the feats of cybercrime Giorgio had fostered over the years, the banks he'd taught her to break into, the passwords he'd laid at her feet, always at her merest suggestion.

'Ah, no. No longer.'

'He's changed jobs?'

'He's become a consultant. Of media and communication.'

'Where?'

'San Marco.'

'The Basilica?' Brunetti asked.

She laughed. 'No, no, the *sestiere*. He's just opened his own office.'

'Office?'

'Yes. Above the Gucci store. He's got three rooms and a secretary.'

Trying for humour, Brunetti enquired, 'He didn't ask you?' Brunetti, truth be told, thought she'd be a better partner than secretary.

'Oh, he did,' she said, using a tone that seemed strangely nostalgic to Brunetti.

'But?'

'But I so dislike that part of the city,' she answered with a faint down-turn of her mouth. 'With the full return of the tourists, it will be impossible to go anywhere near it.'

Brunetti certainly agreed with her, but said, 'Couldn't you have arranged it with him to work from home?'

Her face stiffened, and for a long time she said nothing. 'But I *have* a job, Commissario.'

At a loss for how to respond, Brunetti said only, 'Of course.' Then, returning to Giorgio, no longer of Telecom, he asked, 'What did you tell him?'

'I called and described the problem. Giorgio laughed – gave me just time enough to describe what I'd found – and said he'd take care of it, that it was amateurish, if not primitive.'

Before Brunetti could express his satisfaction, she said sternly, 'I knew all that.' Then, in a firmer tone, she continued, 'It was obvious what it was. All I needed was to know where I could get the counter-weapon to solve the problem.'

'What kind of a weapon?'

'One that sends out a sort of … well, I suppose you could call it a "death ray". Giorgio told me the military is very fond of it.'

Brunetti chose to ignore that and asked, 'What does it do?'

'If you put it next to the device that is listening to you and activate it, the weapon will emit a ray that first upsets, then destroys the other device.' Her pause was a hair's breadth. 'Undetectably. A kind of short circuit, as though it had died a natural death.' She smiled briefly here but went on immediately. 'More interestingly, in its death throes, it will give up the geographical coordinates of wherever the information is being sent.'

'Did Giorgio have a death ray on hand?'

She laughed softly. 'Ah, Commissario Brunetti, you do enjoy making fun of what I do.'

Brunetti could not hide his surprise. 'That, Signorina, is the last thing I'd do.' Then, putting on the voice he used to joke about serious things, he said, 'Your help is for me a bright light in a wicked world.'

Her face lit up. 'My grandmother often said that.'

'So did mine,' he replied, than added, 'but seldom about me.' He paused and added, 'And Giorgio?', eager to hear the rest of the story.

'A young man with a very military bearing, presenting a piece of identification so important that he was immediately accompanied to my office, arrived here the same afternoon and said he'd been asked by a friend to come by and fix something for me.'

'The device?'

She nodded.

'Had he brought you the ... countermeasure?'

'Yes and no,' she said, unable to disguise her irritation. 'He said he couldn't give anything to me, but if I'd leave the office for fifteen minutes, he'd do what was necessary.'

'And did you?'

She nodded. 'I went down to Sergio's and had a coffee, and when I came back, the young man was standing at the window, admiring the view, his hands behind his back and his briefcase on my desk. Closed.'

'His mission accomplished?'

'Yes. He seemed very pleased with the result, thanked me for trusting him and said that before the device was ... taken care of, he'd checked the coordinates of the place it was transmitting to.'

'Ah?' Brunetti whispered, suddenly interested.

She put her hand to her forehead to push back a strand of hair, and he noticed that her fingernails were the same colour as the scales of her jacket.

'Where was it going?'

'Strangely enough,' she said, her voice suddenly grown serious, 'somewhere else in this building.'

Brunetti could think of no adequate response. The police were listening to the police. He raised his eyebrows by way of question, and she answered with a shrug so delicate it hardly caused the scales to ripple.

'He also told me he left the corpse where I'd found it,' she said, pointing under her desk. 'So it will look like a heart attack,' she added with a discreet smile. 'For want of a better word.'

'And Giorgio? Did you thank him?'

'I'll do that later in the week.'

'And until then?'

'I sent him three dozen roses to celebrate the opening of his office.'

'That was very generous of you,' Brunetti observed.

'Very generous of the Questura, actually.'

'Office supplies?'

'They went to an office, didn't they?'

'Ah' was the best response Brunetti could make, then he said, thinking it time to return to a topic that could be more easily controlled, 'I have a few things I'd like you to do.'

Explaining took some time. Although Brunetti had already asked her to look for Fullin's medical files, he had not had time to explain why he wanted to see them. He did so now, explaining Elisabetta's visit and the story she'd told.

Hearing himself summarize the story made Brunetti hear a new, less surprising one. How many times had love and business failed to mix? Had Fenzo not liked something he saw in his father-in-law's accounts? Or had del Balzo rejected some audacious suggestion meant to improve his income? The reason could just as easily be banal: del Balzo had simply grown tired of having the young man tell him how to run his business.

Brunetti explained that the ONLUS had a board of three members, del Balzo, Matteo Fullin, and Luigino Guidone, making no mention of his own primitive attempt to find Guidone.

She nodded and made a few notes, suddenly flipped the pages back, checked something, and then continued. When she finished and looked at him for further information, he said, 'I'd like you to see what you can find out about this ONLUS.' Then, as though pushing a particularly rich dessert towards her, he said, 'It's called "Belize nel Cuore".'

An involuntary and long-sustained sigh slipped from between her lips. She stared at him in undisguised wonder and repeated the name as one would the last words of a prayer, then asked, 'Belize as in Central America?'

'Yes,' Brunetti said.

'Anything you're particularly interested in?'

'I was told that it's a medical charity and works with a hospital in Belize.' Having no more, he stopped.

Signorina Elettra looked up. 'That's all?'

'Yes.'

'Do you know anything about the hospital? How big it is? Who runs it? What it's called?'

Helpless, Brunetti could only shrug.

She raised her head and smiled. 'Ah, Commissario, what delight you sometimes pass on to me.'

He knew her well enough to know she was telling the truth.

'Delight?'

'Yes.'

'Because you get to go ...' he began, but abandoned the sentence for fear of giving her strange ideas.

When his silence had gone on for some time, she looked up and, ever gracious, finished the sentence for him.

'Hunting.'

14

Time passed, and nature intervened in the lives of the people of Venice and, consequently, in the lives of the police. After two days of torrential rain and abnormally high tides, the sirens sounded at two-thirty in the morning, announcing the arrival of *acqua alta*. The implementation of the MOSE tidal barriers was delayed by unspecified 'technical problems', and when they finally did function, the city was already flooded. The subsequent delay in their being lowered trapped the water in the city for extra hours, exacerbating the damage. The following night, the same meteorological pattern was followed: rain, moon, flooding. A new element, however, was introduced: groups of underage boys, now commonly referred to as 'baby gangs', used the night-time chaos to break their way into shops, pharmacies and restaurants that had closed or gone out of business because of the *pandemia* and help themselves to whatever the owners had left behind. If questioned by people passing by, they explained, speaking Veneziano, that they were helping their father or their uncle save the things in his shop from the water, and would the person asking prefer to speak to him instead?

Busy trying to save what they could from their own shops, few people insisted and so left them to steal or destroy what they pleased.

By the third night, the alerted police were patrolling the streets and had arrested at least six different groups, all composed of underage boys. The only satisfaction offered to the police was to call the parents involved, explain what had happened, and ask them to come and pick up their child.

The process proved tedious: some parents were hard to find and had to be called repeatedly; others said they'd be there as soon as they'd called their lawyers; some said they'd be there soon and then did not show up for hours, sometimes not until the afternoon of the following day. None of the latter ever stated outright that their delay was meant to provoke anxiety in their sons, but the parents' coolness sometimes suggested that.

When the boys arrived at the Questura, they had to be put somewhere: most of them were taken to the rooms used to question suspects. Some were taken to the various Carabinieri stations in the city and put in holding cells. One ten-year-old was taken home by two uniformed policemen who were careful to make as much noise as they could when they arrived at the boy's home, leaning on the bell, and when there was finally an answer, shouting into the speakerphone that it was the police and their son had been arrested.

In most cases, the boys displayed a sense of privilege and invulnerability, well aware of how little they risked. Many of them wore Adidas or Nike trainers, jeans that had been strategically ripped or torn, and hooded jackets and vests. Thinking they were unique, they copied one another relentlessly or copied boys they had seen in photos or on the street. Not only did they pursue fashion in their dress: behaviour was also to be copied, no matter the cost to other people.

Yet most of the police, to Brunetti's relief, treated the boys with forbearance. Many of the officers were only a decade older, and others had sons who were the same age as the boys.

But the whole thing took time: endless hours to find a place where they could be taken, to record their details, contact their parents, register their offence and the circumstances of their arrest, and all the while the police knew that little, if anything, would come of any of this.

After the *acqua alta* stopped, other boys preyed on unwatched shops, not because they had an idea of what to do with what they stole but because they didn't have anything else to do to amuse themselves. Finally, one group of them went too far: three of them attacked a man on the street and stole his *telefonino*. The attack was registered by two surveillance cameras; the victim was a tourist. As with other creatures whose habitat is endangered, tourists had become a protected species in Venice, and Patta decided to present himself as a sort of WWF enforcer.

The Vice-Questore chose Vianello to organize night patrols against the baby gangs, which meant the Ispettore's workday had become his work night, leaving him no time to search for information about Signor Fenzo.

During this time, Griffoni was summoned to Milano to give evidence in the trial of a man accused of killing his wife. The magistrate who sent the request said it was likely she would have to be there for two days. Before leaving, Griffoni assured Brunetti, whom Patta had told to take care of her cases, that there was nothing that could not wait until she returned but asked him to read through a stack of ministerial communications and to tell her if anything important was in them.

That left Brunetti and Signorina Elettra with little time, especially after the Vice-Questore asked Signorina Elettra to involve herself in something she described to Brunetti as 'useless but attention-grabbing'. Nevertheless, she did assure Brunetti that, by the end of the week, she would be able to return her attention to Vice-Admiral Fullin and 'Belize nel Cuore'.

With Signorina Elettra occupied on something 'useless' and the two officers with whom he worked best not available, Brunetti was, he realized, essentially alone at the Questura, something that had not happened for years.

Two more days passed. When Elisabetta called on the second day to ask if Brunetti had any news, he temporized. On the third day, after he had been at his desk for only a few minutes, already ploughing through Griffoni's ministerial documents, his *tele-fonino* rang. He saw that it was Pucetti.

'Commissario,' the officer began, 'we're on ...' His voice dissolved, as though disturbed by electrical interference. Brunetti got up and moved closer to the window, hoping this might improve the connection.

'Pucetti?' he said. 'Pucetti, can you hear me?'

'*Sì, Signore,*' the younger man said, paused, and then continued. 'We're at a clinic. The doctor called to report a break-in, so we came here.'

Brunetti listened to Pucetti's breathing. 'What's wrong, Pucetti?' he asked. 'Tell me.'

'There's blood, Commissario. On the floor.' He heard the officer pull in another deep breath. Then, sounding very young, Pucetti said, 'It's all over the place.'

'Pucetti, is anyone with you?' Brunetti asked.

'Only Alvise. And he's outside. He got sick.'

'Anyone else?'

'The Dottoressa.'

'Give her the phone.' He made it a command.

Pucetti hesitated a moment before he answered. 'She's outside, too, Signore.'

'Pucetti, close your eyes and tell me what happened.'

A long silence followed, and then he heard Pucetti's voice, sounding forced and pained. 'She told me she called and reported the break-in. She said she was afraid at first to go inside because she saw blood when she opened the door. But then she said she had to go in and see what was wrong.'

'When was this?'

'Not long ago, less than an hour. The call went to Lieutenant Scarpa, and he said to send two men immediately. Alvise and I were downstairs, so he told Foa to bring us here.' There followed a long pause, during which all Brunetti heard was Pucetti's breathing and, in the background, dogs barking.

'Where are you?' Brunetti asked.

'In Campiello Turella. It's just before you get to Campo Santo Stefano. There's a garden beyond it.' Brunetti had no idea what Pucetti was talking about: there was no Campiello Turella near Campo Santo Stefano.

'Pucetti, where are you? Pay attention. Where are you?'

'On Murano, Commissario. I told you that. Didn't I?'

'You told me now, Pucetti. Tell me what you saw when you got there.'

'The door was open, and the veterinarian was standing just outside, in the *campiello*, leaning against the wall.'

Brunetti waited silently for Pucetti to continue, and after some time, he did. 'She had a dog in her arms, one of those jumpy little white terriers.' Pucetti paused after the name of the type of dog, and then added, 'At first I thought it was dead because it was so still, just hanging there; his head was covered with blood and his ears were covered in bandages. And then I saw the blood on her, on the front and sleeves of her jacket.'

'What did you do, Pucetti?' Brunetti asked, confused by this story that made no sense.

Pucetti said nothing until Brunetti told him to go on. Pucetti paused for a long time, and Brunetti was about to tell him to continue when he started talking again. 'She said ears bleed a lot.' The young officer sighed and took a deep breath. 'So we went in.

'The office was destroyed: computer smashed on the floor, wires pulled out. A cabinet with glass was pushed over, and the glass was everywhere.'

Again, the officer paused, and Brunetti waited. 'Alvise said we should go into the other room: we could hear barking and snarling from there. So we went over to the door.' He paused, and then asked, in his normal voice, 'Can I tell you something, Commissario?'

'Of course, Pucetti. What is it?'

'I was so afraid I pulled out my gun, and then Alvise did, too. And then we went into the other room, but the noise was from only one dog, a giant Rottweiler-looking thing, barking like he was crazy and banging himself against the front of the cage.' Pucetti paused, then added, his voice filled with wonder, 'Only one dog, and he was making all that noise.'

'What else did you see, Pucetti?'

'There were a couple of rabbits and a cat, but the cat was up on the filing cabinet, and that's where some of the noise came from. Grey. I had one like that when we were kids.'

They'd hurt an animal and vandalized the office. Brunetti's first thought was to wonder if this was an escalation by one of the remaining baby gangs.

'What else did you see, Pucetti?'

'I didn't look, Signore. I called you.'

Brunetti held the phone away from his ear for a moment and remembered seeing the second launch docked in front of the Questura when he arrived. He started towards the door and hurried to the stairs. 'I'll be there in twenty minutes. No longer.'

'What do we do, sir?'

'Stay there. Don't answer any questions. Call Foa and tell him to walk with the doctor down to Campo Santo Stefano: there's a bar on the far corner. Get her something hot to drink, but not coffee.'

'Yes, sir. I'll tell him.'

'Stay outside. Don't go inside again.'

'But the animals, Signore?'

'They're safe now. Close the door, Pucetti. Don't let anyone in. Remember, it's a crime scene.'

'Yes, sir. I understand. But what if people ask what's going on?'

'If anyone asks, tell them there was a break-in,' Brunetti said and broke the connection.

Downstairs, he went out to the dock and found Grandesso, a dark-complexioned Buranello who had been with the force for only a few years, wiping the morning's humidity from the launch. Brunetti didn't like riding with Grandesso – didn't much like the man, either – because of the arrogance with which he captained the boat, always using the siren to shove other boats out of the way, never acknowledging – much less returning – the courtesy of other pilots.

'I need to go to Murano, Grandesso. As fast as we can get there.'

'Where, sir?' he asked, stuffing the cloth into the cavity beneath the dashboard.

'Campiello Turella,' Brunetti said, stepping aboard and starting to explain where it was.

'I know it, sir,' Grandesso interrupted, turning on the motor and pulling the boat into a narrow U-turn. They turned into Rio Santa Giustina, emerged into the *laguna*, and shot, siren blaring, towards the other island. When they were approaching the Faro, Brunetti told Grandesso to switch off the siren.

The pilot pulled the newly silenced boat up behind the other police launch and moored it, lights flashing. Brunetti glanced at his watch and saw it had taken less than fifteen minutes to get there.

'Stay here,' Brunetti said, and stepped up onto the *riva*. He turned into the opening of the *campiello*. Down at the end, he saw Pucetti and Alvise standing on either side of a door. If they'd brought a drummer and a band, they might have drawn less attention. Two windows on the other side of the *campiello* were open in spite of the temperature, one on the first floor and one on the second. A woman leaned from the lower window, her hands propped on the sill, elbows stiff. In the other, a woman was visible from the shoulders upwards: she must have drawn up a chair to watch.

Ignoring both women, Brunetti approached the two officers. With unrestrained theatricality, Alvise snapped out a salute, Pucetti raised a hand and said, 'Good morning, Commissario.'

Brunetti greeted them briefly, ignoring both salutes. Then, to Pucetti: 'Where's the doctor?'

'On the way back from the bar, sir,' Pucetti said and, sounding relieved, added, 'She called a friend, who's coming to pick up her dog.' Switching to a more professional tone, he explained, 'Foa said people stared at her because of the blood, so he went back to the boat and got her one of our jackets.'

'Won't that be just as conspicuous?' Brunetti asked.

'You haven't seen the blood, sir. Believe me, the jacket's better.'

No sooner had Pucetti finished speaking than the uniformed Foa and a woman wearing an oversized, thick blue jacket, 'POLIZIA' printed on it in large white letters, appeared in the arch leading to the canal. She carried something that, as she drew near, became recognizable as a dog, probably a Jack Russell, wrapped in a towel, its head protected by a white plastic trumpet. Small and white, it just fitted into her arms, where it seemed to be drugged or asleep. A few brown spots were visible on its head, partially obscured by streaks and patches of blood, a lot of it. Its ears, heavily bandaged, seemed to have been the source of the blood.

Brunetti's eyes moved to the doctor, a tall young woman – were even the veterinarians beginning to look like teenagers? Brunetti wondered – with short dark hair, a prominent nose, and reddened eyes. She was taller than Foa, her height emphasized by her thinness.

Before either of them could say anything, the dog moved nervously in her arms. Looking down at it, she said, 'It's all right, Bruce. Don't worry. Giulia's coming for you.' The dog quieted at the sound of her voice.

She looked at Brunetti, who took the opportunity to introduce himself: 'I'm Guido Brunetti, Commissario di Polizia.' But then curiosity got the best of him and he asked, 'Bruce? As in Bruce Springsteen?'

She smiled, peeked around the edge of the trumpet that was protecting the dog's head, and said, 'Bruce, as in Fogle, I'm afraid. He's my hero.' Seeing Brunetti's confusion, she said, 'He's a veterinarian, not a singer.' Short pause. '*The* veterinarian.'

Something in the woman's tone passed to the dog, who moved around in her arms and started to lick at her hand. Her hands were clean, Brunetti noticed, but the blue jacket failed to cover a broad streak of red on the cuff of her shirt and another in the front.

'A friend is coming to get him,' she said, patting the dog's back with one hand. 'She'll keep him until tonight. There are some things I have to get for her from the clinic.' Calculating that it would be better if she were not burdened with the dog when he spoke to her, Brunetti stepped out of her way and then followed her to the door of the clinic. Alvise saluted them both; Pucetti confined himself to a nod.

As they entered the silent waiting room, a fierce storm of barking erupted in the other room: deep, constant, menacing. The

Dottoressa walked to the door of the second room and stepped inside; Brunetti stayed behind. The barking stopped instantly; Brunetti heard her say, 'Stop that, Zucca. Lie down.' In the silence that followed, Brunetti heard some scratching and then a loud thump. A drawer opened and closed, and then another one. It was only a few minutes before she returned, a paper shopping bag suspended from one hand. 'Zucca's a friend of Bruce's. She had to stay here overnight, so I let Bruce stay with her because she's afraid when she's left alone.' She looked inside the trumpet again and asked, 'Not much of a babysitter, are you?'

She tilted her head back towards the other room and said, 'Zucca's very big, and very sweet, and very stupid.'

'What happened?' Brunetti asked.

'Whoever came in must have brought dog treats with them, just in case the dogs started making a noise.' She looked down at Bruce and said, 'They'd bark their heads off if anyone came in.'

'And so?'

'So the person tossed some treats into the cage. To keep them quiet.'

'And?'

'And they started fighting over the food.' Seeing Brunetti's expression, she said, 'Friends are friends, but food is food.' After a reflexive moment, she added, 'They're no different from us.'

'Flora? Flora?' a woman called from the doorway. Brunetti went out and motioned the officers to stand back, then waved the woman forward. She was about the same age as Dottoressa del Balzo, shorter and rounder. Bruce yipped in delight when he saw her, and the transfer of dog and bag was quickly done. There followed a few moments of instructions Brunetti did not hear, and then Giulia and Bruce started towards the underpass. Just as they reached it, Giulia stopped and turned around long enough for Bruce to give a loud bark, and then they were gone.

Turning to him with no preamble, Dottoressa del Balzo asked, 'Why would someone do this?' as if the police knew special paths into the minds of criminals.

Brunetti had asked himself the same question when he spoke to Pucetti, but now he asked it again and suspected that the answer would be different. Flora del Balzo. Veterinarian on Murano.

'I don't have an answer, Dottoressa, and I won't have one until I know more,' he said.

'There's nothing to know,' she said, speaking slowly and with the emphasis on the last word. Then, as though Brunetti were irredeemably dull, she said, 'This is crazy. Crazy people did this.'

Brunetti thought she was going to cry, but she shook her head and asked him, 'You're a policeman: haven't you ever seen anything like this?'

She was right: Brunetti was a policeman, and he had seen things like this. But with people, not animals.

Ignoring what she had said, Brunetti turned to Pucetti, who was still there, and asked, 'Did you call for the crime squad?'

'Yes, sir,' Pucetti said. 'After I hung up with you.'

'Good.' Then, turning back to Dottoressa del Balzo, he asked, 'Does the door lock automatically when you leave?'

It took her a moment to adjust to the ordinariness of the question, and then she answered, 'Yes.'

'Do you have the keys, Dottoressa?'

Her hands moved towards the pockets of the jacket she was wearing, but the strange flaps confused her and she looked at her right hand, as if it had betrayed her somehow. Brunetti watched her regain her concentration; she reached into the pocket of her slacks and pulled out a ring of keys. Sorting through them, she selected one and passed it to Brunetti.

He thanked her and asked Foa, who was standing behind her, to take her back to the launch and wait: he'd join her in five or ten minutes.

Before Foa could turn towards the canal, she asked, 'Can I go inside again?'

Thinking that she'd already been inside and aware that the crime-scene men would soon be there, Brunetti said, 'It would be better if you didn't go in again, Dottoressa.'

'There's a cat,' she said. There was no hint of compromise in her voice.

Pucetti interrupted here, saying, 'There's a grey one on top of the filing cabinet, Dottoressa.'

Pucetti waited for Brunetti to speak, and when he did not, the officer said, 'Don't worry, Signora. We'll take care of him.' She looked at him as if not understanding. 'I've always had a cat, ever since I was a kid,' he added. 'Do you have spare cages inside?'

'In the closet in the waiting room,' she answered.

'What's his name?'

'Tigre, and he was supposed to go home today.'

'He will, Dottoressa,' Pucetti said. 'We'll take him. I promise.' Brunetti watched her consider the offer: her body relaxed, and he knew she would accept it.

Pucetti must have had the same response. 'Tell me where he lives, and we'll see he gets there.'

It took her a moment to decide, but finally she did. 'They live in the *calle* that begins at Palazzo Boldù, going right as you come out. Their name's on the bell: Zimmermann.' Then, as if still uncertain, she asked, 'Should I call and tell them he's coming home today?'

Pucetti exchanged glances with Foa, who smiled at the doctor and said. 'Not only that, but tell her he'll be going home in a police launch.'

15

Dottoressa del Balzo offered little real opposition when Brunetti insisted that she go back to the launch with Foa and wait for him there. Once they had disappeared under the arch, Brunetti told Pucetti to stop people from going inside, then walked to the door and opened it. From the back room, he heard the dog barking. He looked around. The first thing he saw was the overturned cabinet and the dead computer, its face crushed when it was shoved from the desk.

Choosing to set his feet on spaces free of paper or glass, or blood, Brunetti walked to the door behind the desk and pushed it fully open with his elbow. The noise doubled and grew wilder. There was far more blood on the floor of this room: no wonder Pucetti had reacted so strongly.

The enormous dog had stopped barking and was watching Brunetti. In the voice he had used with his much younger children, Brunetti said, 'It's all right, Zucca. I'm here to see how you are. Everything's going to be all right.'

Brunetti took a step forward and put his foot on something soft. He looked down and saw what he at first thought was a banana peel, but bananas were not grey, nor were they covered with fur.

'*Oh, Gesù,*' he said out loud, and the wild barking resumed. Brunetti ignored the noise: he needed to know what it was. He looked again and then saw the other ear, attached to a rabbit's head that had plastic eyes and a dark plastic nose. One of the dogs had brought his toy with him. So he wouldn't be frightened.

He heard the siren growing nearer and went outside, then into the *campiello*. Soon the crime-scene crew, led by their chief, Bocchese, arrived. Brunetti greeted both officers by name as they set down the cases they carried.

Bocchese approached Brunetti and gave a motion of his hand that served as greeting.

'Is there a place where we can change?' he asked.

'I don't think that will be necessary. The only injury was to a dog, not a person.'

Bocchese, who seemed shorter than he had the last time Brunetti saw him, turned to the men and said, 'You heard the Commissario.'

One of the men set down a large case, opened it and, ignoring the bio suits, pulled out four pairs of plastic shoe covers and the same number of gloves. He handed them to them all.

Brunetti wondered if the others were thinking of how familiar the full protective suits had become in photos and videos in recent years. Not at crime scenes, but surely at death scenes.

'Tell me,' Bocchese said, breaking into his thoughts.

'It's the clinic of a veterinarian. There was a break-in last night,' Brunetti answered. 'Vandalism. Possible theft.'

'What?' Bocchese asked. 'Three of us came out here for that?'

'There might be more behind it,' Brunetti replied.

'That's crazy,' the taller of the officers said in a muffled voice.

Brunetti turned to face Bocchese, extending the two plastic packets. 'I've already been inside. Should I bother with these?'

'That's what the rules say, Guido, so do it, would you?'

Brunetti did as he was told and slipped them over his shoes, the gloves over his hands. Bocchese was already at the door, his men close behind. Pucetti was talking to the tall one but stopped at the door and stepped back to let the technicians enter. Brunetti followed them inside.

'Get pictures,' Bocchese told them. When he saw the traces of blood, he drew in a deep breath and said, very softly, 'Now, was that really necessary?' as though he were reproving a child.

The technicians started spraying the objects that must have been touched: the corpse of the computer, the surface of the desk, the files. When they passed into the other room, the dog erupted into new and more panicked barking.

Brunetti stayed in the waiting room, already regretting having gone inside, perhaps adding to the physical evidence the squad would record.

After photographing the second room a number of times and taking fingerprints from surfaces and objects, the two technicians returned to Bocchese. The noise of the dog subsided immediately, and Brunetti could hear the men speaking in lowered tones, the sound of the spray bottle, footsteps.

Brunetti walked over to the unshuttered window and looked out at the *campo*. He watched as Pucetti and Alvise spoke to the people who came up to question them, pleased at the relaxed posture of the two officers, the ease with which they spoke, and the friendly nods that greeted what they said.

Behind him, the voices grew a bit louder. Something scraped across the floor. He heard a single male voice speak a few short phrases, softly, as though encouraging a colleague to lend him a hand. There followed a few heavy steps, and when Brunetti turned to see what was going on, he saw one of the men holding a cat in his gloved hands. The cat battered its head repeatedly against the cuff of the man's jacket. Finally, it managed to stick its head inside and stopped squirming.

Brunetti went over to the closet on the other side of the desk. He opened it and found three small metal cages, took the one on top and fiddled with the door until it opened. He took the cage back to the technician and set it on the doctor's desk. As if he'd done this before, the technician stuck both hands into the cage, slid back his sleeve and set the cat on two, then four feet on the bottom of the cage. The cat rolled into a ball and stuck one leg over its head.

Bocchese said, 'I think we're done.'

'That was quick,' Brunetti said. Fifteen minutes at most.

The other technician remarked, 'They're animals, Signore.' There was no sympathy in his voice.

'They're also helpless and defenceless,' Brunetti said. It was only a moment later that he realized how much he sounded like his own daughter.

Bocchese made a noise and opened his mouth to speak.

Before he could, the technician picked up the cage and asked Brunetti, 'Your man said he's supposed to take this boy home. Should I give him the cage?'

'Yes, and tell him to have the other pilot – Grandesso – take him there. I'll go back with Foa and the doctor.' Brunetti suddenly realized he'd forgotten about Alvise, a not uncommon event. 'Tell him to take Alvise with them, would you?'

'Yes, sir,' the technician said. He nodded to Bocchese and went outside, carrying the cage.

That left Bocchese and Brunetti alone, their last words echoing in Brunetti's mind.

'What do you think?' Bocchese asked in his normal voice.

'I'd say it was only one person,' Brunetti answered. 'More people would have done more damage.'

Bocchese looked around at the things hurled to the floor, the blood, the files on top of one another. 'Perhaps', was all he said, then turned away, adding, 'I'll take the boys back, but since this is going to be listed as a case of vandalism against property, it's not going to get a lot of attention.'

As they started towards the door to the *campiello*, Bocchese said, 'I've never had anything like this.' He stopped suddenly and turned to look at Brunetti. His face changed as if he were listening to the arrival of a strange idea. 'Maybe because we don't expect these things to be done to animals.' He paused, thinking this through, and then said, 'My God, that means we expect them to be done to people.' He turned his eyes away from Brunetti and considered what he'd just said, then said goodbye and went out into the *campiello* to collect his men and return to the Questura.

Brunetti waited a few minutes until they were all gone, then closed and locked the door. As he pushed down the handle to assure himself it was locked properly, someone called from the opposite building, '*Signore? Signore?*'

Brunetti put the keys into his pocket and leaned against the building. He pushed his head back until it touched the wall and looked up at the first floor, but the window was closed and there was no sign of anyone.

The woman on the second floor, however, was still at hers, and appeared to be sitting. '*Signore*,' she called down a third time. 'Could you tell me what's going on?'

She was elderly, well spoken, polite, and seemed more concerned than interested. 'There's been a break-in, Signora,' he said. She'd soon know everything about it. Neighbourhoods are porous: word travels fast.

'Are the animals all right?' she asked, unable to disguise her fear.

'We'll have to wait and see,' he temporized, reluctant to lie to her but not willing to tell her what had happened.

'Are you police?' she asked.

'Yes.'

'Can I have a word with you?' she asked politely.

'Of course,' he answered, 'but not now. I have to talk to the Dottoressa.'

She nodded, as though she were giving permission for him to do so.

'Could I come and talk to you, Signora?'

'When?'

Brunetti waved his hand towards the clinic, as if to suggest the answer lay there. 'This afternoon,' he proposed and then added, for courtesy's sake, 'if I can.'

'I'll be here,' she said, adding, 'Galvani. The name's under the bell.' Saying nothing else, she pulled the window closed, turned away, and disappeared.

When Brunetti reached the police launch, Foa was polishing the control panel. He must have heard Brunetti's approaching foot-steps, for he stuffed the cloth away and walked to the side of the boat. But the tide had risen since Brunetti arrived, so he needed no help getting aboard.

Brunetti started down the steps to the cabin and saw Dottoressa del Balzo sitting in the farthest seat on the right, head turned away. So as not to frighten her, Brunetti tapped on the window with the back of his fingers, waited until she turned and recog-nized him, then pushed open the door. The warmth of the cabin pleased him.

He heard footsteps above, the noise of something sliding around, and then the motors grew louder as they pulled away from the *riva*. Head bent, he took a place in the middle of the opposite row of seats.

She still wore the police jacket, and Brunetti wondered whether she would take it off when they reached his office. And then what?

'Dottoressa,' he began, studying her face, 'if you agree, we can go back to the Questura now, and we can talk while the memory is still fresh.' As he had in front of the clinic, he spoke in Veneziano, not Italian. He'd found, over the years, that it had a calming effect, especially with women.

'That's all right with me, talking about it now, but I don't think talking's going to help. You saw what happened. Someone broke in and destroyed things. An animal was hurt.' He was struck by how much her voice resembled Elisabetta's, the same tone or pitch or whatever it was musicians called it, and the same wave-like Veneto cadence that was so pronounced when her mother spoke. Her voice tightened and started to wobble. 'My dog.' A flash of red showed on her sleeve as she slapped her hand on her heart.

Brunetti nodded and lowered his head for a moment, as if in thought. Then he looked at her and said, 'I'd like to talk to you to try to find a reason why it happened.'

They had already passed into the *laguna*, and Foa, without having to be told to do so, was keeping to a moderate speed, so they had no difficulty hearing what the other said.

She looked away from him, her glance pulled towards the cemetery, approaching slowly on the left. Brunetti studied her face, looking for more traces of Elisabetta but finding none except their vocal similarity.

'You mean why someone would do that?' she asked. Then, with certainty, she supplied the answer: 'Because he's crazy.'

'And if he's not?' he asked, agreeing with her that it was a man.

'Not crazy?' she asked, as if this were beyond her powers of understanding.

Brunetti said nothing.

He saw the moment when she worked out what he meant and possibility entered her mind: her eyes opened wider, and her mouth fell open just enough for him to see the segmented white line of her teeth. She shook her head slowly, a gesture more indicative of disbelief than negation. 'That's not poss—' she began, but her voice forgot how to finish the sentence.

She turned away from him – or perhaps it was from his words – and, through the back windows, looked at the distant mountains. 'If it wasn't that, then what was it?'

This time it was Brunetti who shook his head. 'As I told you, Dottoressa, I don't know anything except what I saw in your office. I don't know how to explain it, nor do I have any idea why someone would want to attack you.'

She interrupted him. 'I wasn't attacked.'

Brunetti leaned back against the cushions. 'Then can you tell me who owns the practice and who takes care of the animals?'

'I do, of course,' she said, trying to sound indignant. When Brunetti didn't reply, she demanded, 'Why don't you say something?'

'What happened there wasn't done to frighten the animals or their owners, Dottoressa.' He stopped and he waited.

Finally she asked, 'To frighten me?' She tried to sound bold or indignant, Brunetti thought, but fear put a rough edge on her voice. Then, as if to bolster herself, she demanded, 'What gives you the right to say that?'

'I didn't say that, Signora. You did.'

Trying indignation again, perhaps hoping to get it right this time, she demanded, 'Why would anyone do that?'

'That's what I'd like you to tell me, Signora,' Brunetti said. Then, allowing himself to sound tired and impatient, he continued, 'It would save us a lot of time. It will also save you time, Dottoressa. You won't have to be bothered with my questions or disturbed if we decide to have a look at your life to see what might be going on.'

'I don't know what you mean.'

Brunetti's thoughts passed away from her and back to her mother. Elisabetta was a bit of a snob, but she was the child of good and generous people, and that suggested she would be a good and generous mother.

Brunetti looked across at Flora. 'I know your mother,' he said, then stopped to see how she would respond.

She was surprised, no more than that.

'Recently she told me she was worried about you and your husband. She told me he'd warned you that you were both in danger of having something bad happen to you.'

With each phrase he spoke, her face grew tighter, redder, but he had no idea if it was anger at her mother or fear that her husband's warning had come true.

'She had no right to talk to you,' Dottoressa del Balzo said, but it seemed to Brunetti as though she had to force herself to sound angry.

'I'm not sure mothers think in terms of rights,' Brunetti answered.

Before she could reply, Brunetti heard a thundering noise suddenly draw near; the launch swerved to the right, gave a sudden surge of speed, then veered to the left. Thrown off balance, Brunetti struggled upright and looked across at Dottoressa del Balzo, who had somehow managed to keep her place.

The siren gave a long blast, catapulting Brunetti to the door and up on deck. Only metres ahead of them he saw an enormous white launch speeding away.

'Take a picture,' Foa shouted. Brunetti pulled out his phone and took a series of photos of the back of the boat, capturing the red letters: *Gigolo*.

'What happened?' he asked Foa.

'I heard him coming, and when I looked back, I saw how close he was. So I dodged him. Twice.' Then, as an afterthought, 'Bastard.' He pulled the boat's telephone from its place and pushed in some numbers. A man's voice answered, and Foa said, 'Ciao, Lucio. It's Sebastiano. I'm over by Fondamenta Nuove. There's a lunatic loose in a white Riva Bravo. He came up behind me so fast he was there before I noticed him. I swerved away, so I don't know if he wanted to ram me or send a wave over me.' Foa stopped speaking and listened to the other man. 'About twelve metres. Name on the back is *Gigolo*.'

The other voice said something Brunetti could not understand, and Foa answered, 'I think he was trying to frighten me.' The other man apparently found nothing to say to that. 'But I've got a photo,' Foa added, then asked, 'He's heading down toward the Arsenale. Can you send some boats to stop him?'

The other man spoke for a while, until Foa said, 'Could be going out to Certosa, if that's where he's moored. Or San Giorgio, though the boat might be too big for them.' There was another interruption, to which Foa answered, 'No, there's no way he could do that. This boat is big, and it's got double engines.'

Foa turned to Brunetti and started to speak, but the man on the phone said something Foa could not hear. 'Repeat, please,' the pilot said, and when the other did, Foa said, 'Thanks. Of course,' and set down the phone.

'He said he'll send three boats. They'd like your photos.' Then, in a voice that had grown calm, he said, 'I doubt that there are many boats called *Gigolo*, anyway.' After a few shakes of his head, he said, 'You have the number of the Capitaneria?'

Brunetti nodded, found the number in his phone, and sent the photos.

Foa slowed the engine and asked, 'Are we going to the Questura, Signore?'

'Yes, that's best.' Then, thinking of Dottoressa del Balzo, Brunetti said, 'I hope that didn't upset her.'

'Does she live on Murano?'

'No. In the city. But she works on Murano.'

'Then it's not likely to have upset her, Signore,' Foa said as they turned into the Rio Santa Giustina.

'Why?'

'The canal to and from the airport goes past the island, so she's sure to have seen a lifetime's supply of speeding boats.'

Brunetti considered this for a moment and nodded to Foa to acknowledge his wisdom, then went back down to the cabin.

16

When the launch pulled up to the dock in front of the Questura, Brunetti waited until Foa had tied up at the hawser, then got to his feet. He pushed open one of the two swinging doors and held it for Dottoressa del Balzo, stepped up to the deck, then helped her onto the *riva*.

'It's on the third floor,' he told her as they entered the Questura and pointed towards the stairway. 'I'll just be a moment.' Turning back to the officer at the door and speaking softly, he said, 'See if one of the women officers has a spare shirt and jacket – civilian, not police – to lend to Dottoressa del Balzo for a day or two.'

'And if she does, sir?'

'Send them up to my office.'

Munaro saluted, and Brunetti caught up with Dottoressa del Balzo. When they entered his office, he saw it with her eyes: desk, papers, computer, In and Out boxes of files and documents. One cupboard, two chairs in front of the desk.

Deciding it would be wise to make no mention of the jacket she was wearing, he asked, 'Would you like something to drink?'

She had taken one of the chairs in front of his desk and turned to him when he spoke. It took her some time to answer, and when she did, she ignored his offer and said, 'I've never been in a questura before, but nothing I've ever seen on television prepared me for a commissario who offers something to drink.' She smiled as she spoke, and things suddenly became easier between them.

Brunetti ignored his desk and went to the other chair, pulled it a metre away and turned it to face her. 'We don't start with the violence until later,' he risked saying, hoping the absurdity of the remark would calm her.

Her hands released the arms of her chair, and she pulled them into her lap. 'That's certainly a relief,' she said.

'I do need your phone number, however,' he said. 'And your husband's, if you're willing to give me his.'

She considered this for a moment and nodded. He wrote them in his notebook and then, in response to the ease with which she had accepted his joke about violence, closed it and tossed it on his desk.

Brunetti had decided not to record their conversation, thinking this would make it easier for her, so he said only that he wanted her to explain more fully what she had found in the clinic that morning as well as what her mother had been worried about regarding her husband.

Before he could say more, someone knocked at the door, and he called out, 'Avanti,' hoping it would be one of the women officers.

So it proved to be. It was Campi, one of the newest recruits, a young woman just out of school and, from what Brunetti had been told about her, filled with trust in the world and the desire to make it a better place. Not a man given to prayer, Brunetti hoped she would retain some part of that.

'Ah, Officer Campi,' Brunetti said, getting to his feet. He saw that she had a black leather jacket draped over her right arm and a grey sweater in her left hand. A paper shopping bag, from the now defunct COIN, dangled from her right hand.

'Munaro asked me to bring these up to you, Commissario,' she said. 'I hope it's what you're looking for.'

'Dottoressa del Balzo is the judge of that, Officer,' he said, standing aside and waving a hand to present the other woman, who looked confused.

'Are they yours?' Brunetti asked.

The young woman smiled and said, 'I always keep a change of clothing in my locker.'

Brunetti turned to Dottoressa del Balzo and said, 'I thought you might want to change your clothing,' but providing no further explanation.

Before she could react, he started towards the door. 'You can change in here, Dottoressa. I'll come back in a few minutes and we can continue.'

About five minutes later, Officer Campi emerged from his office, leaving the door open behind her. She came up to Brunetti and asked, holding out the bag, 'What do I do with these, sir?'

'Best to destroy them, I think.'

'Even the uniform jacket?'

'Yes. No one would want to wear it if they knew what had happened to it.' From the blank look on her face, Brunetti knew that the doctor had told her nothing. 'Give it to Munaro and tell him to throw it away.'

'Yes, sir,' was all she said. As she retreated, he noticed that she now carried the bag a bit farther away from her body.

When Brunetti returned to his office, the leather jacket hung from the back of Dottoressa del Balzo's chair, and she was wearing the grey sweater.

He returned to his seat and said, 'Perhaps we can talk now, Dottoressa.'

Instead of answering him, she pulled out her *telefonino* and passed it to him. 'Read it,' she said. He looked down and saw a message on the screen.

'He's a reliable man. Trust him.' There was no signature. He handed her back the phone.

'While the officer was giving me the clothes,' Flora began, 'I sent my mother a message and asked her about you. This was her answer.'

'I'm flattered,' Brunetti said. 'It's a long time since we last saw one another,' he said, then quickly added, 'Other than passing on the street, the way one does.'

'I don't remember her ever mentioning you.'

'It was a long time ago, and I was young. We were neighbours.' Then, remembering, 'I think I knew her mother better.'

'My grandmother.'

'Yes.'

'She died only a few years ago.'

'Your mother told me. I'm sorry,' Brunetti said. Then, after a moment's reflection, he added, with great formality, 'She was a good and generous woman.' Brunetti knew they were both stalling, so he decided to precipitate things and asked, waving his hand in the direction of the *telefonino*, 'Do you believe that message?'

'You're a policeman.'

Brunetti laughed in surprise. 'Does that mean you can't trust me or you can?'

She moved around in her chair, leaned back, and turned a bit to feel that the jacket was still in place. Then she turned to him and said, 'I suppose that depends on the policeman.'

She put the phone on her knees and looked at the screen, then looked across at him and said, 'My mother was worried when I told her what happened. She tends to exaggerate.'

Not certain whether she was referring to what she'd told her mother about her husband or to what had happened in the clinic, he asked, 'Are you talking about the … trouble with your husband?'

'It's not trouble,' she said hotly. 'I was worried about him because he's been nervous for some time. And whenever I asked him what was wrong, he told me it was nothing. Only once did he say it was something about work, but that might have been so I wouldn't worry.' She shook her head. 'I don't know.' She sat up straighter and asked, unable to disguise how nervous this was making her, 'What did my mother tell you?'

'Pretty much what you've just told me now.'

'Pretty much?' Her voice was neutral, but suspicion filled her eyes.

'She seemed to believe that his reaction was stronger and he said you'd both be in danger if someone learned what was happening.' It was not until he heard himself say it out loud that Brunetti realized just how vague this was. Then, hoping to surprise her, he added, 'She also said she's afraid he's involved in something bad.' Her mouth fell open, but she said nothing.

Making no acknowledgement of her reaction, he went on, 'She didn't have any idea what that might be.'

In the face of her silence, he continued. 'The only other thing she said is that she thinks your husband is a very good man and could not be involved in anything dishonest.'

'So she thinks he's involved in something bad, but she still considers him a good person who could not be involved in anything dishonest?' she asked, permitting herself sarcasm but keeping anger in reserve.

'So it would seem,' Brunetti answered.

'Do those things sound contradictory to you, Commissario?'

'Of course they do. But people often hold contradictory opinions about other people. Especially if they love them.'

He thought that would prompt her to speak. When it failed to do so, Brunetti asked, 'Did you call your husband?'

She looked up, confused.

'About what happened to your clinic.'

She looked at her phone, then reached back and found the pocket of the jacket and slipped it in there. Now free, her hands went to cover her knees, and looking at her hands and not at him, she said, 'No. There's been no time. The only person I called was my mother.'

'Why haven't you called him, Flora?' he asked. 'You could have done it while you were waiting for me.'

Still avoiding his gaze, she shrugged, made fists a few times, then put her hands back in place on her knees and looked at him. 'Because I'm afraid.' She immediately raised one hand in front of her and said, 'No, that's the wrong word. I'm alarmed and worried. Those things are different.'

'From fear?' he asked.

'Yes.'

Brunetti nodded, and let her answer sit between them for some time before he said, 'What is it that alarms you?'

'That he might have been right, and there's a connection between whatever's bothering him and what happened last night.'

'What sort of connection?' Brunetti asked.

She shook her head. Time passed; suddenly, she looked up at him and asked, 'Do you know Chinese whispers?'

'I beg your pardon?'

'The game. We played it when we were kids. You sit in a circle and someone whispers something to the person next to them, and then that person says it to the next person, who says it to the next, and by the time it's back to the person who said it first, it's not the same thing at all.'

'We called it Chinese telephone,' Brunetti said. 'What about it?'

'That's what happens when you tell people anything. You tell them one version, and after two or more people pass it along, it's changed entirely. That's what's happened here. Enrico told me he was having trouble, and I assumed it was at work, and I suppose I said that when I told my mother.' She was speaking faster and faster as she tried to remember these conversations, and finally she blurted out, 'Or maybe that's what I told her, and she took it more seriously than I did.' She stopped speaking and closed her eyes.

Time passed. She opened her eyes. 'And when Enrico said it had been causing trouble for a long time, I assumed it was something from work: where else could he have trouble?'

Brunetti knew better than to answer this question.

'It doesn't seem a very dangerous piece of information, that your husband has trouble at work.'

'I suppose that depends on the trouble.'

'Do you know what it is?'

She closed her eyes and shook her head slowly. Perhaps she meant it as a negative, but Brunetti read it as an expression of misery at finding herself there, with the police, discussing her husband.

'The only trouble he's ever had was three years ago, and that was resolved.'

'Tell me more.'

'Enrico did the major work in setting up a charity for my father, and then, a few months after it was established and running, he told my father he had done his job and was returning to his other clients full-time.'

When Brunetti said nothing, she added, 'The whole thing had become complicated and took far longer than either of them had planned. It got bigger, and my father hired a secretary.' Her voice quickened as she explained this and, failing to control it, she went on. 'The secretary was paid, but Enrico wouldn't take any money from my father, not even when I told him he should. All the time he was helping my father, he turned down new clients and barely kept up with the ones he already had. Two even left him, he told me.' Her face grew tighter and she said, 'Not that my father ever bothered to ...' She stopped, one word from the cliff.

If Brunetti had been a dog, he would have given a great sniff here, perhaps even begun to pant. His imagination leaped at the resentment in her voice as though it were fresh meat, and that made him something more sinister than a dog. A jackal, perhaps? Some dark eater of carrion.

'Why couldn't he just tell your father he needed an income?' Brunetti asked.

She let out a snort of resignation. 'Because he's a man,' she said with a bitterness that Brunetti could almost taste. 'Because he couldn't admit he was unable to support his wife, certainly not to her father.' She paused and lowered her head, embarrassed to have shown her anger, and added, 'Or maybe he didn't want my father to feel indebted to him.'

She looked at him then and said, using what she probably thought was a normal voice, 'Enrico had no idea it was going to take so long, or I suppose he wouldn't have offered to do it as a favour. For free.' She glanced at Brunetti and added, 'I'd just opened the clinic, and we both really needed the work. And the money.'

When he saw her stretch out her fingers, Brunetti said, 'I understand,' trying to sound as though he believed what he was saying. She put her hands in her lap.

'Have you any idea how your father reacted when your husband resigned?'

She looked off through the window but apparently found nothing interesting because she returned her gaze to Brunetti and said, 'Enrico never told me.' Before Brunetti could say anything, she added, 'And I didn't want to ask.'

Her tone caused Brunetti to put on a concerned expression, thinking it time to ask a diversionary question. 'Has he had trouble with any of his current clients?'

'Not that I know of.'

'With any of the people your father hired?'

She folded her hands together, only to loosen them almost immediately. 'I have no idea.' Her voice was cold, terminal.

Brunetti thought they were heading towards a dead end and so turned into the next side street he passed. 'What I saw in your clinic today was disturbing.'

Her glance was level.

'Could it have been done by one of your clients? Perhaps because of a treatment that failed or an animal that died while in your care?'

She looked at him in confusion, suggesting the impossibility of such a thing. After a moment, however, her mouth dropped open, as though someone had called her a bad name. 'I forgot,' she said. 'It was so crazy I forgot all about it.'

Before Brunetti could ask, she started to speak. 'Some months ago, a woman from Burano brought me a dog she said she'd found on the street. That was supposed to explain why it wasn't chipped and didn't have vaccine records. The dog was in piti-able shape: malnourished, filthy, lethargic.' She held up her hands about twenty centimetres apart and said, 'It was this long, and it weighed... I don't remember, but not even five kilos.' She stopped speaking, as though the memory of the dog was still enough to trouble her. Absently, she added, 'Sweet thing, though.'

'What did the woman want you to do?'

As though having heard only half of what he said, she asked, 'Which woman?'

'The one who brought it in.'

'Oh, of course. She asked if there was anything I could do or if it should be put down.'

Brunetti waited.

'I said I'd do what I could and asked her to call in two days.' She looked at Brunetti and twisted her mouth in what could have been a grin or a grimace of resignation.

'And?'

'And I never saw her again.' After a pause, she said, 'The phone number she gave me didn't exist, and all I had was the dog's name: Georgia.'

'What happened to it?'

'I did an exam, took blood. She had the symptoms of advanced heartworm: swollen belly, lethargy, no appetite, and her temperature was forty.' Then, almost as if he'd asked about his own dog, she added, 'It's passed on by mosquitoes.'

Brunetti realized that the expert in her had taken over, and he could do nothing but listen.

'Just to be sure, I did a heartworm test and she turned out positive, so I put her on a saline drip and started antibiotic treatment.' As though he had asked how long the treatment would last, she said, 'It took more than a month for the worms to disintegrate, but she was tough – must be the Jack Russell in her – and within six weeks she was fine.' Perhaps because Brunetti's concern showed on his face, she added, 'You have to go slowly killing heartworms; if you kill them too fast at the beginning, the dead ones sort of clog up the dog's system and can kill it.'

'Where was the dog all this time?' Brunetti asked, interested now.

'I kept her in the clinic, and when she was feeling better, I had my assistant take her out for a walk twice a day, or I did.'

He didn't want to spend more time on this, so he asked, 'Does this story have a happy ending?'

'Perhaps,' she answered. When Brunetti did not ask, she continued. 'After six weeks, she was a different dog, completely healthy. And she was sweet-tempered, amazing after the way she'd been mistreated, and very affectionate.' Perhaps sensing his growing impatience, she said, 'I met a client on the street, and she told me her dog had died two weeks before, and when she said they wanted to get a new one, I asked her if she'd like to have Georgia.

'She did. I'd already chipped her and given her all the shots she needed, so she went to her new home.'

'Why are you telling me this story, Signora?'

'Because two weeks ago, another woman from Burano showed up, with her son, who seemed like a thug, and told me they wanted their dog. I said I didn't know what she was talking about, and the son insisted I had their dog and they wanted her back. They knew their neighbour had stolen her.'

She shook her head in disbelief. 'The son kept insisting they knew their neighbour had brought it to me, so I took them into the other room and showed them the dogs that were in the kennel. She wasn't there, of course, but they wouldn't believe me and kept saying they knew the dog had been here and they wanted her back.' Her voice slipped into anger and she said, 'You'd think she was winning medals at Crufts, for God's sake.'

'What did you do?'

'I threatened to call the police if they didn't leave.'

'And did they?'

'Finally,' she answered. Then, uneasily, 'But not before saying they'd be back.'

'Did you believe them?'

'That it was their dog or that they'd be back?' She lowered her head in what Brunetti thought was embarrassment and said, 'Both.'

After letting a long time pass, Brunetti asked, 'Why didn't you tell me this before?'

This time, her hands went up in the air in a gesture of help-lessness. 'They seemed like people from another planet. And I decided they shouldn't have a dog. I did.' She paused, and Brunetti quelled his impatience.

'Every time one of them said something, the other repeated it. And they never looked at me directly. Their eyes were always wandering around the clinic. I don't know; it was as though they were trying to decide the price of everything they saw: the table, the cabinets, the instruments in them.'

'Did they threaten you?' Brunetti asked.

'Didn't I just tell you that?' she said impatiently.

'I'm thinking like a lawyer, Dottoressa.' Brunetti spoke calmly and waited until she seemed ready to listen to more. 'Did they say directly that they intended to do you harm if you didn't do what they wanted?' He saw how that changed her expression and so added, 'Or touch you in an aggressive way?'

'All right. You win,' she said and couldn't stop herself from relaxing. 'And I'll add that they didn't frighten me, not exactly, but they were very strange; I'm not accustomed to being around people like that.' Then, as if in response to a request that she explain fully, she added, 'People who have animals tend to be calmer. Especially if they're dog people.' Then, reflecting on this, she added, 'It's cat people who can be strange sometimes.'

However interesting this might be, Brunetti decided to return to the original subject, but before he could, the Dottoressa asked, 'Do you think they could be related to the … attack?'

Ignoring her question, he asked, 'What did they look like?'

She suddenly looked towards the window. His eyes followed hers, and together they watched a cruise-ship-sized cloud float towards San Marco. 'The woman must be in her seventies: dirty grey hair about shoulder length, glasses that magnify the size of her eyes, obvious dentures, and a very strong Buranese accent.' Brunetti waited to see if she recalled anything else. Apparently she did not because she began anew: 'The son might be fifty, perhaps less. There's nothing memorable about him: he's about as tall as you are, only much thinner. Same Buranese accent. Thin hair, dark brown with a lot of white, cut very short.'

'Did one of them seem more ... unstable?' Brunetti asked.

With no hesitation, she answered, 'The mother. He seemed there only to agree with her. Every word. But she was in charge; she kept talking about "my dog".'

Brunetti made no comment.

She raised her hands and let them fall helplessly to her lap. 'I have no idea who it could have been. I looked: no drugs were taken.' Before Brunetti could ask, she said, 'You know addicts break into our clinics, too. The drugs are similar in some cases, especially ketamine and buprenorphine, and the people who steal them all seem to know which ones work best.' When she saw that she had Brunetti's attention, she added, 'They've even learned how to adjust the dosages for a person's weight.'

Brunetti found no adequate comment and so asked, 'Can you think of any other reason it might have happened?'

She sat for a very long time, and he watched her trying to work it out or pretend to look as though she were. He looked away and did not turn back until she started to speak again.

'Perhaps what Enrico said: that there's something he's working on that someone doesn't like.' Before Brunetti could comment, she added, 'But that's crazy. All he's doing is keeping people's books.' Her gaze grew more distracted and she asked him, 'Why would someone not want him to talk about his work?' She let that sink in and then added, 'And why do something to me rather than to him?'

Brunetti decided to take the chance and said, 'It might be a former client. If not yours, then his.'

When she did nothing but shake her head, he realized she was at the point where failure led to exasperation, and then to refusal.

'One more thing,' he said, trying not to voice his own sense of futility at bothering to continue to seek information. 'Has your husband responded strangely to anything in the last few weeks?'

As Brunetti watched, her mouth pulled in, her cheeks suddenly seemed less full, and her eyes contracted as if she were straining to see something that was badly lit. Then she pursed her lips and shook her head, the way one does after saying something stupid. 'No,' she said, but immediately added, 'not really.'

Brunetti smiled and said, 'Tell me,' resurrecting the voice he'd used to cajole his children when they were reluctant to answer a question. For the first time, he noticed three light lines running across her forehead.

Just as he began to think she was going to refuse to answer, she said, almost inaudibly, 'It's something stupid. Nothing.'

'Tell me, Flora.'

The sound of her name apparently trapped her into obedience. 'A few weeks ago, we decided to go for a walk after dinner. It was a beautiful night because of the moon.' Then, with either nostalgia or the irony Venetians often used when acknowledging the beauty of their city, she said, 'Venice by night.' Her smile wasn't really a smile.

'It must have been about midnight. We were walking through Campo Manin.' She looked up and said, 'We were passing the travel agency by the bridge.' Hearing herself, she quickly amended the name to 'ex-travel agency', the usual formula for any shop or office killed by the *pandemia*.

'You know it, don't you?' she asked, this time switching to Veneziano and using the familiar '*tu*'.

'Yes,' he answered, recalling the dusty windows and dead plants, the sun-bleached posters, the general scream of drought and misery that slipped through the windows every time he walked past it.

'We stopped and looked at the brochures that are still in the agency windows.' Then, curious, not stalling, she asked, 'Have you noticed them?'

Brunetti nodded. 'Abandoned on the floor,' he said. 'The grass around all the swimming pools doesn't grow: it just bleaches out more every month. And the palm trees are almost white by now.'

She smiled but did not laugh. 'We were looking at them and asking each other why we used to want to go to those places.' She gave a little faux shudder to emphasize her point.

'And then Enrico stopped talking and stared into the window.' She didn't speak for some time, then resumed. 'It was very strange. He didn't say anything, just stood there and stared inside. All I looked at was his face. It was as if he were watching a film or listening to a conversation in his head.

'After a minute I put my hand on his arm and shook him a little bit, and he looked at me like he was surprised to see me there. I asked him if he was all right, but I think he didn't hear me, or he didn't understand. He looked back inside and then he made a grunting sound, as if someone had hit him. I wondered if he was having a heart attack or a stroke, but I couldn't speak, I was so terrified. Then he stopped and turned and stared at me, and a look flashed across his face that frightened me even more. There was no emotion: his face was dead.

'It frightened me so much that I must have made some sort of noise. Without thinking, I stepped back from him and raised my hands in front of me, and it was as if this broke some sort of magic spell.

'He actually put his hands on the window and leaned his forehead against it, then he made another noise, like a groan. After a while, he looked at me and tried to smile and said we should go home.' She waved one hand in the air as an accompaniment to her words.

'Did you talk about it?'

'I asked him on the way and again the next morning, and both times he said he didn't know what I meant: he just felt weak for a moment, and it was nothing.'

To quiet her hands, she locked them together and set them on her lap. 'You don't know him. Once Enrico makes up his mind, there's no sense in trying to change him. And he made up his mind not to talk about this. But whatever it was, it troubled him deeply.'

'And he was surprised by it?'

She considered this for some time and finally said, 'Shocked, more like.'

'By what he saw?'

'It couldn't have been anything else.'

Long experience had taught Brunetti the signs when a witness's patience was running out: he sensed he had time for one more question. 'Do you think this is related to his work?'

Her gaze indicated that she was already past the limits of her patience, or perhaps it was panic.

With no preparation, she stood. Silent, he pushed back his chair, got to his feet, and moved towards the door. He held it for her to pass through ahead of him. Once in the corridor, she raised a hand and said, 'I can find my way out, thank you.'

He nodded and thanked her for coming, said they would contact her if they learned anything about the attack on her clinic. Then he smiled and said, meaning it, 'I'm glad Georgia wasn't there when they came.'

She had already turned in the direction of the stairs, but this stopped her. She turned towards him and said, 'Thank you. So am I.' And then, as though it were a normal part of her last sentence, she added, 'I don't know what else it could be except his work.'

17

Dottoressa del Balzo had no sooner started down the steps than Brunetti began trying to imagine what her husband could be afraid of. The attack on the clinic showed that Fenzo and his wife had something to fear. Could a warning be any clearer? *The animals now; you next.*

His thoughts were interrupted by the arrival of Pucetti. Brunetti waved him inside, asking, 'How did it go?'

'They weren't home, so I left him with Claudio, at the bookshop round the corner. He said he'd call them and tell them he had the cat.'

Brunetti waved Pucetti to a chair and, when he was seated, asked, 'Did you find the others?'

Pucetti smiled to indicate that he had had some success and said, 'She's in the phone book, so I went to talk to the guys in the Carabinieri station in Campo dei Gesuiti, but they didn't even know who they were. The restaurant in the *campo* is still closed, but the bar across the way is owned by the same man, and it's open. The owner said Fenzo's saved him a lot of money over the last years by claiming expenses and deductions he never knew about and getting him onto the right list of businesses that will be eligible for Covid-loss payments.'

After a moment's thought, Pucetti said, 'It's strange, sir. The restaurant and the bar are the only commercial places in the *campo*, and you know how big it is.' He asked, 'Did ...' but stopped.

'Did what?' Brunetti asked.

'Did the city use to be like that, with real places, where you could buy real things?'

'Like buttons and kitchen pots?' Brunetti asked.

'Yes.'

'You could even find underwear and fresh pasta and flowers,' Brunetti was happy to reveal.

'That's what my mother tells me,' Pucetti said. 'It sounds like a fairy tale.' Seeing Brunetti's expression, he added quickly, 'To me, that is, sir.'

'Yes, it was different,' Brunetti said but was unwilling to continue the topic. 'Thanks for taking the cat back, Pucetti.'

Reading the signal correctly, Pucetti got to his feet. 'You're welcome, sir. Any time I can be of use ...' He stopped in the middle of that sentence, saluted, and left the Commissario to his thoughts.

Sending a cat home on a police launch? Had he really ordered that? He had been aware for months of the invasive lethargy of the *pandemia*, a symptom that seemed to have struck everyone, regardless of whether they'd fallen victim to the other, malign symptoms. Decisions took longer to make, longer to regret having made. Correspondence had slowed, and it took a week to write an email with a simple 'Yes' or 'No'. Recalling conversations he'd had, even the day before, now required effort. But to have used a police launch to return a cat to its owner: this was more than lethargy. It put him in mind of the behaviour of the mother and son who had gone to Dottoressa del Balzo's clinic to retrieve their kidnapped dog. The thought of one old woman led Brunetti to think of the other: Signora Galvani.

Considering her age, Brunetti searched for her in the phone book and found her: Vittoria Galvani, the only Galvani on Murano.

When she answered, Brunetti gave his name and identified himself as the policeman she had spoken to and explained that he had a number of things to do but thought he could stop by to talk to her after launch, although he couldn't give a definite time.

Perhaps, Brunetti thought, time is different for old people, for she seemed not at all troubled by this and said she would be home all afternoon and he could come whenever it was convenient for him.

That agreed, he turned his attention to his emails. Signorina Elettra informed him that both Griffoni and Vianello had returned to work. He immediately called them all and asked them to come to his office to discuss the case they were working on, conscious of his by now automatic neutrality when referring to their expanding interest in the matter.

The first to arrive was Griffoni, in a brown skirt and sweater, wearing black trainers; behind her, Vianello, in uniform. They entered, and while they were arranging their chairs, Signorina Elettra arrived, prompting Vianello to bring over the third chair from its place beside the window. All of them, Brunetti noticed, were carrying folders or papers.

He gave them what he thought was a relaxed smile and said, with no introduction, 'Claudia, would you start?'

She nodded, pulled out a few papers, and said, 'I have del Balzo's bank records. There was nothing unusual until three years ago, when he established the ONLUS and transferred two thousand euros from his own account to Belize nel Cuore's in what appears in the organization's bank records as the first donation.' She turned a page. 'He has no outstanding personal debts, no mortgage on his home. He seldom uses his credit card and never in a foreign country. Since his retirement, he has hired administrators to run his companies and a financial consultant to help him with his investments. Nothing else caught my attention.' She looked at the others in turn, but no one had a question.

Griffoni went on. 'His earnings in the five years before he retired seemed more than adequate, but not exceptional. Because of the variety of his enterprises, his income was always in a state of flux, particularly in the last years.'

She stopped speaking, looked around, then said, 'That's all I have at the moment.'

'Lorenzo, what did you find?'

Vianello, too, had a folder on his knees but didn't bother opening it. 'I asked around. It turns out that I play water polo with someone who worked for him. Managing one of his supermarkets.'

'Water polo?' Griffoni asked, ignoring the supermarkets.

'Over at Sant'Alvise,' Vianello said. Then, as if he were looking for people to join him, he added, 'Tuesday evenings, eight to nine-thirty.'

'And?' Brunetti asked when neither of the women commented.

'And he said he was a good businessman and apparently an honest one.' He paused and added, 'He always treated his employees well: paid half of the fees for the children whose parents sent them to a private nursery.' He looked around and added, 'Most of the workers with children were enrolled.'

Vianello had not finished. 'When I told him about the charity and the money del Balzo's sending to Central America, he smiled and said it's the sort of thing del Balzo would do.'

Vianello pulled his reading glasses from the pocket of his jacket and put them on. 'There's more,' he said and opened the folder, revealing a considerable stack of papers. He removed a few and closed the file.

'He travels a lot, now that he's retired.' Looking down at the paper, he continued, 'He's been to Belize five times since he started raising money for the hospital. Each time he spent more than a month there.'

'How do you know that?' Signorina Elettra interrupted to ask.

'I have his flight dates, but I can't find any traces of him after he arrived in Belize or where else he might have gone, not until his flight back.'

'Surely, there are traces of where he went,' she answered. 'There always are.'

Vianello smiled broadly, set down the papers, and held up empty hands in a sign of helplessness. 'I couldn't find any trace of him.'

In the face of their scepticism, he began to list those absent things: 'No hotel reservations, credit card receipts, no further flights.' He stopped and then added, 'Nor does he seem to have taken his *telefonino* with him on any of those trips. At any rate, the phone was turned off during all five periods.' His audience sat silent, as if in shock at the idea of such a thing.

Before any one of them could comment, Vianello went on: 'I found no restaurant bills or rental cars, no purchases whatsoever. No clothing, no use of a duty-free.'

The Ispettore shook his head and repeated, 'Nothing. It's as if he turned himself off with the *telefonino*.'

Griffoni raised her hand just enough for the others to see the motion, and asked, 'Could he have been staying with friends?'

'Perhaps.' Vianello answered so softly that Brunetti began to suspect he had something to reveal and was enjoying his ability to make them wait for it. 'He didn't use his phone once he left Italy, only sent emails to his wife.' Vianello paused to see if they had anything to say, but no one spoke.

'The day before he left for Belize the last time, he used his credit card to buy a pair of sunglasses at that place near the Ponte dell'Ovo and not again until he got back.' He glanced down at the paper and read, 'Sixty-seven euros.'

He looked around, as if to see wheather he had captured their attention. When he was certain that he had, he pulled, with a magician-like gesture, more papers from the same folder.

'These are the passenger manifests for his flights to and from Belize.'

'All ten flights?' Signorina Elettra broke in to ask, face aglow with pride in his accomplishment.

'Yes.'

'Oh, wonderful, Lorenzo,' she all but cooed.

A very small smile sneaked onto Vianello's face, and he said, 'Strangely enough, on all of those flights, the same person was sitting beside him in first class.'

None of the others spoke for some time, nor did they appear to breathe. Finally Griffoni asked, voice low and reverent, as though she'd just sensed that the blood of San Gennaro had begun to liquefy: 'Who?'

As though he'd just opened the envelope and pulled out the name of the winner, Vianello paused a moment, then announced, 'Dottoressa Innocenza Bagnoli,' and went on to introduce her to the audience: 'Formerly a financial adviser for a bank in Venice that has for some time been under investigation for various offences against banking laws. She lives in Mestre, of all places, and is currently self-employed as a financial consultant and has already begun advising a number of people how best to handle their assets.' He glanced up at his audience and asked, truly puzzled, 'It's interesting that these people never say the word "money", isn't it?'

'It's because the word is vulgar, Lorenzo,' Griffoni said reprovingly. 'Assets, wealth, investments, capital, funds ... and I forget the others. If we were in America, it would be called the "M-word", never to be pronounced, always to be thought.'

Brunetti was suddenly impatient with their playfulness and asked, 'Is Signor del Balzo a client of hers?'

'Yes.'

'For how long?'

'Two and a half years.'

'So after he established Belize nel Cuore?'

'Yes.'

Brunetti had noticed that there were more pages beneath the ones Vianello had already shown them, but chose to let Vianello enjoy his success to the fullest.

'What else have you discovered about Dottoressa Bagnoli?' Griffoni asked, breaking off to raise a fist in the air and punch at the ceiling a few times, a gesture Vianello pretended not to see.

'She is originally from Brescia. She attended the university there and, eighteen years ago, at the age of twenty-seven, received a *laurea magistrale* in ...' Again the Ispettore paused, then very slowly turned to the next page to continue: 'Money, Finance, and Risk Assessment.'

A hush fell upon the assembled supplicants as all of them now saw the sure signs of the approaching miracle. 'Risk Assessment,' Signorina Elettra repeated and then gave an enormous sigh. 'How peaceful and innocent that sounds as it divorces itself from money and finance.' Thrilled, she could do no more than repeat, 'Risk Assessment.'

Griffoni leaned closer to Signorina Elettra and said, 'Bear up, Elettra. I think there's more.'

Vianello nodded and pulled out the final papers. He adjusted his glasses, which Brunetti thought a gratuitous gesture.

'She, as it turns out,' Vianello began, barely able to disguise his self-satisfaction, 'does use a credit card.' He lowered the papers just enough to let them see his eyes and, contemplating his audience from behind his glasses, continued, 'Which is given to her as an employee of the hospital in Belize City.'

Signorina Elettra almost lost control of herself and interrupted Vianello to say, in an awed whisper, 'The charges for which are debited to an account in ...?'

Vianello smiled and picked up her remark by saying, 'Liechtenstein.'

Signorina Elettra would surely have judged any physical manifestation of her delight – say, applause – as unseemly and thus she did no more than lean towards the Ispettore, pat him on the arm, and say, 'Oh, Lorenzo, what a wonderful discovery.' Then, perhaps invoking the spirit of Saint Anthony of Padova, patron saint of lost things, she added, 'Bless you for finding the manifests: that's so terribly difficult.'

Vianello basked in her praise for a moment before saying, 'There's more.'

They sat silent as he went on, attentive as children hearing the story of the babe in the manger for the first time.

'For the last two trips she made to Belize ...' Vianello began, then looked up and said apologetically, 'I haven't had time to check the other trips yet,' before he went back to the previous sentence: 'she travelled with a companion, staying in double rooms in five-star hotels. She also spent a significant amount on restaurants, rental cars – always an SUV or a Mercedes – boat rentals, a few pieces of jewellery, and clothing, including three pairs of Berluti men's shoes.' With a small nod in the direction of Signorina Elettra, his only teacher, he added, 'Size forty-four,' and turned a page.

'During this last trip, she stayed with a guest in a suite at the Four Seasons on the Gulf of Papagayo.' Looking up from the paper, he said, 'That's in Costa Rica. There, she paid not only for the room, more clothing, and more jewellery, but also for daily yoga classes, scheduled at the same time that some other person – whose name does not appear on any of the registration forms – took scuba lessons, for which she paid.' He stopped speaking and handed some of the papers to Brunetti, retaining two sheets for himself.

Brunetti smiled at Vianello, glanced at Signorina Elettra, and said, 'Lorenzo, you are a compliment to those who have taught you.' When his words had stopped sounding in the room, he waved a hand towards the remaining papers and asked, 'And those?'

Vianello shook his head. 'It's the hotel registration. I've tried everything, but I've had no luck.' He added, as though he were embarrassed by his failure, 'I've had no time. I've been out at night, hunting drug dealers and children, and during the day I try to sleep.'

Signorina Elettra turned towards him and said, sounding nervous, 'Would you mind if I had a look?'

'I hoped you'd offer,' Vianello said gratefully and passed her the two remaining sheets of paper. 'It took me half the night to find the manifests, but the hotel records are impenetrable.'

'Yes, they're hard to locate,' Signorina Elettra agreed.

Vianello lowered his head in defeat.

'Don't worry,' she reassured him. 'I have a friend who works in Lausanne, in the hotel business. It shouldn't be hard for him to find the name of the other person in the double room.' Then, primly, she added, 'The guards might be sloppy about checking passports at the borders, but the Four Seasons is not.'

And how does she know that? Brunetti asked himself, but he chose, instead, to ask her, 'What have you discovered about Signor Guidone?'

His question freed Signorina Elettra to add her mite to the collection plate, which she did by telling them that the only trace of him she had found was an obituary in the *Giornale di Vicenza* announcing his death two years before, *'dopo una lunga malattia'*, the accepted euphemism for cancer. She chose to read them the rest. "'For decades, his kitchen machine and cutlery shop in Piazza delle Biade was known and sought out by professional cooks and all those interested in the preparation of food. He will be deeply mourned by his nephew, Avvocato Luca Guidone, also of Vicenza.'" She paused to show her respect for the dead, then added, 'I took the liberty of calling Avvocato Guidone, who explained that his uncle was an old friend of Signor del Balzo and, yes, had been asked to sign a document of some sort in the year before his death.'

Silence fell upon them, until Brunetti, playing devil's advocate, said, 'We still have no proof that del Balzo is anything other than what he appears to be: a man who wants to help his fellow man.' Before any of them could contradict him, Brunetti repeated, 'Proof.'

Griffoni interrupted to say, 'Wait until we see if the money's going to the hospital, Guido.'

'I think we can dismiss that possibility,' Signorina Elettra observed.

'With what proof?' asked Vianello.

'You've given us a suggestion of the proof, Lorenzo,' she said. 'Yoga classes.'

'A magistrate might not agree with you,' Vianello admonished her.

'Nor a judge,' agreed Brunetti.

Ever practical, Griffoni interrupted the speculation to ask, 'What do we do now?'

Brunetti looked at the others before saying, 'So far, we've found evidence of a possible case of fraud. We'll have no idea of the dimensions until you,' he began, returning his attention to Signorina Elettra, 'have a look at the financial records of Belize nel Cuore: who has given them money and how much? Who in Belize receives and distributes the money they're given, and where do they send it?'

He saw that she had flipped over one of the papers she had and was taking notes. He paused until she stopped writing, then asked, 'Do you think you can do this?'

'It might take a day or two,' Signorina Elettra answered, tapping the erasered end of her pencil against the paper. 'If it's a small project, then it's unlikely they'll have adequate protection.'

'Against what?' Brunetti asked.

'Me.'

18

Brunetti was struck by the vainglory of that single word, 'Me.' Fast upon that, the realization swept over him that this entire enterprise was driven by the same sense of vanity. Real crime was rare in Venice: the worst problem they had was a handful of bored adolescents using the cover of night to break into shops long closed by the *pandemia* to steal, or vandalize, merchandise in which they had little interest. In pharmacies, they could steal drugs, but what would they take from a kitchenware store or a shoe shop? Youth had no need to conquer the storerooms of maturity: it would all come to them in time.

Seeing his distraction, the other three began a whispered conversation, leaving Brunetti to his thoughts. All of what they'd done resulted from his sympathy for someone from his past, and all they'd discovered was that her husband was an adulterer and the director of a dodgy charity. For almost two weeks, he had involved his friends in the pursuit of something that was clearly the business of the Guardia di Finanza.

He had worked them all into a corner where they were now trapped in possession of information that was not in their remit: probable financial crime and tax evasion. As members of the Polizia di Stato, they were obliged to investigate the break-in at Dottoressa del Balzo's clinic, even though the thieves hadn't even bothered to open the drugs cabinet, but the investigation of the other possibilities of crime they had come upon belonged to the Guardia di Finanza.

Brunetti thought of something Paola said whenever she was presented with the possibility that she had taken the wrong path or had gone too far, whether it was the discovery that she was going north to get to Rome or had added a cup of sugar instead of a spoonful to the tomato sauce: something about it being as tedious to return as to go on. Here, Brunetti found himself faced with a similar dilemma. How to pass the investigation to those whose job it was? How to admit an error to his colleagues without embarrassing, even dishonouring, himself?

His attention drifted back into the room; the others sensed its return and stopped talking.

'Is there anything else we should all know?' he asked.

Signorina Elettra raised her hand and held up a finger.

'What is it, Signorina?' Brunetti asked.

She opened her folder and pulled out a piece of paper and then another. She did not look at them as she said, 'You asked me to look into Vice-Admiral Fullin's medical history.' Brunetti nodded, and she went on. 'That was some time ago.' She shifted in her chair. 'My search was slowed down by the need to enter military files. I'd never ... consulted them before, so it took me some time to understand the system and how best to ... examine it.'

She allowed herself to glance at the first sheet of paper. 'He was diagnosed with the early symptoms of dementia six years ago, the diagnosis slowly shifting to Alzheimer's after two years, as the symptoms became more pronounced. That second diagnosis was confirmed at a military hospital in Rome, where he could have remained. His family declined and brought him home, where they insisted he would be more comfortable. This is now his sixth year with the disease, with no improvement noted, only a slow decline.

'I mention that phrase "slow decline" because his doctor has noted that, even now, at times he seems no more than slow to respond as his eventual responses indicate that he has been following the conversation. In his case notes, his doctor described it as *"un giorno sì, un giorno no"*, which is confirmed by everything his family says about his behaviour. He has good days, and he has bad days.'

Griffoni gave a deep sigh, so deep it called the attention of everyone in the room to her. A long time passed before she said, 'Well,' as though the question mark had been half erased, but she had no idea of whether it was meant to be there or not.

Brunetti knew what she was asking and suspected that the others did as well. He considered the unspoken question and realized that he wanted to be free of this, wanted to turn the whole thing over to the Guardia di Finanza and be done with it.

It had become too complicated; too many people had appeared in the cast list. What had started with the possibility of a dishonest accountant had morphed into a story that had expanded to include the beaches of Costa Rica, a degree in risk assessment, and a demented Vice-Admiral who enjoyed looking at medals, watching a war DVD, and listening to his grandson read him stories of exploits at sea.

Before Griffoni could repeat her semi-question, Brunetti got to his feet. 'I'd like to wait a few more days. Before we pass this to the Guardia di Finanza, I want to talk to my friend. She was worried that people would learn about her family, but it's impossible to avoid that now. She came to me because she saw this as a family problem, and she trusted me not to involve the police in any official way.'

He leaned forward and shoved some papers to the other side of his desk, suddenly aware of how much the information given in confidence by a friend had metastasized into a tangled mess of obligations and speculation.

The others got to their feet, all silent. He had said nothing about what he would like Vianello and Griffoni to do, leaving it to them to follow their curiosity and continue, or to stop spending their time doing a favour for a friend of a friend.

They filed out silently; Brunetti could not recall a meeting ever having ended in such a solemn manner. When he was alone in the office, he pulled out his phone and dialled the number Elisabetta had given him. She was eager to meet so that he could tell her what he'd learned.

Elisabetta's voice grew tense. 'Flora's told me what happened in her clinic.' She paused, as if to give him the chance to say something, but he chose to remain silent. 'She wants me to go there with her this afternoon.'

Brunetti had no objection and said, 'It's no longer a crime scene.' Then he added, 'Perhaps we could meet before you go?'

'Where?'

'What about Rosa Salva?' he suggested. It was in the *campo* below her home, so nothing would be easier for her. 'It should still be warm enough to sit outside.'

After a moment, she said, 'That's fine. What time shall we meet?'

'I could be there in fifteen minutes,' Brunetti said.

'Perfect,' Elisabetta answered, and replaced the phone.

Elisabetta was there when he arrived, sitting at one of the central tables. He wondered if this choice was a holdover from former times, when a free table was hard to find and those sitting at the outer ring of tables had tourists continually walking by.

There were precious few passers by, and those who did walk through the *campo* looked like Venetians going about their business. The large umbrellas were still in place among the tables, but they were furled, awaiting more sun and a rise in temperature.

Brunetti slipped through the chairs and said her name. She looked up and smiled, the sun behind her, casting her into a less revelatory light. Today she wore a navy blue jacket, a white shirt with a scarf at the neck that Paola had taught him to recognize as Hermès, jeans, and white sneakers. An inattentive glance would describe it as 'casual wear', whereas a practised one would instantly see a cost sufficient to maintain a small village in Uttar Pradesh for a month.

He looked around for a waiter, then sat down. 'Thanks for coming,' he said.

She smiled back. 'I should thank you, Guido. I'm sorry if I sounded stiff on the phone, but this attack on Flora's clinic has ...' She glanced up at the waiter, who had arrived silently at Brunetti's left.

They both ordered coffee.

'It's crazy. It was a crazy person: that's what Flora said, and it's what I think, too. She said it looked like ...' she began, but let the sentence trail away. She shook her head, and Brunetti assumed she was trying to shake away whatever had happened at the clinic.

Brunetti nodded and gave her a highly edited account of what they'd learned. Once he'd eliminated references to Belize nel Cuore, there was very little to tell her; he suggested that the cause of the difficulties between Flora and her husband was nothing more than the ordinary problems married couples have, and tried to flatter Elisabetta by saying that she would certainly understand the secrets of her daughter's heart.

'After checking as much as I could,' Brunetti said, careful to speak in the singular, 'I've found nothing that would explain your son-in-law's nervousness.' As he spoke, he was already planning how he could manage to hand her husband over to the Guardia di Finanza. Better for her not to know. Better for her never to realize that it was her concern for her daughter that had led her, like Pandora, to open the lid and let it all escape.

The coffee came; Brunetti poured in a packet of sugar and noticed that she did not. They both sipped. Brunetti lowered his cup and added more sugar, then finished the coffee in one sip. Elisabetta looked into hers, swirled the coffee around a few times, and then drank it quickly. She lowered the cup and stared inside at what was left.

To distract her, Brunetti said, 'I think you're supposed to read tea leaves, Elisabetta, not coffee dregs.' The speed with which she set the cup on her saucer surprised him, but not as much as the glance she shot at him, unfiltered and angry.

Elisabetta moved back a bit in her chair to escape the rays of the sun that were slowly moving across the *campo* and her body. She pushed up the sleeve of her jacket and looked at her watch. This cued Brunetti to call for the bill, which came quickly: he paid and left a euro on the table. He got to his feet and shoved the plastic chair – hating it as he hated all plastic chairs – under the table, trying to hurt it or at least make it yelp.

Standing, she raised her hand in farewell, but while it was still in the air, she said, voice hesitant, 'Maybe you could take another look at his work for Bruno, Guido?' He had never heard her use such a plaintive tone before, so dissonant with the manner of the Elisabetta he remembered.

'At what, the charity?'

'Yes,' she answered in a firm voice. 'I'd do it myself,' she started, giving a self-deprecating sniff, 'but I wouldn't know how to begin.'

It sometimes happens that pavements are cracked or badly made and one's foot lands a few centimetres lower than the previous step. There's no danger of falling: it's never much of a difference. But there is always the slight jolt of something unexpected, unanticipated, uneven. And then one registers the new height.

Brunetti had the same surprise at the waif-like tone Elisabetta had used, appearing helpless so that the nearest man would jump to her service. She had come to him, asking for help to keep her daughter safe, and now it seemed to Brunetti that she sought to unleash him to investigate her son-in-law, or even her husband. Was he meant to leap to her aid?

He fought to put an easy smile on his face and asked, making it sound like an idea that had suddenly come to him, 'Perhaps I should speak to your husband?'

'What for?' she asked sharply, but Brunetti had turned away to look at the statue of Colleoni, as though not much interested in his own question.

Her recovery was quick. 'I mean, what reason could you give?'

'Oh, I don't know,' Brunetti mused. 'I could always say my father-in-law was interested in the charity and wanted me to find out more about it.' When she didn't respond, he returned to his contemplation of the statue and said, as though her silence had cancelled out his suggestion, 'I've always thought this the most beautiful *campo* in the city.'

He stepped away from the table and said, 'It was good to see you again.' Then, knowing how much people like to hear it, he added, meaning it, 'Your daughter is a fine woman.'

She took a step away, ignoring his compliment, then turned back and said, 'Yes, perhaps call him.'

He smiled and waved and started across the *campo*, in the direction of Rialto, aware that she had left unclear whom to call and what to say.

19

He walked to Fondamenta Nuove and took the 4.1 to Murano, got off at Colonna, crossed the first bridge, and walked up towards Campiello Turella. He turned into the enclosed space and went over to the building that faced Dottoressa del Balzo's clinic.

He rang the bell for 'Galvani' and was immediately buzzed in. As he approached the second-floor landing, he saw a thin, white-haired woman standing in front of an open door. 'Signor Brunetti?' she asked. She wore a dark green woollen sweater so thick it reminded him of what la Contessa had said about hating the cold.

'*Sì*, Signora Galvani,' he answered, stepping up to the landing. 'Thank you for agreeing to speak to me.'

Her glance was neutral, her eyes bright with intelligence. 'I offered to speak to you, if memory serves,' she said, speaking Italian and not Veneziano with a clarity and beauty he had not heard for years, articulating every syllable, sounding every vowel, and making clear every double consonant she used. He stood, transfixed by her speech as another man would have been transfixed by a woman's beauty or another man's strength.

'That's correct. Thank you for reminding me,' he said.

'I might be an old woman, but I like to think I am still a good citizen.' Then, stepping back inside the apartment, she told him to come in. Following her, he noticed that she limped a bit, favouring her right leg, or knee.

They came into a high-ceilinged room that looked out on the *campo* through four large windows. In fact, two rooms must once have run the width of the building, but had been united into one at some time in the previous centuries. There was a piano – it looked like a concert grand – off to the left. No sheets of music were in evidence. The top was closed and covered by the same sort of silver grove of picture frames that grew on the Fullins' cabinet. The one closest to the edge showed Signora Galvani at least half a century before, next to her a very handsome man who gazed upon her as though nothing else were worth the bother.

Ignoring the photo and the instrument, she walked over to the first window on the left and gestured to Brunetti to join her. When he did, he looked down at the *campo* and saw the front door of the clinic and had a view down the *calle* running between it and the next building.

With no introduction, the woman said, 'It's a dead end. It allows access to the side door of the clinic and, farther down, to the door to the apartment on the top floor.' She took a few sliding sidesteps to her right, stopping at the last window, Brunetti at the one before. 'From here you can see – perhaps it's better from where I am – into part of the reception area where the doctor talks to the owners of the animals. That's her desk and chair and the chairs for the people who bring their animals in. They're treated in the back room, through that door to the right of her desk. But I suppose you saw all of this when you were inside.'

'Yes, I did, Signora, but it's interesting to see it from up here.' Then, because he was curious, and because she might have seen the strange couple who came to complain about their stolen dog, he asked, 'Do you spend much time looking at the animals and their owners?' It was surely more polite than asking directly if she spied on her neighbours.

She turned to him and, without smiling, said, 'I'm afraid I don't pay much attention to that part of the world, Signore.' In response to his unspoken question, she continued, 'I prefer to read, and I like to read by natural light.' Then, smiling, she added, 'That explains my proximity to the window, not nosiness.'

She placed her hand on a large blue upholstered chair that stood with its right arm to the window. The sun had faded the entire right side of the chair as well as the inner upholstery of the opposite arm. Two stacks of books that held one another steady stood beside the chair, pieces of paper sticking from most of them, sometimes more than a few.

'But please sit down,' she said, moving towards the chair and indicating a smaller, less accommodating one that stood near the piano. Brunetti picked it up and moved it closer to her, setting it down a metre away but facing her. It was only then, when she folded them on her lap, that he saw how her hands had been ravaged by arthritis. The knuckles were the size of cherries, the fingers, in contrast, as thin as twigs and just as prone to turn at crooked angles. He looked away, not wanting to be seen staring, and asked, 'What is it you wanted to tell me, Signora?'

'I am an insomniac, Signor Brunetti,' she said with the same actor-like clarity. 'I am seldom free of pain,' she added with no special emphasis, hands motionless. 'The night is a bad time for me, and so I often try to read. To distract myself, as it were.' She paused and, seeing he had no questions, continued. 'Some years ago, the city installed far too much night-time lighting. Everywhere.'

Brunetti nodded in full agreement. She was Venetian, so it was not necessary to point out that this was for the tourists.

'In this particular *campo*, it is so bright that I am able to read by the light provided by the city.' He nodded to show that he was paying attention.

'The night of the ...' she began, and he waited while she selected the word she thought most appropriate, '... vandalism of Dottoressa del Balzo's clinic, I was in this chair, reading.'

Readers like to know what other people read, and so Brunetti asked, 'What were you reading, Signora?'

She was obviously delighted by his question, perhaps doubly so because he was a policeman.

'Alda Merini. Do you know her work?'

Brunetti, who had admired this poet's wit and astuteness since his student days, replied, '"I'll always refuse the Nobel Prize because Norway is so cold."'

'Ah,' the old woman said, her face warming with new interest in this man. 'Not everyone likes her poems.'

'I'm sure she'd take that as an enormous compliment,' Brunetti said, and then, 'You said you wanted to tell me something, presumably about what you saw that night.'

'I've been going on, haven't I?' she asked, and Brunetti nodded and smiled at the same time, as would a priest being asked to absolve a delightful sin.

She sat up straighter and said, 'It was a bit past three, and I had begun to nod, which is the sign that tells me I'm tired enough to be able to sleep, when I heard footsteps in the *campo*.'

She saw Brunetti's attention focus and added, 'Believe me, Signore, this is not a *campiello* where people come home at three in the morning.'

'I'm sure.'

'Feeling a bit guilty that I should be curious – the old lady spying on her neighbours – I told myself I could turn my head but could not stand to peer down because to do so would be to cross a line.' She stopped speaking here and gave him a look that clearly asked for his opinion.

'Of course.'

'But I cheated.'

'Good.'

'I allowed myself to push up on the arms of the chair and look down.'

'What did you see?'

'A woman standing in front of the clinic.'

'What did she do?'

'She just stood there for a few minutes. After a while, my hands hurt, and I had to let myself down into the chair.'

Brunetti nodded.

'So I changed the rules again and stood up. She had her back to me. There was no chance that she'd see me.' A long time passed before she continued. 'Then she moved off to the left. No hesitation: she knew where she was going.'

For fear of breaking her momentum, Brunetti decided not to ask: it proved a wise decision, for she continued. 'She walked down the *calle*.'

This time, not bothering to announce a further change to the rules, Signora Galvani said, 'I opened the window so I could hear if she did anything. For a moment, I wondered if she had gone in there to relieve herself: men often do, but she did not seem the type of person to permit herself to do such a thing.'

However interesting the reason for her judgement might have been, Brunetti remained silent.

'I heard a door open, and then, through the window above the door, I saw light come in from the back part, where the animals are. I closed my eyes for a moment because of the street light, and when I opened them again, the light was gone, and the only light inside was what filtered in from the street lamps.

'I went back to my bedroom to get my other glasses, the ones for distance, but I couldn't find them in the dark. Before I could turn the light on, I heard a sort of crashing noise: it sounded like glass. And then another thump. When I got back to the window,

I heard a dog start to bark, then another one. It was very loud and – I admit – frightening.

'At last the barking stopped, and there was no more noise. I stayed at the window and after a few minutes the woman came out of the *calle* and into the *campo*. And then ... and then,' she began, raising one of her ruined hands to her face, 'she looked up, and I think she saw me at the window. I stepped back so quickly I bumped into my chair and fell back into it. By the time I stood up again, she was gone.' She wound down and stopped.

Brunetti waited and did what he always did when he had to stop himself from speaking: he started from one and counted to himself, hoping something would happen, the person would speak, the messenger would arrive with news of who had won the battle.

But none of this happened, and so he stopped counting at twenty-seven and finally asked, making his voice as neutral as he could. 'Who do you think it was?'

Signora Galvani hesitated for some time before she spoke, 'She resembled Dottoressa del Balzo's mother,' she said at last, and returned to her chair.

Surprised, Brunetti asked, 'How is it that you know the doctor's mother?'

'I had a cat, and last year it got sick, and my daughter came and had a look and told me it was probably his kidneys. She told me I should take him to the Dottoressa, who was just across the *campo*. So that's what I did, and the doctor told me my daughter was right. He was nineteen, so I wasn't surprised, but still, we'd been together a long time, and...' Signora Galvani glanced at Brunetti and said, 'It wasn't easy to decide, but the Dottoressa said it was best.' She paused to look at him, and he gave a small, resigned smile.

'After she did it, she said that she had someone who would take care of things.' When she saw Brunetti's face, she said, 'His body. What to do with it.'

He nodded.

'So she let me go back into the room where ... where he was, and I said goodbye, and when I came back into the other room a woman was standing there, and the Dottoressa introduced me, saying she was her mother.'

She rubbed at her eyes and said, 'I was still crying. I know that's silly, but nineteen years ...' She used the back of her right hand to wipe her eyes and went on. 'That's why I'm not entirely sure it was her mother, because I was crying and did no more than glance at her and leave.'

'Would you recognize the woman you saw in the *campo*?' Brunetti asked.

'But that's the same as asking if I'd identify her mother, isn't it?' she asked.

'It is,' Brunetti admitted.

'I told you: I can't be sure. Besides,' Signora Galvani added, 'it doesn't make any sense. Why would her mother go in and damage the place?'

'You've heard what happened?' Brunetti asked.

'Yes. Everyone in the neighbourhood knows by now: things broken, one animal hurt.' She leaned to one side of the chair and propped her head on her hand. 'No mother would do something like that. Would she?'

'It's hard to believe,' Brunetti offered in lieu of an answer.

'Besides, how would she get here?' Signora Galvani asked, beginning to sound defensive. 'She'd have to fly,' she said. 'There's no way she could get here at that time of night.'

He stood slowly, not wanting to do anything that would suggest he was not convinced by her defence, such as mentioning the Notturno Murano that left from Fondamenta Nuove every half-hour all through the night.

'Thank you nevertheless for your time, Signora,' he said, trying to finish the conversation. When he saw her start to lean forward, as if to tip herself up from her chair, all thought of safe distancing fled and he impulsively offered her his arm, fearing that he'd hurt her if he took her by the hand. She latched on to his forearm with both hands and used her momentum to haul herself up from the chair.

'May I?' he asked, as he passed the pile of books.

Confused, she could only ask, 'What?'

He had stopped near the piled-up books and said, pointing to them, 'Have a look.'

She stepped back and tilted her head to one side, as if he'd put on, or taken off, a costume. 'Of course.'

He squatted down so that he could see the titles. Most of it was poetry, some in translation, some in the original language. How strange, he thought, that this seems to me such an accurate way to assess a person's soul. Reading from the top, Brunetti saw Donne and Bishop in Italian; Bachmann and Rilke in German; Dickens and Wharton in English, Flaubert. And last, a dog-eared copy of Dante. Brunetti looked up, unable to disguise his surprise at finding the Petrocchi edition and unable to resist the temptation to take it in his hands. From above him, she said, 'Well, he's the base of everything, isn't he?'

Brunetti smiled, defeated, and stood, having found only the common thread of genius to unite the books.

'Well,' she asked, 'did I pass the test?'

Thinking that he was here because he had accepted his duty to help the daughter of someone who had been good to him, Brunetti said, 'If there was a test, Signora, you'd already passed it by defending the mother of someone who was good to you. The books are only a sign of why you did it.'

20

On the vaporetto back to Fondamenta Nuove, Brunetti checked the timetable and found, as he knew he would, the circular Notturno that left every half-hour through the night and stopped at all of the Murano stops before returning to Fondamenta Nuove in exactly thirty minutes. So Elisabetta could have got there and could have been the person to vandalize the clinic. But why vandalize the clinic of her own daughter? The person with a grudge was the woman from Burano, convinced that Flora had somehow stolen her dog.

A message from Bocchese peeped its way into his phone. 'There are scores of prints, both human and what I believe to be animal. The report's on your desk, but I'll save you the time you'd spend reading it: there is no way to determine who had been in that office without taking prints from all of her customers. And their animals.'

He moved downstairs to the forward passenger compartment, where the noise of the engines would be less, and searched for the phone number of Belize nel Cuore, berating himself for not having done this sooner. He dialled the number and was greeted by a pleasant female voice saying, 'Good afternoon, Belize nel Cuore. How may I help you?'

Speaking in Veneziano, he said, 'Good afternoon, Signora, this is Guido Brunetti, I'm an old friend of Signora Foscarini, and she's made me interested in your charity.' This was certainly true.

'That's very good to hear, Signor Brunetti, and in what way may I be of service to you?'

'My father-in-law has asked me – since he consults with me about his gifts to charity – to speak to someone there who could give me more detailed information about Belize nel Cuore.'

'Is this with a view to a contribution, Signore?'

'Eventually, I hope,' Brunetti said in the most optimistic, positive voice he could muster.

'I see, and what did you say the name of your father-in-law is?'

'I didn't say, Signora,' Brunetti told her. It wasn't exactly a reprimand, merely a remark that carried a certain weight.

'Ah, I see,' she said, sounding suitably chastised.

'I would, of course, give it to someone who could provide me with more detailed information about the organization.'

'Could you hold on a moment, Signore?' she asked.

'Certainly,' he answered, warmth returning to his voice.

He heard a click, and then he heard the motors of the boat slow and slip into reverse as they reached the Fondamenta Nuove stop. Holding his phone to his ear, Brunetti climbed the steps and followed the other passengers off the boat. He walked down towards the hospital and paused at the edge of the *riva* to look across the Adriatic at what many people still referred to as 'ex-Jugoslavia', as though it were too much trouble to remember the many names of all those countries that had been carved out of the old bloc. Only the tops of the mountains were visible. Brunetti had no idea which country the mountains were in. Albania? No, that was far to the south, opposite Puglia. That left either Slovenia, which had a tiny bit of coast, or Croatia, which was much longer. Probably Croatia.

'Signor Brunetti?'

'*Sì*,' he answered.

'Our Director is here and said he'll speak with you.'

'Oh, how very kind,' Brunetti said warmly.

'One moment,' she said and was gone, replaced by a click, another one, and then a male voice saying, 'Good afternoon, Signor Brunetti. This is Bruno del Balzo. I believe we might already know one another. Didn't my wife and I have a coffee with you at Didovich some years ago?'

'Indeed,' Brunetti said, then risked, 'I'm flattered you remember.'

'Of course I do,' del Balzo said in a voice that expanded in pleasantness. 'Elisabetta has mentioned you over the years. Even though you and I met only the one time.'

'I'm delighted that she would,' Brunetti said, sounding quite as though he meant it.

'My secretary said you were interested in Belize nel Cuore.'

'Not for myself, Signor del Balzo,' Brunetti clarified in his most straightforward, never-tell-a-lie voice. 'It's my father-in-law who's interested.' Because he was speaking to a Venetian, Brunetti did not think it necessary to provide his father-in-law's name.

'Really?' del Balzo said. 'And why is that?'

'He told me he was talking with some friends at the Circolo dell'Unione, and one of them started lamenting the state of the world.' The elderly gentlemen of the Circolo were much given to lamenting, Brunetti knew.

'Ummm,' del Balzo murmured.

'Another man – I think Orazio said he was a retired military officer – told him to stop complaining and do something.' Brunetti stopped and said, 'Well, it ended up that this man spent some time talking about your organization, which he apparently praised and recommended to Orazio.'

'That would be Captain Pederiva, I believe,' del Balzo said. 'He's been a supporter since the beginning.'

'Orazio didn't tell me his name, only that he was quite liberal in his praise of you and your organization.'

'And this is why you're calling?' del Balzo asked, ignoring the praise.

'Yes. Orazio asked me to speak to you and tell him what I thought,' Brunetti said with the simple clarity of the honest man. 'I suppose he thinks policemen have some sort of radar vision into people's thoughts.' He had decided that Elisabetta would probably have long since told her husband the story of the upwardly mobile Brunetti brothers: one the chief radiological technician at the Ospedale Civile and the other a commissario of police. Thus for Brunetti to refer casually to his profession at this point was unnecessary, especially if he was wearing the cloak of respectability conveyed by il Conte Falier's interest in Belize nel Cuore.

It was some time before del Balzo answered, but finally he said, 'It's very wise of him to ask you.' Then, his voice growing more serious, he went on, 'I've been in charge of my own small effort for only three years, but during that time I've heard things that make me suspect that many charities set up to help people in the developing world are ... perhaps not what they appear to be,' he concluded, making it clear he did not want to cast aspersions on his colleagues. He paused and said 'Um' a few times, an indication of his reluctance to give examples.

Brunetti let some time pass before he spoke again. 'Actually, he's interested that another Venetian is doing such an exemplary thing: that's why he's asked me to speak with you about Belize nel Cuore.' Brunetti had worked out a system in which he was to be rewarded with one glass of grappa after dinner for each time he managed to say Belize nel Cuore without sarcastic emphasis on the last word.

There was an even longer pause before del Balzo said, sounding pleased, 'I'd be delighted to speak to you.' Again, a pause, then he said, 'We're just now beginning a programme to construct a new pediatric clinic. Perhaps we could talk about that?'

'I'd be very interested,' Brunetti said. Then he added, giving a tiny yank on the leash, 'I think my father-in-law would be as well.' Behind him, a vaporetto misjudged its trajectory and hit the main landing with a solid thud that Brunetti could feel through his feet, even at this distance.

'Good heavens, what was that?'

'The Number One with what sounds like a new pilot,' he answered lightly. Then, before del Balzo could enquire, Brunetti explained, 'I'm at Rialto,' thinking that one badly piloted vaporetto would sound like any other. 'I had to see someone, and now I'm deciding whether to go home or go back to the Questura.'

Del Balzo cleared his throat and said, sounding decisive, 'Why don't you come along now and we can talk?'

Brunetti used a more serious voice to say, 'That depends on where you are, I'm afraid. I have to meet someone at . . .' he began, taking a look at his watch, '. . . at six.'

'We're in San Giovanni e Paolo,' del Balzo said, adding, as if Brunetti wouldn't have known it, 'you could be here in ten minutes.'

Brunetti remained silent for some seconds and then made the sort of quick grunt one makes when discovering something. 'That should work. Where are you? Which house?'

Del Balzo told Brunetti what he already knew and said he looked forward to seeing him.

Brunetti decided there was time to have a coffee at one of the bars at the *imbarcadero*, then walked along the Fondamenta dei Mendicanti, which took him straight to del Balzo's front door.

He found Belize nel Cuore on the list of names, rang, and was buzzed in.

In all the years he'd been curious about the apartment on the top floor, Brunetti had never been able even to peer into the entrance hall. When he pushed back the door and found the light switch, he saw a row of heavily grated windows on the right side, running along the canal. The paving stones were the common black and white chequerboard, the chandeliers in need of cleaning, and there were signs of water damage on the wooden panelling of the walls.

He approached the stairs and saw that they had probably been there from the time of construction, the original sharp angle along the centre of every stone worn into a shallow curve by centuries of shoes and boots. He walked quickly to the first floor, feeling something close to pride that these stairs had been here so long and were still being worn away by the feet of Venetians.

As he approached the first landing, a light splashed out from an opening door, and he looked up to see a dark-haired, middle-aged woman a few years older than he standing just inside the apartment. 'Signor Brunetti?' she asked.

'*Sì*,' he answered as he reached the landing.

She wore a grey woollen dress that came to the middle of her calves, black shoes with low heels, and a welcoming smile. '*Prego*,' she said and stepped back from the door. He passed in front of her, careful to say, '*Scusi, Signora*,' and she closed the door after him.

'If you'll follow me, Signore, I'll take you to the Director.' She turned away with surprising grace. Seeing her from the back, he noticed how very thin she was, with hips as narrow as her shoulders and legs that seemed little more than bones covered with a thin film of skin.

She led him down a short corridor, which he thought was taking them back towards the *campo*. She stopped in front of the door at the end, knocked twice, and went in without waiting for an answer. She stood back, and he again excused himself for walking in front of her. She left and closed the door.

Bruno del Balzo sat at a desk with his back to the window, allowing the guest the sight of the entrance to the Ospedale Civile, something most people saw only from the ground. Here, even though he was only one floor higher, Brunetti was conscious of how the perspective changed from this vantage point but did nothing to alter the perfect asymmetry of the façade.

He recognized del Balzo instantly: the tight cloud of white hair was, in Brunetti's experience, unique in the city, not so much because it was white but because it was so impenetrably thick and curly. Del Balzo got to his feet and came around his desk to offer Brunetti a relaxed smile and wave him to a chair.

'Good afternoon, Commissario, and thank you for coming to see me at such short notice,' he said as he returned behind his desk. He seemed younger than he had the only other time Brunetti had spoken with him: apparently retirement agreed with him.

'I should thank you, Signore. I like to be of service to my father-in-law. It's very seldom that he allows me the pleasure of doing him a favour, so of course I came at the first opportunity.'

Del Balzo smiled and, waving towards a trio of upholstered chairs that stood in a small U to the left of the desk, said, 'Let's be comfortable and see if I can give you enough information to take back to il Conte.' He walked over to the chairs and stood by the one on the right, more or less shepherding his guest to the chair opposite him, which gave that person the same view Brunetti had seen upon entering. He sat and noticed that, by leaning forward even a bit, his view to the right brought him the façade of the Basilica.

'This is perhaps the most glorious view a person could hope to have,' Brunetti said with the force of truth and, equally unusual for his professional persona, sincerity.

'And the views of the Grand Canal?' del Balzo asked, a way of letting Brunetti know that he knew who his father-in-law was and where he lived.

'Equally glorious, but too much like postcards, I'm afraid.'

Del Balzo failed to prevent himself from laughing, and when he stopped, he said, 'I hope you've never expressed that opinion to your father-in-law.'

'If I had,' Brunetti replied instantly, 'he would have had me transferred to Sardinia, and I wouldn't be sitting here.'

'But you are,' del Balzo answered and added, 'so the least I can do is give you information about Belize nel Cuore.'

'Il Conte will be pleased.'

Rising to his feet, del Balzo said, smiling, 'Let me get you the brochure we've made.' He went back to his desk, opened a drawer, and took from it a small booklet the size of a magazine but far thinner.

He came back and handed it to Brunetti before returning to his seat. On the cover was a photo of the front of a modern, four-storey building. The entrance was through a pair of wide sliding glass doors, white marble Doric columns on either side and above them a sign, 'St Peter's Hospital', written in English in red letters on a blue field bordered on top and bottom with narrow strips of red. Brunetti had done a bit of looking and so recognized the resemblance to the national flag.

A large lawn filled with palmy-looking trees and others he did not recognize expanded in front of the building. To the left of the hospital, he saw a decorative palm surrounded by dizzyingly coloured flowers.

He opened the pamphlet and found the names of the chief medical officer, the chief doctors of the various clinics, and a staff of more than twenty doctors. He paged through it and found the usual photos of doctors' offices, an operating room with some sort of operation in progress, three white-suited people – one a woman – encircling the draped patient, private rooms, two-bed rooms, a large laboratory with white-jacketed technicians busy looking into their microscopes, a spotless kitchen, and what seemed to be a communal room for patients, all of them looking healthy and happy.

It was the same sort of thing he'd seen in the past, whether from a hospital, nursing home, or a private clinic. The text spoke of 'the highest standards', 'our dedication to patients' well-being', 'Ministry of Health approved', things like that. The racial diversity of the people in the photos was almost perfect: half black, half white.

Brunetti looked up at del Balzo and smiled. 'I'm seeing the Faliers this evening, and I'll give this to my father-in-law.'

He paused and allowed himself to move about nervously in his chair before saying, 'My father-in-law is, however, also curious about the tax ramifications of any donation he might make to your organization.'

'Of course, of course,' del Balzo agreed. 'And he's very wise to consider this.' He pushed himself back in his chair and crossed his legs, something Brunetti had often observed people do as a sign of confidence, as though ease of posture were ease of conscience.

While del Balzo spoke, Brunetti turned off his ears and observed the speaking man, a habit he had developed during years of interrogating suspects, listening to witnesses, or sometimes hearing his children explain their school grades. Usually, some uncontrolled part of the body – a foot, a finger, or even a nose – gave evidence of the state of affairs inside the speaker; further, the non-listening listener could not be lulled by flattery or charm, nor by persuasive numbers. He simply watched a person, looking for evidence that what they were saying was not what they knew or believed.

The eager-faced Brunetti, undistracted by words or meaning, watched, and soon enough he noticed the way del Balzo used his thumb to move his wedding ring in a circular path around his finger.

After a few minutes, he tuned back in to del Balzo and heard him say, 'So he would be allowed – I don't know if he is interested in this – to subtract a part of the amount of the donation from his taxable income.'

Brunetti looked up and gave a broad smile to signify how interesting he'd found everything del Balzo had told him. 'I'd say everyone would be interested in that, wouldn't you, Signore?' he asked, smiling in his friendliest manner.

'Indeed,' answered del Balzo with a similar smile. 'He'd also be helping a good cause. I've visited the hospital many times, and I've always been impressed by their seriousness.' Then, almost reluctantly, as though these words were being driven from his mouth by the obligation always to tell the full truth, he said, 'Of course, the level of the medical treatment is not on a par with what's given in, for example ...' and here he waved a hand in the general direction of Mestre, leaving Brunetti interested about why he did not point across the *campo* to the Ospedale Civile.

'That can't be expected,' del Balzo continued, 'even though many of the doctors have studied in Europe.' He gave himself a little shake. 'But, compared with the other hospitals in Belize, indeed, St Peter's provides superb medical services of all kinds.

'I confess I'm not a doctor,' del Balzo continued, 'so I can't give a professional judgement that has credibility, but the hospital has a very good reputation among the professional classes, and it's always passed its government inspections with the highest assessments.'

Brunetti nodded, as he thought he was meant to do.

'Well,' he said, holding up the brochure, 'do you think you could have someone send my father-in-law any documents you think relevant ... including those government reports?' Brunetti was careful to make them sound like documents in which the truth was reflected, or at least documents in which his father-in-law – at Brunetti's suggestion – could place his trust.

Del Balzo smiled again and said, 'I have a complete dossier: it must run to thirty pages. Everything's in there, including the certifications from the Ministry of Health and the plans for the pediatric clinic. I'll ask my secretary to send it tomorrow.'

'Fine. You could send it directly to my father-in-law. I'll tell him tonight that it's on its way.' Then, risking a bit of humour, he added, 'If that can be said about anything entrusted to the post office.'

Instantly alert to the suggestion, if deaf to the irony, del Balzo said, 'I had thought of sending it as an attachment to an email.'

'Ah, of course,' Brunetti said with an easy smile that attempted to disguise his embarrassment. 'I'm afraid I'm locked in the past about some things: when people use the word "send", I still think of the post office.' Del Balzo's smile was indulgent and forgiving. As ever, Brunetti was pleased at how easy it was to convince someone of his stupidity.

Brunetti got to his feet, smiling, while still wondering how it was that del Balzo knew il Conte's email address.

Conscious that their conversation had never strayed beyond the limits imposed by addressing one another as '*lei*', Brunetti said, 'That would be very kind of you, Signor del Balzo,' addressing del Balzo formally.

Del Balzo stood and accompanied Brunetti to the door. When they got there, del Balzo said, 'I look forward to hearing from Conte Falier,' avoiding the need to choose between formal or familiar, but leaving no doubt about his good feelings.

21

After dinner, when the kids had disappeared into their rooms to do their homework, Brunetti asked Paola if she had the time and patience to listen to him while he recounted everything that had happened since his old friend Elisabetta had sought him out at the Questura with the story of her daughter's marital tensions.

He tried to observe chronological order as he explained things to her, but it soon seemed to him that the plot of this story – if it had one – resembled the path of the metal balls in the pinball machines that had stolen so many hours of his youth. He remembered releasing the ball towards the top of the glass case and watching it start to roll down the playfield through the oblivion that awaited it everywhere. There were flippers and bumper rails that could save the ball from disappearing down the many holes in the playfield: skilful players could save it by swift and accurate moves; audacious players banged on the sides of the case or, in some instances, lifted the bottom of the case to turn the ball back towards the top. He remembered that the game, filled with uncertainty and triumph, had thrilled him. Until one day it didn't, and he stopped playing.

Elisabetta had pulled back the plunger by coming to see him, releasing the ball that he had come to identify as Belize nel Cuore. It had been deflected on its way to the bottom, first by a kicker, a Vice-Admiral who drooled, and then by a bumper, a man who had signed a document and died. And then a new ball had shot out, going to vandalize Flora del Balzo's clinic, unstopped by flippers, bumpers, or kickers. Something was wrong with the playing field, and Brunetti had a strong desire to walk to the bottom of the board, pick it up, and give it a good shake.

When he had finished telling the first story, he went back and added the story of the blood-covered dog and stated his belief that Elisabetta's daughter had no idea what was going on, other than that her husband was stressed to such a point that a tourist brochure had upset him. That necessitated his having to tell her about Fenzo's reaction when he'd looked in the window of the ex-travel agency in Campo Manin.

'There's more,' he said, sipping at the grappa he had earned that day, 'but those are the major events.'

Pouring herself a whisper of grappa, Paola, who always wanted to understand what drove a plot, asked, 'Why is all this happening?'

That stopped him. After a moment's thought, he answered. 'My guess is that it somehow gets money out of the country.'

Setting her glass down, she said, 'Tell me.'

'It's something Henry James never wrote about,' Brunetti said, trying to lighten the mood. He set his glass beside hers.

'I will not rise to the temptation you create with that remark,' she said.

Paola leaned forward to tip the last drops of grappa into their glasses. She held up the empty bottle. 'God bless Endrizzi,' she said and set it on the table.

After some reflection, she said, 'I'm an academic, so all I know about moving money out of the country is that my father trembles if he has to transfer more than ten thousand euros to any foreign bank account. He says it can set off flares, and that's nothing he wants to do.' She pulled her feet up beside her on the sofa and said, 'I suppose so much cash is floating around now that most things go unnoticed until you send a hundred thousand euros to your own account in the British West Indies.'

Brunetti didn't comment. Instead, he pushed back his sleeve and asked, 'Would you like to go for a walk?'

'It's after ten, Guido.'

'You afraid of being mugged?'

'Very funny. Where do you want to go?'

'Campo Manin.'

She was on her feet in an instant, heading towards the door.

It took them fifteen minutes. They walked around the Cassa di Risparmio, its ugliness diminished – but not erased – by the darkness, and walked along the buildings on the left of the *campo*. To Brunetti, though he did not say this to Paola, it resembled attending an autopsy, or, more accurately, walking into the morgue at the Ospedale. In Campo Manin, the bodies of dead shops lined the way to the canal. There was a dead Middle Eastern fast-food place, a dead sporting goods shop, a dead clothes shop with two dead mannequins in the window, and, at last, the dead travel agency. Luckily, shops didn't have toes, for then each of them would have had a tag tied to their left big toe listing their name, age, and presumed cause of death. Those here in the *campo* had all died of Covid.

The mannequins in the travel agency still wore bathing suits and sandals, although months in the sun had caused their skin to begin to peel and gather at their feet in small piles of greyish paint. Brunetti had brought along a torch and he shone it through the window, hunting for the brochures he was sure he'd seen there. Finally he found them, drawn close to one another in death, having crawled halfway to the safety of the shade provided by a desk. They lay there, flat, flagellated by the sun: Greece, with a sea bleached almost white, three albino Kuwaiti camels, photos of either ghosts or clouds in some nameless place on the cover of a brochure that had landed closer to the *campo* and had thus spent more hours in the sun over the months, and finally a four-storey white building set behind a palm-studded lawn, a faded sign above the door declaring it to be the Hotel des Bains, with twin automatic glass doors and on either side of them marble Doric columns.

He kept the torch on it so long that Paola finally asked, 'What's that?'

He switched off the light and put it back in his pocket. 'Proof.'

Brunetti lay awake much of the night, trying to think of a way to make real his remark to Paola that the photo of the hotel now disguised as a hospital – or perhaps, more accurately, a hotel Photoshopped into a hospital – was proof of the real function of Belize nel Cuore.

It was with this project that Enrico Fenzo had begun his career as a *ragioniere*, asked to help set up a charitable organization, and what client more trustworthy than a relative? Brunetti wondered when Fenzo had first begun to suspect that all was not light and flowers in the business of his father-in-law. No wonder Fenzo had stopped working for del Balzo. Unable to tell his wife what her father might be up to, Fenzo could only gently pry himself loose from del Balzo and hope that the passage of time would erase any memory of his early involvement with the foundation. As he listened to the bells tell him of the passage of time, Brunetti remembered the photo on the tourist brochure and asked himself why Fenzo had panicked at the mere sight of it.

He drifted towards sleep, but then the memory of Vice-Admiral Fullin came to his bed. Something lingered in Brunetti's memory about the Vice-Admiral, the man who seemed to come and go, turning from a blankly staring statue of a man who, however slow of thought and action, was still present and aware of what was going on around him.

Surely he had recognized that the medal Brunetti had worn was military, as were his own. There had been a host of them, Brunetti recalled, in the photo of the Vice-Admiral in full uniform, all but cascading down the front of his uniform jacket. Brunetti had always admired the uniforms of the Navy: how clever of them to choose white, the better to display the pretty trinkets for which so many exchanged their lives.

The idea of white took Brunetti's thoughts to other white things: snow, doves, brides, paper, aspirin. He opened his eyes and backed up his mind: paper. Paper. Letter. Girolomo had kept the pieces of the letter that had provoked his grandfather to rage against his friend and fellow officer, Capitano Pederiva. Brunetti turned to look at the clock and, sure enough, it was three. Had any other time ever revealed itself when he looked at the clock in the night? Did alarming news and emergency calls ever come at a different hour? He remembered reading that Mandelstam had kept a packed suitcase by the door, always, waiting for the arrival of the KGB, who always came at night. And who had come.

What a fool he had been not to ask the young man if he had kept the pieces of the letter. He flipped onto his stomach and draped his arm over Paola's back, not at all afraid that he would wake her. Vice-Admiral Fullin could anchor his destroyer in the Grand Canal at the end of their *calle* and fire a 21-gun salute to the city, and Paola would remain enwrapped in the sleep of the wise and just.

At nine, Paola brought him coffee, intruding into his slow-waking mind by saying, 'I'm going to the market by Piazzale Roma; is there anything you'd like for dinner tonight?'

It was too soon in the day to think of dinner, so he said, 'Anything you like, Paola.'

Paola slapped her hand to her chest and choked out, 'What's wrong with you?'

'What?' Brunetti asked, beginning to be alarmed.

She removed her hand, saying, 'In all these years, this is the first time I've known you – when given the chance to choose what to have for dinner – to decline to do so.' She turned and left.

Were other men subject to this continual abuse? he wondered. In their own homes? Indeed, in their own beds? He laughed out loud and, still laughing, went down to take a shower.

He looked out of the window before he dressed and then, to be certain, opened the door to the balcony before choosing what to wear. The chill that greeted him made him alter his first choice and select a dark blue suit he'd found in Milano some years before, when he had briefly escaped from the afternoon session of a meeting chaired by the American consul on the danger of terrorist attacks on the civilian population of Italy.

He'd walked into the shop, tried it on, and boldly pulled out his credit card to pay for it, certain that the price would be more than covered by the lavish cash per diem the Americans were willing to pay to induce Italian police commissari to attend their conference. Because he thought of it as his 'American suit', he always wore a white shirt and red tie with it.

Before he left, he called la Contessa and asked her for the *telefonino* number of Girolomo Fullin, giving no explanation. He called and identified himself, then asked the young man if he had kept the pieces of the letter he had taken from Captain Pederiva. Of course, he'd hold the line and wait while Girolomo had a look.

Girolomo's phone made a noise when he set it down but he was quickly back, saying he'd found it, in four pieces, a bit crushed and worn, but still legible.

'You haven't read it?' Brunetti asked.

There was a moment of what Brunetti would later realize was stunned silence before Girolomo said, 'It's not addressed to me, Signore.'

'I see,' Brunetti said softly. 'If I assure you that I want to see the letter in order to help your grandfather and perhaps save his honour, would you give the pieces to me?' Young people, Brunetti knew, believed in things like a man's sense of honour.

He could all but hear the young man calculating, running through everything he had heard about or observed in Brunetti, assessing the weight of la Contessa's confidence in him. Because Girolomo was young, it was not a long time before he said, 'Yes. Would you like me to bring it to you, Signore?'

Without explaining his reasons, Brunetti said, 'Yes, please. That's very kind of you. 'Could we meet in Caffè del Doge in ten minutes?'

'Yes,' Girolomo said. 'I'll see you there.'

Before leaving, Brunetti made a quick call to the brother of a friend of his and asked if he could look into the Navy files for the *telefonino* number of a Captain Pederiva of Venice, retired. When Timoteo agreed, Brunetti asked if he could send the number in a message.

'Nothing easier,' Timoteo said and hung up.

Because there was still time, Brunetti took the stairs slowly and peered into the mailbox in the entrance hall. Their box appeared to be empty, but that was more often the case these days. Whose letters will we read, he asked himself, in days to come? Perhaps we won't miss them, after all. He thought of something Seneca had written in one of his letters, advising us that it wasn't until we had began to go without things that we realized how unnecessary they were.

They had not gone to the cinema during the entire period of the *pandemia*, and he certainly had not missed it. For weeks, they had been without newspapers and had read them online. The schools had been closed for months, and the children seemed no less clever. All the city really missed were the tourists.

He turned into the caffè, almost empty at ten. He recognized Girolomo standing at the counter. He approached and stood next to him, ordered a coffee, and asked, 'How is your grandfather?'

The younger man picked up his coffee but set it back untouched. 'Today promises to be a good day for him, thank you.'

'It must be terrible for your grandmother,' Brunetti said. Then, after his coffee had been delivered, he added, 'My mother was in the Ca' di Dio for some time.'

'It's a hotel now, isn't it?' Girolomo asked, then sipped at his coffee.

Brunetti stopped himself from asking in return, 'Isn't everything?' and, instead, chose to nod. 'She was happy there. At the beginning. The sisters were very kind to her. They always were. But she changed.'

Not wanting to think about that any more, he said, 'It started out as a hospice for pilgrims to the Holy Land.'

'When was that?' Girolomo asked, sounding interested.

'In the twelfth century, I think; maybe before.'

Girolomo raised his eyes and looked around: the tables, chairs, an enormous coffee machine, two soccer shirts on the wall. 'And here we are, almost a thousand years later, in the same city, drinking coffee.' Looking down, he saw that his was finished and slid the cup and saucer to the far side of the counter.

A copy of that morning's *Gazzettino* lay folded on the counter. Girolomo pulled a dark red plastic file folder from inside the newspaper and handed it to Brunetti, saying, 'I didn't want it to suffer any more damage.'

Brunetti took the folder without opening it and thanked the young man, then asked, 'What shall I do with it after I've read it?'

'If it's something you think my grandfather would want to have, you could give it back to me.'

'And if not?'

'If it doesn't concern him, you can keep it or give it back to the Captain. He's the one who brought it to my grandfather's, so it was probably sent to him.' He paused and gave Brunetti a long look before he said, 'There's something you should perhaps know. When I led the Captain out of the apartment, he was crying.' He paused and asked the woman behind the bar for a glass of water and said nothing until it came.

Girolomo drank it quickly, then went on, 'I'd never seen a man cry before. It was as if he was angry and ashamed at the same time.'

Brunetti, who had seen many men cry, nodded.

'All he said, again and again, was, "I didn't know. I didn't know," but he didn't say what it was he didn't know, and I was... afraid to ask him.'

Before Brunetti could think of anything else to say, the young man slipped the folder back into the newspaper and slid it across the counter to him, saying, 'The newspaper will protect it. I've read it.' Then, with a smile, he added, 'I was here for five minutes, waiting for you, so I had enough time.' He wished Brunetti a pleasant day, left some coins on the counter, and walked out into the *calle.*

22

Impatient, Brunetti took the Number Two and got out at San Zaccaria, even though he knew the trip would be no faster this way. At least the vaporetto gave him the feeling of speed, which is what he wanted. He barely noticed the perfection of the morning, so intent was he on finally getting some evidence that was different from the various versions he'd been given of what people had done and why they did it.

A letter was open to interpretation, surely, but at least it was a text where the words themselves would not change because someone remembered them one way, someone else another. Although he had been married for decades to a woman who saw most texts as ambiguous and in need of interpretation, Brunetti had retained his impulse towards more literal interpretations.

He went immediately to his office and closed the door behind him. He put the newspaper on his chair and tried to make order on his desk. He slid all of the documents and folders to the back, turned his computer screen so that it ran parallel to the sides of his desk, and shoved everything else aside, clearing out an area about the size of a fully opened newspaper.

He set the folder in the middle of the empty space, placed the newspaper on the floor, and sat. He slid the pieces of paper onto his desk and dropped the empty folder on top of the newspaper. The letter had been ripped into four pieces, almost equal in size. Although he knew it was foolish to concern himself with any fingerprints that might be left on the paper after the pieces had passed through so many hands, he still picked up each piece by the very edges to see that they were printed on one side only. That being the case, he set them on their backs and studied them. They lay there like four pieces of a giant, rectangular potato chip, each with two smooth edges, two rough; all wrinkled.

It was simplicity itself to reassemble the letter. Four corners and a few dozen lines of text: he easily fitted it together.

The return address surprised him: Palazzo Dandolo, Campo SS. Giovanni e Paolo, and gave a very high house number in Castello. Channelling his mother in moments of great surprise, Brunetti whispered, *'Maria Vergine,'* for it was the address of the offices of Belize nel Cuore as well as of Signor Bruno del Balzo.

He looked at the place where the address of the receiver would have been in a formal letter, but there was only the salutation *Dear Giovanni*, presumably the first name of Capitano Pederiva.

He read on.

I hope this letter finds you well and busy with your memoirs. I want to encourage you in this worthy endeavour because I think it is important that an account be given of the dedication of men like yourself who have worked so selflessly for the good of our country. For decades you were a part of that service, rising through the ranks until you achieved your life's goal, to be a Capitano, a leader among those who work continually to bring safety and security to our citizens.

As you know, the long career of our mutual friend Matteo Fullin shows how he, too, was interested in bringing safety and security to others. At this time in his life, the focus of his concern has shifted to the citizens of Belize, a country he holds dear to his heart. I visited him yesterday, and we spoke, for Matteo still has many hours when he returns to the energy and power we have admired in him for so many years.

I told him of my plans to expand the hospital, of which you are such a loyal friend, and he encouraged me to ask for your help in this project. He praised your generous spirit in a way I shall not reveal to you for risk of causing embarrassment. There are few people Matteo admires more than you, both for your service to the Navy and for your remarkable generosity.

When I saw him, he seemed in very good health and, as ever, enjoys the care, love and protection of Antonia. With all my heart and in the fullness of my friendship and respect for both of them, I wish them a safe and calm future.

In hopes of hearing from you soon, Giovanni, I remain,

With respect,

The signature at the bottom was a simple: *Bruno.*

Brunetti recalled the brief account Girolomo had given of the scene he'd interrupted: the shouting Vice-Admiral tearing a piece of paper from the hands of his friend, raging, Lear-like, at some betrayal he could not name, perhaps could not even comprehend clearly. How much of the letter had he understood? Had his friend read it to him? Or had it sufficed to see del Balzo's signature on a letter making reference to him? Or to see any letter about the charity of which the Vice-Admiral was a founding member?

The reason for his behaviour could easily be explained as an explosion of the random waves of dementia that flowed through the Vice-Admiral's mind. His family said he still had 'good days', when he was like his 'old self', but what did that mean? When had his 'old self' last been seen? And what constituted a 'good' day?

Brunetti looked at the letter and saw that it was dated the month before. That was before Elisabetta had come to speak to him and before the vandalism of Flora del Balzo's clinic. He had not yet heard from Signorina Elettra, so he had no idea of the nature or extent of the donations made to the charity. Brunetti thought of those donations, long since spent on yoga lessons and scuba classes, not to mention a few pairs of 2,000-euro Berluti shoes. Could new shoes, he wondered, drive a man to risk so much: his oldest friendship, marriage, respect, honour?

The letter had made him nervous, and he glanced back and read it again. This time he noticed the conflict between its stodgy formality and the fact that it used the informal 'tu'. 'That's not possible,' he whispered to himself, not in combination with the stiff, artificial language and the awkwardness of the reference to old times. Would a man, even a businessman, write to an old friend in this manner?

His phone rang: the display told him the call was coming from Signorina Elettra's *telefonino*. 'Yes?' he answered.

'Good morning, Commissario,' she said. Brunetti could hear, in the background, a man's voice on a scratchy loudspeaker making some sort of announcement. He heard 'Roma' and 'one hour and—' and then the scream of a whistle.

'Are you at the station?'

'Yes. A friend of mine is arriving this morning, but the train's been delayed.'

'Can I help in some way?' he asked, thinking that it would be possible to send Foa and the launch.

'No need to, Signore. There's already a boat waiting.'

'Ah,' he said with careful neutrality, asking nothing.

'I wanted to tell you to look in your outbox, under the brochure for new guns.'

As if he had been ordered to do it, Brunetti stood and leaned towards the back of his desk and removed the brochure without bothering to study the dark grey pistol on the cover. Underneath was a collection of papers sloppily clipped together. He removed them and read the title on the cover page to her: "Incidence of Theft of Livestock (Including Domestic Fowl) in the Province of Venezia, 2016–2018.' Is this what I'm looking for?'

'Yes, Commissario,' she said, then made a shushing noise that allowed him to hear, from somewhere beyond her, 'Arriving on *binario* three, Freccia Rossa from Rome, with one hour and forty-three minutes delay.' When the voice finished, Signorina Elettra's returned. 'You were eager to see it, sir. I won't be in for the rest of the day, so I thought I'd camouflage it and leave it on your desk.' Before he could answer, she was gone.

He put the pieces of the letter back into the plastic folder and slid it into his drawer.

Returning his attention to the report on the theft of domestic animals, he removed the paper clip and title page, set them aside, and was left looking at a page that showed three columns headed 'Date', 'Amount', and 'From'. He quickly flipped through to the last of six single-spaced pages and found the date of the most recent entry: two months earlier.

Flipping back to the first page, he saw that on the same date in March that the organization papers for Belize nel Cuore were signed, the first donation of 2,000 euros was followed by del Balzo's name and address. A week later, 350 was donated by a man living in Cannaregio. The next was recorded after another two weeks, 200 from a woman living in Castello. Small sums kept trickling in: fifty euros, twenty-five, thirty, a hundred, sometimes more, but more often less.

Not a very propitious start, although if the money was going to a poor country, perhaps it would do more good.

Towards the end of the year, after receiving 1,000 euros from Giovanni Pederiva, address in San Marco, Belize nel Cuore received the sum of 2,000 euros from Innocenza Bagnoli, resident in Brescia. Brunetti looked at the date of her contribution, pulled his notebook from his pocket, and wrote it down, then continued reading.

Two months later, a man in Caltanissetta donated 3,000 and a month later, 13,000 arrived from a notary in Brescia. On the same page, there were three more sums originating from men resident in Brescia and Vicenza for 22,000, 19,000, and 24,000.

He skimmed through the pages, recognizing none of the people who had made donations to Belize nel Cuore. When he arrived at the bottom of the last page, Brunetti pulled out his phone, found the way to make it serve as a calculator, went back to the first page, and slowly began to enter any donation that exceeded 500 euros.

When he flipped over the last page and put in the last sum, Brunetti paused a moment before pushing the = key, having long since lost track of the total that he was amassing.

Saying '*Bingo*' out loud, he pushed the key, glanced away so as not to have to accuse himself of cheating, and said, 'Four hundred thousand.' Only then did he allow himself to look at the total.

Seven hundred and sixty-two thousand euros.

'Goes a long way in Belize, that sort of money,' he told himself, though he suspected very little of it had been spent in Belize.

He drew another folder from his drawer and slipped the papers dealing with the theft of livestock in the Veneto into it and shut it in the drawer.

He swung the screen back to its proper place and retrieved the keyboard. Whispering a silent prayer to the goddess of technology, who, for all he knew, might well be Signorina Elettra, he opened his server and keyed in the name 'Innocenza Bagnoli, financial consultant'.

And waited to see what the computer had to tell him.

A red light began to flash at him from the centre of his screen. *Check email. Check email. Check email.* The message could not have been clearer. He tried to ignore it and clicked on his server, whereupon the message repeated itself, this time in protective-vest orange: *Check email. Check email. Check email.*

Defeated, he clicked once on the flying bird – he hoped not one listed in the report of stolen fowls – and his email opened, presenting him the possibility to open only one, flashing red in the inbox. Only one person could be responsible for this, so he opened it without his common fear, at the first sign of techno-obstinacy, that the computer was about to explode.

Dear Commissario, she wrote, *I wanted to save you time and delay as you searched for information about Innocenza Bagnoli. (This email cannot be read by any computer but yours.)*

There is an attachment containing everything I've been able to find. I hope it is useful to you.

There was no signature.

He clicked on the icon and waited while the attachment opened.

There were two pages, starting with Bagnoli's first position, as a secretary at a brokerage house in Brescia, where she had worked for three years, without promotion or a salary increase.

She had left brokerage for banking and accepted an offer from a bank in Venice, where she'd worked as a financial consultant for three years. There was some uncertainty about the reasons for her departure, although a not-disclosed sum had been paid to her by the bank when she left.

Soon after, according to a flight manifest from United Airlines, Signora Bagnoli had flown from Venice to Belize City, via

Frankfurt, with a flight time so gruelling that Brunetti almost felt pity for her, crushed into a seat in economy. Yet a month later, somehow now promoted to Dottoressa Bagnoli, she had returned to Venice first class, putting an end to Brunetti's spontaneous sympathy.

Within two months, she had opened an office as a financial adviser in Campo Santa Marina. One of her first clients was Bruno del Balzo, who lived not far from her office. Five months after becoming a client, del Balzo – three and a half years retired from the direct handling of his enterprises – hired Dottoressa Bagnoli as publicity director of Belize nel Cuore, which so far had had very little success in fundraising. Soon thereafter, donations began to improve and del Balzo began his twice-yearly visits to St Peter's Hospital in Belize.

As Brunetti had anticipated, there was no signature on the attachment.

Brunetti scrolled back and, taking his notebook out of his pocket, wrote down the dates and highlights of Dottoressa Bagnoli's career.

He decided to try to transfer the email to his file for 'Restaurants', but not only would it not move, but, as he highlighted it so as to be able to move it, it blinked red three times and disappeared, not at all to his surprise. Well, Elisabetta had been assured that nothing would go into a computer, although he doubted that Signorina Elettra was included in this agreement.

23

Some messages had come in while he was reading the file; he looked at them now. The first was Pederiva's phone number, which Brunetti dialled without bothering to look at the other messages.

After four rings, 'Pederiva.'

'Captain Pederiva,' Brunetti said, 'this is Commissario Guido Brunetti. I'm an acquaintance of Vice-Admiral Fullin.' He paused there to allow the Captain to acknowledge or question this.

'Yes, Girolomo and his grandmother have both spoken of you.' Pederiva had a low voice and the cadence of a person who preferred speaking Veneziano.

Resisting the temptation to move into the informality of dialect, Brunetti continued in Italian. 'I hope they spoke well of me.'

'Both of them did.'

'I'm relieved to hear that, Captain. Girolomo told me about your last meeting with his grandfather; it sounded as though del Balzo's letter pushed him beyond bearing.' Brunetti abandoned all formality here and said, 'That shouldn't happen. Not to a man like him. He's very—'

The Captain broke in to say, 'I served under him for four years, and he made me the man I am. He shouldn't have—' His voice tightened off his words, leaving Brunetti with only the sound of his rough breathing.

'Would you tell me what happened, sir?' Brunetti asked.

He heard the sound of wood scraping on something, and then the Captain gave a grunt of relief, perhaps as he sat. 'The letter I received from del Balzo, asking for a contribution, sounded strange to me, so I took it to Vice-Admiral Fullin to ask him if he'd said those things.'

'Did you ask him or did you read him the letter?'

'Does it matter?' the Captain asked.

'It might. Do you remember, Captain?'

After a very long pause, the Captain said, 'I think I might have read him some of the letter, Commissario.' Then, in a rougher voice, 'Certainly not the beginning and what was said about my memoirs.' He stopped and Brunetti could hear him grasping for control of his voice.

'The whole letter sounded false, made-up: del Balzo has him saying things he'd never say. Matteo would never tell me what to do, tell me who to give money to. He was a discreet man, and he never talked like that.' Brunetti was saddened by Pederiva's use of the simple past tense when speaking of the Vice-Admiral, but he kept that reaction in his heart.

'Matteo would never say those things about me, never,' he said, as though Fullin had betrayed a trust by saying he was a generous man. 'Stupidly, I read him the part where del Balzo tried to convince me to continue contributing to his charity, and that's when Matteo began to shout.'

'What did he say?' Brunetti asked.

'"He tricked me," and "Thief," even "Traitor."' Brunetti heard what sounded like a sob, quickly stifled.

'Could he have meant anyone else?' Brunetti asked.

'No. He knew who wrote the letter. Then he grabbed it and ripped it apart.'

'What happened then?'

'Before I could say anything, Girolomo came in. He'd heard the shouting, so he came to see what was wrong and took the pieces of the letter from his grandfather. He helped him sit down, and then told me it would be better if I left.' Brunetti heard the deep breathing and, not wanting the old man to cry, or worse, be heard crying by another man, changed to a brisk and efficient voice and said, 'Thank you, Captain. What you've told me is very important.'

'He's my friend,' Pederiva managed to say, sounding very weak.

'And you're his, Captain,' Brunetti replied softly, but before he could offer more comfort, the other man broke the connection.

He replaced the phone and went to stand at his window. How was it, he asked himself, that Vice-Admiral Fullin had come to believe that Bruno del Balzo was a liar, a thief, and a traitor? Was this not the same man whose integrity he had vouchsafed by signing the founding documents of his charity? Even though dementia had laid waste the mind of the man making the accusations, Brunetti had learned enough in recent days to believe that Fullin's accusations were not necessarily untrue because of that.

He should, Brunetti knew, take what he'd learned to a magistrate and have a formal charge made against del Balzo, although this would effectively take the case from Brunetti and give it over to the Guardia di Finanza. But where was the evidence to support a formal charge? And had he not promised Elisabetta that this would be kept private?

Brunetti's thoughts were interrupted by the sound of the motor of a passing taxi; he turned away from the noise to return to his desk. Pulling out his notebook, he found Fenzo's number, dialled it, and waited. After the third ring, a man's voice answered. 'Fenzo.'

'Signor Fenzo,' Brunetti said in a neutral voice, 'this is Commissario Guido Brunetti.' He paused to give the other man time to reply.

'The man Flora talked to.'

'Yes. We spoke at some length.'

'She told me.' Fenzo's voice was formal and reasonably pleasant.

'I called because I'd like to speak with you, as well.'

'About the break-in at Flora's clinic?' he asked, his scepticism audible.

Brunetti paused a moment. 'Hardly. I'd like to speak to you about the setting up of your father-in-law's charity.'

'Belize nel Cuore?' Fenzo asked as though he were speaking the name for the first time and didn't much like the sound of it.

'Yes,' Brunetti answered.

'Why do you want to talk about it?'

Brunetti suddenly realized that a man such as the one he had come to believe Fenzo to be would respond best to the truth. 'To find a way to keep your wife from being damaged by what's going to happen to her father.'

This, Brunetti thought, was the point where Fenzo would refuse to speak to him or not.

And so it proved. 'Where would you like to have this conversation?'

'Would Campo San Vio be convenient?' Brunetti asked. He knew there were benches there where they could sit and not be overheard, and it was not far from Fenzo's office.

'I planned to go home early today, but I could meet you there at three.'

This agreed, Brunetti broke the connection.

*

When he left the house after lunch, he looked at the time and saw he had only twenty minutes to get to Campo San Vio. He did the calculations – geography, time of day, foot traffic – and turned left into Rughetta. He set himself on hurry.

He was three minutes early and breathing heavily when he came down the bridge into Campo San Vio, another of those strange *campi* in which there was almost no commercial enterprise: a shop selling Murano glass to his right and, a bit ahead, a pizza takeaway. Because the church was Anglican, Brunetti did not consider it a commercial activity.

He looked to the left and saw a man in a light tweed coat sitting on one of the benches, reading what looked like *Il Sole 24 Ore*.

Brunetti walked over and stood in front of the seated man, casting a shadow so that the other would not have the sun in his eyes when he looked up. 'Signor Fenzo?' he asked.

Fenzo closed the newspaper and got to his feet awkwardly.

It was only then that Brunetti saw the cane leaning against the side of the bench. 'Shall we stay here?' Brunetti suggested, and when Fenzo nodded, he flicked aside the back of his coat and sat at some distance from him.

'Thank you for agreeing to talk to me, Signor Fenzo.'

He was a handsome man, with brown eyes and very thick eyebrows. His nose tilted a bit to the left. His gaze was open and direct.

'I agreed to meet you, Signor Brunetti, not necessarily to talk to you,' he said, trying to smile.

'True enough,' Brunetti admitted. He crossed his legs and leaned against the back of the bench, then used his hands to rise up and shove himself farther back. When he was comfortable, he turned to Fenzo and said, 'Elisabetta came to the Questura – our families were … neighbours when I was in school years ago – to tell me she was worried about Flora.'

'What?' Fenzo asked, staring at Brunetti. 'Worried about Flora?' His face had contracted, his eyes narrowing, mouth tightening. 'Worried about what?'

'You, it seems,' Brunetti answered. 'That you might harm her.'

This time, Fenzo shook his head, seeming put beyond words. 'That's crazy,' he finally said. 'She knows that's crazy.'

'It was Flora who told her she was worried about you,' Brunetti said, watching Fenzo's reaction. His expression didn't change, but he raised his right hand in a sign of exasperation, the kind of gesture a person makes when words have proven useless.

'And Flora also told her you'd warned her not to say anything about your job.'

Fenzo lowered his eyes and stared at the pavement, then shook his head quickly from side to side, as if trying to clear it of something that was clinging to it.

'That's not what I said.'

'But you did say something about your job? Something that might have alarmed Flora?'

This time, Fenzo propped his elbows on his knees and cradled his head in the curved stand he'd made for it with his hands. 'I told her that something had gone wrong with some work I'd done in the past and that worried me.'

'Elisabetta also told me that you'd said it might be dangerous for both of you if you talked about it.'

Fenzo froze, his face still lowered and invisible to Brunetti. He ran his fingers through his hair and sat up straight, palms pressed flat on either side of him. 'I think I said something about there being trouble in it for us if I ended up being mixed up in it. Something like that. I wanted to reassure her I wasn't being moody or secretive, that there really was something to worry about.' He paused and looked at Brunetti. 'I suppose I hoped this would make her more patient with me.' He smiled after he said that, and shrugged.

'What do you mean when you say you might be mixed up in it?'

'Can you tell me how much you've learned?'

'For some time, my colleagues and I have been looking into the charity you helped set up.'

'What have you learned?' Fenzo enquired again in a tight voice.

'There is the hospital that seems not to be a hospital.' Brunetti paused and glanced at Fenzo to see his reaction.

Fenzo nodded as though he'd just been told something he needed to think about. 'Why do you say that?' he asked.

'Because I've seen a photo of the same building,' Brunetti began, 'dressed more in the fashion of a hotel.'

Fenzo nodded again. 'Yes, I saw that. Hotel des Bains.' Then, after a moment, he risked saying, 'It's far more impressive as a hospital.'

Brunetti asked, 'Do you have any idea how they managed to make it look like a hospital? And the patient rooms and operating rooms, and all the machinery?'

'I suppose they got the photos from the internet.'

'The sign?' Brunetti asked.

'Photoshop, I'd guess,' Fenzo answered.

Suddenly curious, Brunetti asked, 'Is there in fact a hospital?'

'Yes. It does exist.'

'Where?'

'In Belize City. And its name is St Peter's Hospital.'

'What does it look like?'

'Like a rundown, understaffed, not-very-clean hospital that tries to provide basic care to the people of the city. Who sometimes have beds to sleep in, sometimes don't.'

They were interrupted by the arrival of a young couple, probably tourists, who approached the bench slowly, almost timidly, obviously wanting to sit down. Seeing them, Brunetti took out his wallet and removed his warrant card. The young man approached him, strangely diffident, his backpack in his hand.

Brunetti held up the card and said, '*Polizia.*' The young man jumped back, took his partner's hand, and pulled her in the direction of the Accademia Bridge.

'You seem familiar with the hospital, Signor Fenzo,' Brunetti continued. 'Have you ever been there?'

'No, no,' Fenzo said. 'I know because the hospital director sent me photos when Bruno was thinking of making an agreement with them.'

'Photos of the conditions you described?'

Fenzo nodded. 'I think they were embellished, but not like now,' he said with a wry laugh. After a moment's reflection, he added, 'In a way, the photos probably helped: we saw how much they needed our support.'

'Do you know why your father-in-law chose that clinic?'

'His parish priest put him in touch with the chaplain, Padre Filippo, an Italian missionary.'

'And the director?'

'His name was Erian Martínez-Pérez. We exchanged a number of emails and spoke on the phone a few times. He seemed a competent person.' Fenzo paused and then added, bitterly, 'It doesn't matter, anyway. He's not there any longer.'

'What happened?'

'He resigned. I was told he disagreed with some policies of the new administration.' He paused there, then added, 'He stayed on until things were moving smoothly between the hospital and the charity. Then he left.'

'And who replaced him?'

'I don't know, Commissario. I'd stopped working on the project by then.'

'For any reason?'

'If you've spoken to my wife, you know it's because I'd already opened my own office, although I'd neglected it during the time it took to establish the charity.' Fenzo moved around on the bench, pushing himself up with both hands and then letting himself back down, almost as if he were trying to invent a new sort of exercise.

'Was there any other reason you stopped working for your father-in-law?'

'No,' Fenzo said, perhaps too quickly or too firmly.

'You simply left it to him to run the charity and went back to your own clients?'

'More or less,' Fenzo said, raising himself up again but this time holding himself suspended for a few seconds before letting himself drop back on the bench.

'That's the first evasive answer you've given me, Signor Fenzo,' Brunetti said calmly.

'I know. I've never been good at evasion.'

'So then, tell me the truth.'

'That is the truth. I left ...'

After a long time seemed to have passed, Brunetti asked, 'You left, because ...'

'It's more like, "I left, but ..."' Fenzo said.

'Would you explain that to me, please?'

'I told Bruno that I'd keep an eye on the books for him if he wanted me to. I knew, even as I made the offer, that I shouldn't do it. But he's Flora's father, and he'd need help or he'd make a complete mess of it.'

'And so?'

'I stayed on for a few months, keeping an eye on things. After about six months, he said he felt competent enough to do it himself.'

'Was he?'

'Not in the least,' Fenzo said hotly.

'Did you suggest another *ragioniere* who could help him?'

Fenzo gave this question some thought and finally said, 'No.'

'Why?'

'Bruno had already found himself another ...' Fenzo stopped speaking for a moment, and Brunetti turned to watch him search for the proper word.

When it seemed that he was not going to finish the sentence, Brunetti asked, 'Found a what?'

'Financial counsellor,' Fenzo said, pronouncing the English words with an accent Brunetti thought he was exaggerating.

'Do you know his name?' Brunetti asked.

Fenzo laughed, scooched down on the bench, put his head against the back, and laughed again.

When he stopped, Brunetti asked, 'What did I say that amused you?'

Like a man so tired he wanted nothing more than to be left in peace to go to sleep, Fenzo turned his head back towards Brunetti and said. 'I used the English words "financial consultant" and you asked if I knew his name.'

'That's true,' Brunetti said.

'But you've spoken to both my wife and my mother-in-law, and one of them is sure to have mentioned that the "consultant" is a woman.' Fenzo paused for a long time, still looking up at Brunetti from his headrest at the back of the bench, smiling in such a friendly way as to make Brunetti nervous. 'If I might take the liberty, Commissario, I'd point out that this is the first evasive thing you've said to me.'

Brunetti sat quietly and Fenzo, like a sepulchral statue, half lay on the bench until, perhaps tired of the game, he sat up straight and said, as though it were a curse, 'Innocenza Bagnoli.'

24

Fenzo suddenly got to his feet but made no immediate move. After some time he bent over, picked up his cane, and limped over to the edge of the water, left hand stuffed into the pocket of his overcoat, and stood gazing across at Palazzo Barbaro.

A vaporetto slid past from the right, then both of them could hear the motor disengage, reverse, and then the thump of the boat at the Accademia as the pilot made a sloppy landing.

When Fenzo came back and sat down again, keeping the cane stretched out in front of him, Brunetti asked, 'Can you tell me how this works? And what happens to the money?'

Fenzo smiled with no sign of happiness. 'I can tell you about how the money travels.' Having said that, he glanced at Brunetti again and gave a real smile, as if relieved finally to be able to talk about this to someone.

'In the beginning, we transferred what little we raised to the hospital's account, and we were sent emails – some of them very charming, some even with photos – of what was done with the money: a new refrigerator to keep blood samples in; three

hundred pairs of surgical gloves; packages of gauze and bandages. It stayed like that until I left.'

Brunetti suddenly realized the sun was gone, and they were
sitting in the shade. Fenzo, too, had noticed and started to speak
more quickly. 'Some months ago, I was sent – I'm sure by mis-
take – a copy of the previous two months' accounts between
Belize nel Cuore and the hospital. The hospital acknowledged
receiving more than eighty thousand euros and sent receipts to
show where the money went: a new ambulance – they specified
that it was used – the first two months' salary of a newly hired
pediatrician, at least I think it was a pediatrician. A doctor, at
any rate. Repairs of medical machines and equipment, and I
can't remember the rest. They were sent as proof of how the
money was being spent.'

'Proof?' Brunetti asked.

'Evidence, at any rate,' Fenzo admitted, then added, 'Not that
it matters. They were fake.'

'Have you any idea of where the money actually went?'
Brunetti enquired, then failed to prevent himself from adding,
'Or still goes?'

Fenzo pulled the collar of his coat up around his neck and
stuck his hands in his armpits. 'If you'd asked me that two years
ago, I would have said I had no idea.'

'And now?' Brunetti asked, telling himself not to move or look
as though he was aware of the cold that was beginning to lay
itself across his back.

'I have a friend who works for – don't hold this against me,
please' – Fenzo interjected with a real smile – 'for the Guardia di
Finanza. He's in Novara, but he said that doesn't make any difference: the procedure is standard. Anyone who wants to can
start a charity, an ONLUS, and try to save the world. Most are
legitimate, but some are not. The ones that aren't usually have an
agreement with someone working in the administration of a

foreign institution: school, hospital, university. That person agrees to keep a small part of what's sent to them by the charity.' Fenzo stopped here and raised his chin to enquire if Brunetti was following. After Brunetti nodded, Fenzo added, 'Many of these people actually pass their part of the money on to their institution. Some don't.' Brunetti nodded again.

'The Guardia di Finanza doesn't have the manpower to get involved for anything under thirty thousand euros, so usually less is sent. But let me use thirty thousand as an example because the calculation is easier to make.' Brunetti nodded again to show what an attentive pupil he was, which prompted Fenzo to add, 'Bear in mind that the supposed donor is already getting a tax reduction because of the amount sent, so instead of paying tax on, say, a hundred thousand euros, he's paying on seventy, and that also puts him in a lower bracket, so he's paying a lower percentage on his earnings.'

'Where does the money go?' Brunetti asked.

'The hospital, after keeping whatever fee they've agreed on – probably three or four thousand – makes two transfers to accounts in safe places like the Emirates, the Cayman Islands, or any of a number of countries. The first – another three or four thousand – goes to the account of the director of the ONLUS, and what's left, perhaps twenty-four thousand, goes to the account of the person who made the original donation.' Then, in the manner of an accountant striving at clarity, Fenzo added, 'All of this varies, depending on what sums have been agreed upon.'

'I had no idea it was so ... businesslike,' Brunetti said.

'Well, to the people who do it, it is a business, and a very big one. As with any other business, there have to be rules, and people can't cheat,' Fenzo said seriously, as if he were explaining the rules of piquet.

'Don't you find that perverse?'

'I'm describing it to you, Commissario,' Fenzo said briskly, 'not passing judgement.' Seeing Brunetti's expression, he gave a sly smile and asked, 'And which of us wouldn't want to pay less in tax?'

The accountant waited to see if Brunetti had any other comments, and when it seemed he had not, Fenzo stretched out his legs and began bouncing his heels on the pavement, one after the other, as one does when a bus is late. 'It also gives the donor about twenty-four thousand untaxed euros to spend on what he likes without having to worry if the Guardia di Finanza will start asking questions about where he's getting the money for those pretty things.'

Brunetti believed Fenzo, had no reason not to. But to go to that trouble for so little: he could not understand such a thing. Two weeks of scuba lessons, even on the Gulf of Papagayo, hardly seemed worth it. A taxi approached from the right, possibly from one of the hotels. Both men watched it disappear under the bridge; when the sound had disappeared, Fenzo said, 'I'd like to say one more thing, if you don't mind.'

'Of course.'

'I think Bruno started with good intentions.' Hearing this, Brunetti resisted the impulse to ask, 'Doesn't everyone?' and instead asked, 'Why do you say that?'

'He worked hard from the time he was a young man, and he knew the ethical cost of what he sometimes did.' Fenzo paused to better order his words, and while he did, Brunetti considered how a person could best survive in a world where increased profit and lower costs were the pillars upon which success was built. How strange, he reflected, that both he and Fenzo had fathers-in-law who had triumphed in commerce yet had daughters who had fled their fathers' worlds, taking up professions distant from the commercial sphere and marrying men who viewed their fathers-in-law's achievements with dispassion and little admiration.

When Fenzo still did not speak, Brunetti prodded him by asking, 'Why do you say that?'

'Because when I was helping him set up the ONLUS, he talked about how important it was that he do some good in his life while he still could.' Fenzo raised his hands in the air and let them drop. 'But he's almost seventy, so I suppose his thoughts would turn that way.' He considered that for a moment and said, 'He meant it; he really did. He wanted to do one good thing while he still could.' Fenzo let another long silence pass, and Brunetti decided not to speak.

Finally Fenzo said, 'He wasn't lying, not at the beginning. I'm sure of that.'

It was clear to Brunetti that Fenzo believed what he was saying.

Fenzo spoke with equal certainty when he went on to say, 'But he's thrown all that away.'

25

'And the reason?'

'Innocenza Bagnoli,' Fenzo said with no hesitation, as if this were a perfectly normal and understandable answer. 'That's obvious to anyone.' Brunetti remained silent, hoping it would induce Fenzo to tell him more.

Apparently it did. 'She was recommended to him by a friend who said she had helped him with his investments and was very good and very serious. Bruno was looking for someone to help manage his investments because he didn't want to spend his retirement worrying about money the way he had in the past.' Fenzo paused, as if unable to prevent the irony from taking over his voice, and said, 'He wanted a different kind of life.'

He looked at Brunetti directly: two men hearing this same old story and not certain whether they should weep or laugh and still uncertain about whether they could do so in the company of the other.

'Presumably, his life is different now,' Brunetti risked saying, then added, to show he was not prodding, 'now that he's retired.'

'To say the least. He spends two months in Belize every year, telling Elisabetta that he wants to see the good he's doing. He sends back photos of himself in the wards, talking to nurses and doctors and patients. There are photos of him with politicians: the mayor, the Minister of Health, then with some of the foreigners who live there and who donate to the hospital. He even sent her photos of the place where he lives when he's there: some sort of guest house where he has a bedroom and a study. Very spartan.' Fenzo raised his hands in a gesture of utter helplessness.

'Does Elisabetta ever go with him?' Brunetti asked.

'She went once,' Fenzo said. 'The first year. And she hated it. When she came back, she said it was dirty, she didn't like the food, and she didn't much like the people. She refused to go to see the hospital after Bruno was told there was an outbreak of scabies. He went, but she refused.'

Suddenly Fenzo got to his feet. 'I can't stand the cold any more, and I've told you most of what I know.'

'Which way are you going?' asked an amiable Brunetti. 'I'm sorry I didn't think of meeting inside. Now that we can, I mean.'

'Back to Accademia to get the vaporetto,' Fenzo told him. He bent and picked up his cane.

As they walked, Brunetti asked, 'Tell me a bit about Elisabetta. I've seen her on the street a couple of times a year for ages. But I have no idea about her life.'

'There's not much to tell,' Fenzo said. 'She spent a few years at university, studying art history. Got a job in a gallery.'

'Did she have a career?' Brunetti asked.

'Not really,' Fenzo answered. 'She met Bruno and married him, and then she had Flora and stopped working. She decided she'd stay home and raise her.' Fenzo's steps slowed and he said, sounding more reflective, 'It's a shame she didn't go back to work.'

'Why?'

'Because ... I'm not sure how to explain this,' Fenzo said and stopped in front of the bar on their left. He put both hands on the handle of his cane and leaned his weight on them. 'Bruno and Flora became all she had, and she was very ... protective of her ... well, of both of them. When Flora finished the *liceo scientifico* and said she wanted to study in Bologna and become a vet, Elisabetta had a kind of ... I don't know. Maybe it's best to call it a bad period and leave it at that.'

'Bad in what way?' Brunetti asked, not at all prepared to leave it at that.

Fenzo started walking again, very slowly, perhaps to give himself time to think of an answer, perhaps because his leg hurt. 'I don't know. She and Flora have alluded to it, but neither has ever told me exactly what happened. All they've ever said was that she was unwell for a time.'

Before Brunetti could question him again, Fenzo quickened his pace, doing his best to keep ahead of Brunetti.

Brunetti allowed Fenzo to stay in front while he considered the new light this information cast upon Elisabetta. He could not remember ever having been introduced to her friends, which the young Brunetti had attributed to the difference in their ages, or their class: she had certainly seemed displeased any time she'd found Brunetti chatting with them on the steps or outside the house. He realized only now how strange that had been, especially for such an attractive girl who'd had so many friends, friends to spare.

Fenzo must have tired of the pace he'd set himself because he slowed down, and Brunetti took the opportunity to catch up and walk beside him, saying nothing. Fenzo slowed even more and began to favour his right leg. After a moment, he came to a stop and lowered his head, saying, 'I always try to deny it.'

'Deny what?' Brunetti asked, thinking that the other man wanted to reveal something about his wife or her mother.

Instead, Fenzo raised his eyes to Brunetti's and said, 'My leg. It's been like this since I was a teenager. I was up in Alto Adige and fell into a hole.' Seeing Brunetti's expression, he said, 'Just stupid, bad, dumb luck. It was bad, and I had a bad doctor – I know people always say that – and it was set badly and—' He stopped abruptly and shrugged, then held up his cane to show it to Brunetti. 'I think she likes the fact that I use a cane.'

'What?' Brunetti asked, completely confused.

Fenzo held it up higher and said, 'I think she sees it as proof that there's something wrong with me, and Flora will eventually go back to her.'

Brunetti failed to find an adequate response to acknowledge that he'd heard. Unprompted, his imagination presented him a picture of Elisabetta sitting immobile in the centre of a circle, utterly still, while other figures moved closer to her and then away. That vision led his memory to his *liceo* class in philosophy. There, he had learned about the 'unmoved mover', which could, at will, put other things, gods, or beings into motion while remaining unmoved itself. His professor had traced the concept back from Thomas Aquinas to Aristotle with a great display of erudition, or perhaps only of memory – his professors had a habit of equating the two – that had impressed Brunetti but had failed to convince him.

He saw Fenzo remove one hand from the handle of his cane and set off again towards the Accademia. Brunetti walked to his right at a slow pace, asking himself if Elisabetta were, somehow, the unmoved mover in all that had happened.

At the corner, Fenzo turned right and bumped into Brunetti, who had not been aware that the other man was making the turn, so distracted by his thoughts that he'd kept heading straight towards the wall of the Accademia.

Startled, Brunetti looked up and, seeing the wall and the water of the Canal, returned his attention to Fenzo. 'Sorry,' he said. 'I was thinking about something.'

Fenzo nodded and smiled. 'It happens.'

They said goodbye at the vaporetto stop, nodding pleasantly and not shaking hands. He waited until Fenzo disappeared into the *imbarcadero*, not bothering to look back, and then Brunetti started towards home, thinking of how far Fenzo would have to walk to get to Fondamenta Nuove, wondering how much pain he was willing to endure to live in the city.

He walked past the antiques shop that il Conte had always referred to as 'la Standa di Venezia', an insult that had lost its force because the supermarket of that name had left the city decades before and only people Brunetti's age or older were still sure of where the stores had been or of the jumble of things that had been found there.

What was the Latin? he asked himself as he walked. Not far from the Italian: *'primum movens'*.

Well, if Elisabetta were that force – and he conceded that her behaviour had seemed pretty much motionless – she had certainly set things into motion.

As he continued towards home, he fitted more and more pieces together: without pointing Brunetti's suspicions towards the ONLUS, Elisabetta had merely made it inevitable that he would examine it by talking about Fenzo's fears and the danger he thought they were in. Sooner or later, Brunetti's attention was bound to be pulled towards Belize nel Cuore. He slowed to a stop, much to the irritation of the man behind him, who muttered something about *'maledetti turisti'* and stumbled around the motionless Brunetti, who had just realized how he'd been pointed towards the ONLUS, given one last tap on the back and let go to careen towards and around it.

He resumed walking, wondering what Elisabetta had discovered, and how. He doubted that the money laundering would bother her; after all, if her husband did it, then it would profit her, too. She might well not know that the donations were going astray and that very little money reached the hospital, but even if she did, Brunetti doubted she'd be troubled by this.

It was when Brunetti thought of the wreckage and blood he had seen at her daughter's clinic that he raised his eyes from the pavement in front of him and was surprised to find himself in Campo San Barnaba. Habit had led him in the wrong direction, and he was heading for home instead of returning to the Questura.

He turned into Calle del Traghetto and walked quickly down to the *imbarcadero*, where he managed to jump onto a departing Number One just as the sailor was sliding the railing closed. As the boat headed towards San Marco and the Bacino, Brunetti pretended that the buildings were moving themselves to the left, reeling themselves by with their usual chronological chaos: Gothic shoulder to shoulder with late Renaissance, which rested comfortably against Byzantine, only to be interrupted by a small canal, after which erupted an enormous hotel, and then a broad garden still filled with roses climbing up a badly restored Baroque wall. By what rule of sanity, he wondered, could this be normal?

The words 'sanity' and 'normal' brought him back to the attack on the clinic and the signs of rage he'd seen there. His original impulse had been to ignore the possibility that Elisabetta was capable of such a thing, but what Fenzo had said about her response to Flora's decision to go to university in a different city had opened up new possibilities about her character.

There was also – and far more persuasively – the possibility that Signora Galvani, even without her glasses, had recognized the person in the *campo*, but, lacking absolute certainty, had refused to identify her.

But why? But why? But why? he asked himself. Why frighten her daughter with the break-in? Why leave the wounded dog? And why do it at a time when the break-in would only call attention to Flora and, by extension, her family? Not sane behaviour, not normal.

He cast his memory back to the conversation that had begun all of this. When speaking of the people who helped her husband run the charity, Elisabetta had mentioned a woman living in Mestre – of all places – but claimed she'd never met her. That might be true, but why would she know the woman lived in Mestre when she seemed to know nothing about the secretary or the girl volunteer? Or care?

The vaporetto pulled up to the San Zaccaria stop and Brunetti got off, still brooding. He tried to think of someone who might know more about her, but he could think of no one who, in all these years, had mentioned her name to him. So much for his belief that everyone in Venice was but a phone call away from the beginning of a trail of acquaintanceship that would lead to anyone or everyone.

As he reached his office, he remembered telling himself, when he first spoke with her, to treat Elisabetta as he would anyone else he questioned. He had not. He had immediately given credit to what she'd said, believing that what she told him was true and bore examination, not questioning.

Where should he have begun? Where could he find traces of her past? He sat at his desk and stared out of the window, telling himself to think like a policeman and not like someone who had to do a favour for an old friend because her mother had been kind to his.

He leaned forward and switched his screen into life. He keyed in her name, 'Elisabetta Foscarini'. He did not know her date of birth, but perhaps the computer was in a clement mood.

He found references to two Elisabetta Foscarinis, one who connected with a print in the collection of the Correr Museum of the 1749 reception for the duke and duchess of Modena, and another, who sounded very much like the first, who seemed to have been both the widow of Pietro Foscarini and subsequently the mistress of his brother, Doge Marco Foscarini.

Suspecting that neither was likely to be of use to him, Brunetti turned his attention to a more current source of information: the already digitalized record, going back thirty-three years, of criminal charges entered into the official register of the Questura. When that proved not to contain Elisabetta Foscarini's name, he turned to a file that Signorina Elettra had sent him and which he had hidden in his computer under the title she had given it: 'A Brief History of Topiary Animals in British Landscape Architecture'. The contents were other, for it contained the complete digitalized records, dating back sixty years, of the children's court in Venice.

Although the file had been in his computer for a year, Brunetti had never had the need, nor the courage, to look at it. He had always felt a particular abhorrence for crimes of whose victims were children; equally horrid to him seemed the crimes committed by children.

He found her in the early years, first mentioned aged eleven, when a classmate's mother reported to the police that Elisabetta had repeatedly threatened her daughter and accused her of trying to steal her friends.

Two policemen had spoken to Elisabetta's father and mother at home, and the matter had ended there. Brunetti reflected on this and decided that the threat must have been taken with some seriousness for two officers to have spoken to the parents, thus exposing them to the risk of the neighbours speculating about a visit from the police.

Brunetti found two subsequent entries from when Elisabetta was fourteen and sixteen. Two boys in her class had had to restrain her from attacking her history teacher, a middle-aged married man, for having praised the work of a classmate while giving her paper a barely passing grade. Less than a year later, she had been seen running a key along the side of a motor scooter parked on the street on the Lido. The scooter, the police reported, belonged to a fellow student of Elisabetta's who had twice accepted her invitation to spend a day at the *capanna* her family rented each summer at the private beach of the Excelsior Hotel on the Lido. And had then declined a third invitation.

A passer-by had confronted her, demanded her name, and gone home to call the police. This time, things had been settled between the police and the boy's family, although Elisabetta was warned that from the age of eighteen she would be in danger of being arrested as an adult and subject to far more severe measures.

The warning must have been enough to have kept her from ever being arrested as an adult. Or, Brunetti reflected, it might have done little more than make her more cautious.

Regardless of what she had done, what remained was the common motivation: Elisabetta was not to be ignored. When she was, her responses escalated from threats of violence against a person, to an attempt to inflict it, and then to the destruction of property.

Could his mother have known this? he wondered. He had often heard her praising Elisabetta when they met on the street or on the stairs. His father was impervious not just to Elisabetta's charms but to her existence.

Curious about this, he called his brother, Sergio, and they exchanged commonplace questions and answers about their families and work, after which Brunetti asked, 'Do you remember Elisabetta Foscarini?'

It took Sergio a moment to ask, 'In Castello? Upstairs?'

'Yes.'

He took longer to answer, perhaps trying to understand why Guido would be curious after all these years. 'Why do you ask?'

'I'm involved in something that might concern her, and I wondered what sort of person you think she might be. Or have become.' This question seemed allowable under the rules he'd agreed to with Elisabetta, though Brunetti realized he didn't much care about that any more.

'You didn't know her very well, did you?' Sergio asked, and Brunetti began to suspect he had been wise to make the call.

'No, I didn't. She's five or six years older than I am, so I always thought of her as somehow being above me,' Brunetti said, beginning to suspect only then how eagerly Elisabetta herself had contributed to this feeling.

'An idea in which I'm certain she joined you,' Sergio said in a tight voice.

Brunetti was surprised at the heat with which his brother spoke. 'I never saw that in her,' he said, considering the possibility. 'Why do you say it?'

'Because she thought she was superior to everyone: her parents, you, me, our friends, *Papà*, even to *Mamma*, if you can imagine such a thing.'

'But *Mamma* was ...' Brunetti began, but stopped himself. He would not call his mother a saint, would not sink into cliché with his own brother, who knew their mother better because he had known her longer. 'She was a good woman.' It was the best that his surprise allowed him to come up with. Recalling his mother's remarks about Elisabetta, he said, '*Mamma* liked her.' He said it as though citing the Sibyl.

After an extended silence, Sergio finally said, 'Guido, you're the one who's always saying how important language is, how important it is to express things accurately.' When Brunetti found nothing to say, Sergio prodded him. 'Aren't you?'

'I suppose so. Why do you ask?'

'Because *Mamma* never said nice things *about* her. She said nice things *to* her, and I won't insult you by explaining the difference.'

'But why did she say nice things to her?'

'I imagine it was because, if she didn't, Elisabetta would invent something nasty to tell her mother about you.'

'Why would she do that?'

'Because her mother liked you. Well, she liked us all, but she seemed to like you best, or at least Elisabetta suspected she did.'

'I never realized.'

'If she could hide it from her own daughter, she could easily hide it from you, Guido, don't you think?' Sergio paused for a long time, then finally said, '*Mamma* saw it.'

'What, that Signora Foscarini liked me?'

'Yes.'

'I had no idea,' Brunetti said quietly.

'You weren't meant to, Guido,' Sergio explained with the protective calm he sometimes used when speaking to his younger brother. 'I've always believed Elisabetta thought she owned people and they had to put her first, or love her most: her parents, her friends, us. Everyone.'

'And if they didn't?' Brunetti enquired, although the police reports had already answered that question.

'She'd find some way to punish them,' Sergio answered, then added, 'I'm glad we moved.'

'To that apartment in Santa Marta?' Brunetti exclaimed, recalling the small room they had shared; two tall boys with their feet hanging over the sides of the bunk beds, no place to study, little light, perpetual damp.

'It was freedom for me,' Sergio said, sounding relieved, even after all these years. 'No questions about where I'd been, or who

I'd been with. Or where you were.' When Brunetti added nothing to this, Sergio asked, 'Don't you remember?'

'No. Was it Elisabetta who asked?'

'Of course. She always wanted to know who our friends were, who we studied with, went to the beach with.' Sergio let some time pass and then added, reflectively, 'Maybe she didn't do it with you because you were even younger than I was. But she always asked when she saw me in the *campo* or coming into the house. God, it was like living in a police station at times.'

Brunetti laughed at this and said, 'Police stations are much worse, believe me.'

'Why?'

'Because they don't have Signora Foscarini's cooking,' Brunetti said, then waited to hear Sergio's laugh, and hung up when he heard it.

26

Brunetti propped his head in his hands and whispered, barely audibly, *'Dio mio,'* suddenly aware that it was his own master hand that had created all of this. If he had done what any careful policeman would have done and told Elisabetta he was not a private investigator, and that if she wanted things to remain private, that's whom she would have to talk to, he wouldn't have ended up in this trap. Instead, Paladin for a woman who had died years before, he had stepped up and raised his hand, saying, 'Oh, do please let me take care of it for you, Signora. Your mother was a saint, and I'll never be able to pay her back for her kindness to me and my family, so do please let me break the rules and risk my career to help you.'

He had, in short, done precisely what she knew he would. He realized now that Elisabetta's intention had been more likely to direct him, not towards her son-in-law and some vague harm he might do her daughter, but to Belize nel Cuore and thus to her husband and the money flowing out of Italy. Ultimately, however, Brunetti suspected he was being nudged towards the woman she had somehow found out about, yet another in the line of people who had stolen the attention that rightfully belonged to Elisabetta.

Brunetti doubted Elisabetta was smart enough to have planned this with chess-like strategy, aware of where each new move would lead. She had no plan, only impulse; she might well not even have had a carefully calculated target, only the lust to punish. Revenge, that deformed child of Justice, fed itself with blind desire, incapable of seeing what was ahead, caring nothing about means or method, about what it left destroyed in its wake. Only vindication and suffering mattered and would, in some bizarre way, make everyone involved realize that it was Elisabetta who mattered most, who was most worthy of attention and love.

In his career, Brunetti had seen many instances of this same wild contradiction of love and destruction, and it had always frightened him because of its irrationality and incurable selfishness. He had seen a man step over the body of a woman he loved to punish the man she loved, and he had known a mother who killed her children to punish their father for loving them more than he loved her.

Because Elisabetta had come to him clothed in the trappings of old friendship, he had not paid sufficient attention to her behaviour, nor seen how his path towards Belize nel Cuore had been so brightly lit.

He remembered something he had once read, and he smiled. The Jesuits, it was often said, boasted that if a child was given into their care for their first years – the number was variable – that child was theirs forever. Thus, confession and the desire for it were deeply rooted in his spirit, however much he disliked that truth. He picked up the phone, dialled Griffoni's number, and asked her to come down to talk to him.

It didn't take him long to explain to her what he had discovered, and now he sat silent, waiting for her to decide his penance.

Without revealing what lay behind the topiary animals in English landscape gardening, he had told her everything he'd learned about Elisabetta, including what he'd read in her juvenile records.

She sat, pushed back in her chair, eyes closed, her lips pressed against the tips of her linked fingers. As he watched, Griffoni crossed her extended legs at the ankles and raised them up and down a few times. She finally lowered her hands and pushed herself upright, looked across at Brunetti, and said, '*Stamm nguaiat.*'

'Which means?' Brunetti asked politely, recognizing the dialect but not the meaning.

'That we are in the shit.'

'I thought as much.'

'Well, we are.'

'Thanks for using the plural.'

She smiled. And said, perhaps by way of consolation, 'If we look at it legally, however, I don't think we've done anything serious.'

After considering this, Brunetti said, speaking slowly as he thought his way through it, 'We've questioned only a number of people, looked into records and files, and are preparing a report about the possibility of fraud and tax evasion.' After saying this, he looked across at her and said, 'I'm waiting for one of us to dismiss it all as a day's work.'

'Well?' she asked. 'Do you think we could get away with it?'

'Since we're the only people who know what the evidence is, I suspect we could, at least for now.'

'We'd be aiding and abetting a crime.' After saying that, Griffoni went silent on him; he watched as she ran through what they'd done and said in pursuit of evidence, whom they'd spoken to, the documents they'd looked at. After a time she gave a deep sigh and said, 'We've left too much behind us. If anyone ever takes a look at this Belize thing, our fingerprints are on it, and we'd be asked about it.'

'That's what I was afraid of,' Brunetti admitted.

She shifted in her chair, not nervously so much as to give her body something to do while she tried to think. 'How much real evidence have we got?' she finally asked.

Brunetti pressed his palms on the surface of the desk and stared at the space between them. 'There's our initial interview with her,' he said, thanking the gods of caution that had suggested inviting Griffoni to come down to speak to Elisabetta with him. 'I've spoken to her daughter, her son-in-law, and her husband, as well as some people who know them.' He thought of the break-in at the clinic and added, 'But I spoke to them after the vandalism, so there was reason to do so.'

She nodded in approval at the removal of the first obstacle and asked, 'Where did you find the information about creating an ONLUS?'

'It's all available on official websites.'

Griffoni considered this for some time and finally said, 'It would be normal for you to find out about her family to see if there was a link to the break-in.'

'Yes.'

'And the information about Signora Bagnoli and their trips to Costa Rica?' She paused a moment and then added, 'And the credit card charges?'

That stumped him for a moment, but then he realized that the information was divided among them, like disparate pieces in a puzzle, making no sense until someone with a picture of what they were trying to put together saw them and understood. Until then, they made no more sense than the few pieces of paper sitting in his drawer.

'There's no need to worry about that,' Brunetti said, quelling the impulse to open his drawer and see if the papers were still there.

'So what can we do?' Griffoni asked.

'Something or nothing,' Brunetti said.

'Shall we eliminate the "nothing" right now and not waste time thinking about it?'

He nodded again.

'There's no need to deny that we spoke to her,' Griffoni said. 'I understood she was an old friend of yours, and you wanted my opinion.'

'The break-in at Dottoressa del Balzo's clinic's been reported, and everything we've done since then could be the result of that.'

Both sat in silence, looking for the easiest and least destructive way out of this.

Finally Brunetti said, 'We could simply feed them to the Guardia di Finanza.'

A sudden silence fell between them, but they were content to let it extend as they considered the events surrounding Elisabetta and her claims.

It was Griffoni who finally broke the silence, saying, 'There's one thing I've never understood.' Restless, she moved again, this time leaning forward and folding her hands, then trapping them between her knees. 'It's not as if del Balzo's making a fortune on this. If he gets a few thousand euros for each large donation he accepts and transfers – and I'm inventing that number – what can he make, thirty or forty thousand euros a year?' She looked over at Brunetti, who acknowledged the sum with a nod and a shrug.

'What can they do with it?' she asked, sounding exasperated by her own inability to understand. 'It's outside of the country, sitting in an account in the Cayman Islands, or wherever they're sending it.' When Brunetti did not respond, she went on, her confusion growing more audible with each sentence.

'I've no idea what a person can buy in the Cayman Islands, so I don't know why they go to all this trouble to send the money abroad. How in God's name will they spend it?'

Brunetti looked across at his friend and saw a beautiful woman who had little need of make-up, dressed in a pair of blue Diesel jeans and a dark green sweater. She wore white Stan Smith's without socks. This perhaps explained her difficulty in recognizing what was obvious to Brunetti: people wanted luxury, wanted to enjoy the sense of superiority bestowed by wearing, eating, drinking, driving what was perceived as being the very best by the people they knew. 'The best' remained the standard description, although the separate objects filling those slots differed according to class, age, education and the world in which they displayed their possessions.

Brunetti knew, and knew that Griffoni did, as well, that a great deal of the money seeping out of the country through the conveniently malleable loopholes left open and unprotected by a cooperative government was used by the sharks of evasion to pay for drugs, guns, and women, much of which ended up in Italy. Compared to them, del Balzo was nothing more than a tiny fish who filtered miniscule bits of krill or picked up the scraps that slid from the teeth of the large predators.

In that instant, Brunetti began to feel something akin to pity for del Balzo, for none of this was really about money. Del Balzo certainly had earned enough to pay for his own Berluti shoes. Brunetti thought of the other mathematics, the difference in age between del Balzo and Bagnoli of almost twenty-five years and of the things that came with that difference: younger, softer skin; round, firm breasts. Like so many others arriving at the age when work ends and things began to fall apart – family, teeth, friendships, eyes, knees – del Balzo had found the elixir of youth, which was only a euphemism for sex with a much younger woman.

27

Brunetti slept late the next morning and thus had no chance to look at *Il Gazzettino* until he'd hung up his coat and was sitting at his desk. He spread it out and paged through the first section, skipping anything to do with politics. He read a few of the headlines and two of the articles, one of them about the trial of the Navy captain arrested the previous year for having sold NATO secrets to a military attaché at the Russian Embassy, and the other about the continuing investigation of the disappearance of the wife of a banker in Rome.

He closed the first section, slid it aside, and glanced at the first page of the 'Venezia' section, and there he saw a photo of Vice-Admiral Matteo Fullin in full uniform, white hat neatly tucked under his arm. The photo must have been taken thirty years before, when the Vice-Admiral was in the flush of powerful manhood: the epaulettes on his shoulders were impressively far apart, his massive chest covered with medals far more striking than the paltry thing Brunetti had worn to show him, his face strangely sensitive, with full lips and a thin nose, eyes looking boldly forward, as if at some distant prize he was about to win or at an enemy he was about to destroy.

And above it, the headline, in the manner of the *Gazzettino*, screamed at the reader: ANOTHER CRIMINAL SAILOR? Later, he would compare the experience to what it must be like to open a letter bomb: you think it is going to be one thing, then it blows up in your hands. There followed an account of the raid by the Guardia di Finanza on the suite of offices of Belize nel Cuore, located in the fourteenth-century *palazzo* of its director, Bruno del Balzo, a well-known Venetian entrepreneur. Documents were confiscated, computers and hard discs were taken from the building by the officers of the Guardia di Finanza for close examination of what was suspected to have been a carefully constructed tax fraud that had been going on for years. Brunetti looked at the second, smaller photo, took a more careful look, and noticed that the building from which the officers were carrying the computers was not Palazzo Dandolo. He sighed and continued to read.

The journalist reminded the reader that this apparently well-orchestrated fraud followed close upon the arrest of the captain suspected of treason for the sale of secret documents to the Russians and the suspicious sale of two frigates to Egypt for a sum calculated to be between 250 and 500 million euros LESS (the newspaper permitted itself the use of capital letters here) than the price the Navy would pay for the same ships. Could this be, the journalist went on to speculate, a sign of deep-rooted problems in the Marina Militare? Problems so grave that few people would have the courage to point them out.

Vice-Admiral Fullin (retired), whom the Guardia di Finanza had named a 'person of interest', sat on the board of Belize nel Cuore, an international charity that worked in the developing world. Indeed, he was one of the founding members. The article reported that the Vice-Admiral had, for some time, been encouraging his retired former shipmates to contribute to this charity, a judgement that one of those former officers referred to as 'hypocrisy and dishonesty on the part of someone who is no better than a "pirate in a white uniform", disgracing the noble record of la Marina Militare while living out his retirement in one of the most famous *palazzi* in the city.'

Brunetti was distracted by the low moaning sound emerging from his own mouth. How in God's name had this happened, and how had the information passed to the Guardia di Finanza?

He stared at the photo of the Vice-Admiral, certain the article was an attempt to find a soft target. Given the bad press the Navy had had in the last months, there could be no easier villain than a vice-admiral, especially one who lived in a *palazzo*. The journalist seemed to believe that part of del Balzo's guilt was evident from the fact that he lived in one; thus it was only a short step to incriminate the Vice-Admiral for the same offence.

He opened his drawer and saw the folder, pulled it out and opened it. The papers were all there. He heard a noise at the door to his office and looked up to see both Vianello and Griffoni. He waved them in. Vianello closed the door after himself. Neither of them, Brunetti was glad to see, had the newspaper, nor did either carry any documents.

When they were sitting in front of him, he asked, 'Well?'

Vianello crossed his arms, and Griffoni crossed her legs. Neither, it seemed, wanted to be the first to speak.

Brunetti decided to do it for them. 'I saw it only ten minutes ago, when I got here.'

Vianello nodded and said, 'Me too. I went up and got Claudia.'

'And we decided we needed to talk about this,' she concluded, making an all-encompassing gesture with her arm, as if to include everything that had happened since Elisabetta came to the Questura to see her friend Guido Brunetti.

Brunetti waited, and Griffoni went on. 'I've tried to remember everything we did – at least anything that can be traced – and all of it, except the original conversation ...' she said, placing heavy emphasis on the word 'conversation', '... happened after the break-in at the vet's place. So,' she added, 'everything we did and all the information we sought can be explained in light of that clearly criminal act.' Before Brunetti could mention his visit to the Fullins, Griffoni said, 'In the unlikely event that your mother-in-law and her friends are ever asked about your visit to the Vice-Admiral, I'm certain they will have no memory of it.'

Brunetti stopped himself from remarking that she would have made a wonderful defence lawyer and said instead, 'That still doesn't tell us how the Guardia di Finanza suddenly learned about this, nor how the newspaper had so much information.'

'How did they find out that Fullin was on the board, for instance?' Griffoni went on.

Vianello turned to her and said, 'All anyone would have to do is take a look at the foundation charter for Belize nel Cuore. His name is there, and the papers are open to public examination online.'

'But a person would look for them only if they had reason to take a careful look at Belize nel Cuore. I want to know why someone – perhaps a journalist – would begin asking questions about it,' she persisted.

Brunetti took a deep breath and continued, having had time to think about the article and what news it actually conveyed. 'Let's try to unravel this. How much information does the article actually reveal? It mentions Fullin, del Balzo, and Belize nel Cuore.' Vianello opened his mouth to speak, but Brunetti kept talking. 'But it offers no real evidence, only rumour and suggestion.'

Both looked across at him, curious now.

Brunetti pulled the open newspaper towards him and looked at the article again. 'Listen,' he said. 'The papers confiscated from the office were "suspected to be" evidence of fraud. Then there's mention of the captain who sold papers to the Russians and the frigates that got sold to Egypt at fire-sale prices.'

He looked at them and said, 'Both irrelevant. They do nothing but toss some mud on the white uniform Fullin is wearing.' His eyes returned to the page and continued down the column. 'Fullin is a "person of interest".' Looking across at them, he asked, 'What's that supposed to mean?'

Neither responded; Brunetti continued down the column. 'He was a founding member of the charity.' Glancing first at Vianello and then at Griffoni, he said, 'Until there's proof of fraud, whether he was or was not a founding member is meaningless.'

Again, silence. 'Then there's the statement from some unnamed person who calls Fullin a pirate and suggests his crime is made worse by the fact that he lives in a *palazzo*.' He paused for a moment, then added, 'I've visited a lot of people who live in famous *palazzi*, and some of them were living in places that were falling apart from neglect or were about fifty square metres.'

He took another deep breath and, with an embarrassed glance back to some of the ideas he'd voiced as a student, said, 'It's not a crime to live in a *palazzo*.'

As if it were an unruly animal, Brunetti shoved the newspaper aside. 'There's nothing in there that could be admitted as evidence in a criminal case. There's no proof of a crime, only a description of the intervention of the Guardia di Finanza and an accumulation of rumour, irrelevance, and vague suspicion.' Then, before either one of them could beat him to saying it, Brunetti told them, 'If this is the evidence they have, it's worthless.'

'So why did we come down to talk to you?' Griffoni asked.

'Does that mean you believed it?' Brunetti asked.

She shook her head. 'No, I didn't – not that Fullin was guilty of anything. But I wondered why the Guardia di Finanza would descend from the heavens on del Balzo, just at the time we've all been chasing after information about him.'

Vianello broke in here to say, 'Well, that's obvious enough, isn't it?' Finding himself instantly the subject of their stares, the Ispettore asked Brunetti, 'It's your friend, isn't it? She set you rolling down the hill, and when you said you had nothing to tell her, she got in touch with the Guardia – probably anonymously – and told them to have a look at Belize nel Cuore.' He paused and looked at Brunetti, then at Griffoni. 'One way or the other, she wants her husband to be punished.'

When neither of them answered him, Vianello said, sounding aggrieved, 'I thought it was obvious. She came to see you and talk about the danger to her daughter to set you sniffing at his so-called charity. And when you failed to deliver his head on a plate, she tried the Guardia di Finanza.'

Brunetti thought this was true. 'Nothing else explains it.'

'Love turned sour?' Griffoni asked.

'We've all seen cases,' Brunetti said. No one at the Questura liked to respond to a domestic violence call because often at least one of the participants was beyond reason by the time the call came.

'So what do we do?' asked the ever-pragmatic Vianello.

'I suggest we get on with our normal work and let the Guardia di Finanza go ahead with the investigation of Belize nel Cuore,' Brunetti said. 'I spoke to Signor del Balzo about his son-in-law, not about the charity,' he reminded them.

'And the attack at her daughter's clinic?' Griffoni asked.

'It shows all the signs of being a random act of vandalism, probably by one of the so-called "baby gangs",' Brunetti answered, pleased with how plausible he could make it sound and relatively certain that no one would think to question Signora Galvani.

'What about the victim?' Griffoni asked.

'Which victim?' Vianello asked.

Before she answered that question, Griffoni put her palm over the photo in the newspaper.

'Vice-Admiral Fullin.'

28

Hearing Griffoni call things honestly, Brunetti realized how much he had hoped to make it all disappear, had hoped that the word 'pirate' could somehow be airbrushed from the headline, the name Fullin altered or perhaps made to disappear from the article. The insinuating tone would change, and the next journalists would make clear that Fullin's role was exclusively honourary and that he had nothing at all to do with the running – for good or ill – of the ONLUS. And everyone who read the subsequent articles would immediately wipe from their memories the false revelations about Vice-Admiral Fullin and realize that he was a man who had dedicated his life to the Navy and the defence of his country.

Griffoni was right: Fullin was the victim in all this, and likely to remain so because reputations were not redeemable. Fullin would lose his good name, and even after retraction, proof of innocence, apology, it would never be as it had once been. After the Guardia di Finanza finished with del Balzo and made public the secrets of Belize nel Cuore, Fullin would be recalled as 'that Navy officer' – no, not the one who sold the papers to the

Russians, the other one, the one who had the *palazzo* and was mixed up in that scandal with the hospital in Benin, or was it Belgrade? Try and persuade people they'd got it wrong.'

Brunetti looked across at Griffoni, who sat silent, implacable. He nodded in the general direction of the newspaper. 'Fullin can't see that.'

'What if he already has?' Griffoni asked. 'Would he understand it?'

Brunetti tried to remember the room where he'd met the Vice-Admiral. He could recall no magazines or newspapers, only the photographs of former times and – the thought came to him – former rules. 'Even his grandson isn't sure what he understands. Or doesn't.'

The silence they shared expanded until none of them seemed willing to break it. Finally, getting to his feet, Brunetti said, 'I'll go and try to talk to them. To him. At least warn them about the article.'

Griffoni started to speak, 'Do you want ...?' but failed to find the rest of the words.

'No,' Brunetti said, speaking with the voice of hope. 'It will be less upsetting if someone he's already seen talks to him.' Then, before either of them could say it, he added, 'If he remembers me.'

Outside, he found Foa in the cabin of the launch, sitting near the door, intent on *La Nuova Venezia*. The pilot looked towards the sound of footsteps on the deck, got to his feet when he saw Brunetti coming down the steps, and pulled open the door.

'Could you take me over to Palazzo Albrizzi, Foa?'

The pilot closed the paper and tossed it onto the seat. He put on his hat, touched his fingers to the brim in a gesture meant to be a salute, then squeezed past Brunetti and up the stairs.

Brunetti, who usually enjoyed any ride in a boat, no matter how short, for the view it gave him of the other life of the city, sat where Foa had been and picked up the newspaper. The story was not hard to find: with it came the same photo of the Vice-Admiral's stern face and medal-strewn chest, and a similar headline, although this one had discarded the question mark and so could came closer to a direct accusation: RETIRED ADMIRAL CO-FOUNDER OF CHARITY INVOLVED IN INTERNATIONAL FRAUD.

The story below the headline was all but a paraphrase of the *Gazzettino*'s: only the order of the insinuations was changed, as though the journalists had had the same crib sheet to copy from. Fact was as absent here as it had been from the other article, although the phrase 'person of interest' was used. The sale of the documents to the Russians and the frigates to the Egyptians made their appearance before giving way to the letter of denunciation from the unnamed shipmate who pointed out that the Vice-Admiral dared to live in a *palazzo*. All that was missing was 'pirate in a white uniform', which Brunetti had found particularly inventive, however vile.

Raising his eyes from the page, Brunetti saw that they were passing the university and wondered what Paola was doing. He glanced at his watch and saw that she would be teaching now. He hadn't asked her, last night, what she was going to be discussing today, but it was likely to be one of those books that revealed the secrets of human behaviour.

He remembered, years ago, trying to tell her that they did the same thing, he and she: they tried to discover why people did things. They listened to people talk about themselves and others, and they realized that some of them were, and some were not, telling the truth. They realized further that some people said things that were not true because they'd been told them by people who were lying or mistaken. The last time they'd talked about this, Brunetti said that what his daily routine lacked was the luxury of a reliable narrator. Paola did nothing more than smile.

His reverie was interrupted by a slowing of the motor and then a sudden shift into reverse, which brought the launch to a stop that kissed the *riva* lightly and let Brunetti step up easily. 'I don't know how long I'll be,' Brunetti said.

'That's all right, Dottore. I've got the newspaper.'

'I left it back there,' Brunetti said, pointing into the cabin. Then, 'Thanks.'

Foa waved at the brim of his hat, tossed the hawser onto the pavement and climbed up to slip it through the thick metal ring that served as a stanchion. When the boat was moored, Foa said, 'I'll go have a coffee, if that's all right, Dottore.'

'Oh course, Foa,' Brunetti said and turned to the door of the building. It was only then that he realized he had not called, but had assumed the older people would be at home.

He looked at the bells, saw the names of two former doges. He saw the Fullin bell and rang it once, waited what seemed a long time and pressed it for even longer.

'Fool,' he called himself under his breath and rang a third time, leaning heavily on the bell. A loud noise from the speaker startled him – a slammed door? – and he took a step backwards. The noise came again: it could have been a fall or a blow.

'What is it?' he shouted into the metal grille of the speakerphone. The noise continued, and he thought he heard a man's voice, deep and bellowing.

'Stop,' a woman's voice pleaded, then grew louder and cried, 'Help!'

'Police, police,' was the only thing Brunetti could think of shouting. 'It's the police.'

The noises continued, seeming to move farther away from the phone. The door snapped open. Brunetti pushed it back and heard it slam against the wall, but he was already on the way to the stairs. It would be faster.

He took the first two flights two at a time, then dropped his pace to a single step as he continued running up, turning and starting again, hauling himself with the help of his right hand pulling on the railing. Then another turn again and up, trying to keep track of the floors as he climbed. At the bottom of the final flight, he was forced to lean down and brace his hands on his knees, gasping, his legs already beginning to tremble with the strain.

He shoved himself up from his knees and ran up the final flight, stopped at the door of the Fullin apartment and kicked at it. He heard the shouting from within, made a fist and slammed it against the door, and again, and again.

It was opened by Signora Fullin, who was startled by the sight of the man at her door, then seemed to recognize him and fell with her back against the wall.

'Stop them, please make them stop,' she said.

Even as she was saying that last word, the noise continued to rumble down the hall towards them: male voices, two of them, both shouting. One pleaded, 'Please, please stop,' while the other, deeper, continued to mix animal moans and undecipherable words.

Brunetti ran towards the back of the apartment, to the room he had visited. The door was open and Brunetti flung himself inside, trying to stop his momentum by grabbing the door frame with one hand.

Two chairs lay on their backs; standing to their left he saw the Vice-Admiral. His jacket hung open and one part of his shirt had been torn loose from his trousers. A second pair of hands were locked together in front of him, one hand clenched to the other wrist, both arms imprisoning the Vice-Admiral's. Brunetti could see only those alien hands and, behind and beside the Vice-Admiral, a pair of legs braced on either side of him, the better to anchor the person holding him from behind.

A male voice came from behind the Vice-Admiral, repeating what sounded to Brunetti like a children's nonsense song, until the words became meaningless noises.

'No. No, *Nonno*. No.' The Vice-Admiral struggled, but Brunetti could see there was little energy left in the old man. Again, the soft cantilena, a voice striving to sound normal in the midst of this madness. 'No, no, *Nonno*. No.'

The old man looked at Brunetti, his face twisted in confusion and rage.

'Fullin!' Brunetti shouted in his loudest voice. The old man stopped twisting and trying to pull his arms free. He stood stock-still and attempted to straighten up.

'Fullin!' Brunetti shouted again. 'Stand at attention.' The Vice-Admiral's face became a mask of confusion, his eyes shot around the room, only to rest on Brunetti again.

'You heard me!' Brunetti said. The word came to him, and he used it, 'Cadet Fullin, *attenzione*.'

Fullin said, in a voice made small by fear, '*Sì, Signore*.'

The person who stood behind the Vice-Admiral must have felt the release of tension in Fullin's body, for Brunetti saw the hands separate and then disappear. A moment later, Girolomo Fullin took a step to his grandfather's right; Brunetti had a fantasy that he was seeing Girolomo as he would look as an old man. In a lower but no less angry voice, Brunetti said, '*Riposo*.'

Freed, the Vice-Admiral stood upright and snapped out a salute, put his arms behind his back, no doubt with locked hands, and moved his right leg precisely twenty centimetres to the side. He had turned to stone, frozen in the routine he'd known all of his professional life: obey orders, wait for the next one, obey that one.

Brunetti looked at Girolomo, fearing that the shouting had been only the verbal part of the trouble between him and his grandfather. 'Are you all right?' he asked.

The younger man nodded, standing as dazed and silent as his grandfather. He raised his hands to his face and, in the manner of a child, covered his eyes with them.

'Can you tell me what happened, Girolomo?' Brunetti asked.

From behind his sheltering hands, Girolomo nodded. 'He came here,' he began.

'Who?' Brunetti asked.

Instead of answering, Girolomo pointed in the direction of the two overturned chairs. Brunetti glanced at them, looked back at Girolomo, confused about what he meant, and looked again. It was only then that he saw the foot lying on the floor behind one of the upturned chairs.

Brunetti took three quick steps towards the man lying on the floor. As if he'd heard Brunetti coming, the man began to moan. He was on his back, so it was easy for Brunetti to recognize Bruno del Balzo lying there. Eyes closed, mouth slack and partially open, head turned a bit to one side, nesting in the white cushion of his hair. Del Balzo could have been asleep, were it not that people did not set themselves down to sleep on a blood-soaked cushion.

Brunetti took his phone and dialed 119; it rang only twice before it was answered. 'This is Police Commissario Brunetti. I have a seriously injured man at Palazzo Albrizzi and need an ambulance. Now.' Before the operator could begin with the usual reasons for any delay, Brunetti said, 'This is Code Red, and I'm giving you ten minutes, no more. Get an ambulance here. Third floor.'

Before the operator said anything, Brunetti ended the call.

He knelt next to del Balzo, careful to keep his hands in the pockets of his jacket, and looked more closely at his face. On the right side of his forehead there was something Brunetti thought was a dent, although that word rang strangely when describing a human skull.

But there it was, a triangular wound about a centimetre deep, the apparent source of the blood. Helpless in the face of the blood and the moans of the man below him, Brunetti could think of nothing to do but to reach for the wrist at the end of the outflung arm and feel for a pulse. He felt the throb of blood under his fingers, pulled his hand away, and got to his feet. He saw a plaid wool blanket lying over the back of a chair. He shook it out and spread it over del Balzo.

He went over to Girolomo, who was propped against the back of an easy chair, turned away from the injured man.

'Tell me what happened,' Brunetti said, careful not to put his hand on Girolomo.

'I went out for a coffee, and when I came back,' Girolomo began, speaking in a hoarse voice as if fear still held him by the throat, 'even in the lift, I could hear the shouting before I got here. I didn't know what it was. I thought it might be trouble with a workman: the people next door have had problems with their electrician for months, and they've had shouting matches with him before.

'But when I got out of the lift, I heard it coming from here.' Girolomo paused and looked at his feet, then went on. 'When I came in, my grandmother was trying to hold his arm, but he kept shaking her away. The other man was shouting. It was like a madhouse: *Nonno* kept shouting at him that he was a traitor, a thief, a swindler. And the other man kept saying he wasn't: he was the one who'd been cheated.

'*Nonno* had a newspaper in his hand. I don't know where he got it: he doesn't read any more. But he kept looking at it and shouting. The man said it wasn't true, and he could prove it, but then *Nonno* shouted out the word "pirate" at him, and hit him across the face with the folded newspaper.' Brunetti noticed that as he spoke, Girolomo's hands contracted around the padded back of the chair.

Girolomo's voice changed and he started speaking very slowly, with careful precision. 'It looked like one of those old historical movies, where the men throw down handkerchiefs and then have to fight a duel. *Nonno* didn't touch him with his hands. He just said, "Pirate" and swung with all his strength and hit him in the face with the newspaper.

'He fell backwards a few steps, like he was dancing, and then his foot got twisted in the carpet, and he fell against the credenza.'

'You saw this?' Brunetti asked.

'Yes. All of it. It was horrible.' Girolomo looked at Brunetti, and said, 'What's worse is that I could think it was funny.' He shook his head, confused and horrified at himself.

Both of them were silenced by the far-off shriek of an ambulance.

Brunetti made the calculation, following the boat in his mind: it would take another four minutes. He put his hand on Girolomo's shoulder and detached him from the chair, propelling him to the door of the room, where he pushed him back against the wall and told him to stay with his grandfather. Brunetti went out into the corridor.

Girolomo's grandmother was still standing beside the entrance door, eyes closed, lips moving in what Brunetti realized must be prayer. He approached her quietly and began speaking when he was still a metre from her. 'It's all right, Signora. Your husband is with Girolomo. An ambulance has come for the other man, who isn't feeling well.' He stopped in front of her, touched her hand, and waited until he was sure she understood who he was and what he was saying. He took her arm, opened the first door he saw, led her to a chair, and helped her sit.

'Wait here for Girolomo, please, Signora.'

When she nodded, he returned to the corridor: he heard noises at the end. He opened the front door just as two white-jacketed medics spilled out of the lift, a stretcher between them. They followed Brunetti towards the injured man and quickly moved the furniture to get to him. They placed him on the stretcher and carried him quickly out to the lift. Brunetti ran down the stairs and reached the bottom just as the lift opened and the men started towards the ambulance.

Foa was standing next to it, talking to the pilot, but broke away when he saw Brunetti emerge from the building. 'What is it, Commissario?' he asked.

'A man fell, hit his head.'

'Fell?' Foa asked.

'Fell,' Brunetti repeated.

Foa seemed satisfied with the confirmation and said, 'The pilot told me it took them twelve minutes to get here.' He shook his hand in the air in front of him, as though it had been scorched by the heat of the ambulance's motor. 'From the Ospedale.' After a reflective pause, he added, 'I don't think I could do that.' Then, after a moment, 'Will you be going back to the Questura now, Commissario?'

'No, not now.'

'Then where can I take you, sir?'

Brunetti hadn't thought of it until Foa asked, but when he heard the question, he also knew the answer. 'Campo San Giovanni e Paolo.'

29

As the launch took him towards Campo SS. Giovanni e Paolo, Brunetti considered how easy it would be to confront Elisabetta without telling her that her husband was in the hospital, but he realized this was beyond his capacity for deceit.

Elisabetta's story of Fenzo's behaviour had given Brunetti a place to begin, but events had soon spun out of control. Like a delivery truck jumping its brakes and starting to roll downhill had come the vandalism at the clinic and Fenzo's explanation of the money trail. With rising speed, the perfidious Dottoressa Bagnoli and the tragic Vice-Admiral Fullin had arrived to play their parts.

He rested his head against the back of the padded bench, glanced to the right, and watched the backs of houses slip past the launch. He turned and looked ahead and saw the façade of the hospital growing larger.

Brunetti got to his feet quickly and went on deck. 'Foa, you can stop here,' he said, as they came alongside the steps leading up to the *campo*. The boat glided to a halt and he stepped up onto the *riva*. 'You can go back. I may be some time.'

The door to the *palazzo* was only a few metres from him. He rang the bell at the top of the panel, waited, rang it again.

'*Sì?*' a woman's voice asked.

'Elisabetta, it's Guido Brunetti. I'd like to talk to you.'

'Is Bruno with you?' she demanded.

'No.'

'Why are you here?' she asked in a voice now touched by fear.

'I need to talk to you,' he said, and when she did not answer for some time, he added, 'About Bruno.'

The door snapped open. He crossed the entrance hall, started up the stairs, and passed the offices of Belize nel Cuore without hearing any sound from within. When he tried to move faster, his legs gave him silent opposition, and he slowed his pace. Pride prevented him from using the handrail.

There were only two doors on each floor, to the right and to the left, suggesting that the apartments were enormous or that there was another entrance to the part of the house that did not face the *campo*. He noticed, by the time he reached the third floor, that this was a building with rules. In front of each door there was a rectangular beige coir mat, nothing else.

As he paused on the fourth landing to regain his breath, the door on the right was pulled back, and Elisabetta took one step towards him before stopping, her hand half raised to her mouth. The words seemed to come from a machine: 'What is it?' It had been less than a month since she came to talk to him at the Questura, but her face, indeed her whole body, appeared to have shrunk, as though they had passed through a longer time.

A preamble would only upset her more, he reasoned, and so he said it clearly, 'Your husband's been injured.'

Over the years, he'd delivered this news to many people: some grew pale, some red-faced, some slapped a hand to their mouth, others stood still and gave the impression they did not understand the word 'injured'. Elisabetta belonged to this last group.

She stared at him, shifted her glance to the wall behind him, then took a faltering step backwards and steadied herself with a hand on the frame of the door. He watched as she tried to work things out from the word 'injured,' searching for the events that might have taken place in the time since she had last seen her husband.

She took another step back into the apartment, and for a moment Brunetti feared she was going to close the door in his face, but she didn't, nor did she move again.

'Elisabetta,' he said in a neutral voice, 'I think we should talk.'

It took the words some time to slip through whatever silent noise was deafening her, and then she took another step back and – still incapable of speech – waved him into the apartment. She turned and weaved down the corridor like a drunkard, pausing to brace a hand against the wall every so often; Brunetti closed the door and followed her.

Elisabetta turned right into a sitting room; he recognized the glass-fronted cabinet from Elisabetta's home in Castello, all those years ago. Beyond the long line of windows, he saw the profile of Colleoni and his horse and, beyond them, the façade of the hospital, but he didn't pay them much attention. He followed her with his eyes until she lowered herself into a chair, her back to the windows. Brunetti walked to a chair beside her, pulled it farther from her and angled it so that he could see her in profile and not be distracted by what lay beyond the windows.

'Where is he?' she asked in a small voice.

'An ambulance took him to the hospital,' he said, waving a hand toward the building on the other side of the campo so that she would not be confused and mistakenly believe him to be in Mestre.

She closed her eyes and nodded a few times, as though she'd known that this was going to happen. Not when or how, just that it would. 'Tell me, please,' she whispered, lacking the energy for more.

'He tripped and fell and hit his head,' Brunetti said truthfully.

'Where?'

'Where he went when he left here.'

'To see that man who signed the papers?' she asked.

'Vice-Admiral Fullin?'

'Yes.'

She lowered her head but held her hands taut on the arms of the chair.

'Bruno wanted to explain,' she said, voice barely audible.

'Explain what?' Brunetti thought it safe to ask.

'The article. That he had nothing to do with it.'

'In the newspaper?'

She nodded again.

'Tell me what happened, Elisabetta.'

She looked across the room at a dreary still life, filled with flowers and small insects crawling on the table that held the vase. When she spoke, she sounded entirely matter of fact, as though discussing the weather. 'Ever since he retired, Bruno goes down to the *edicola* by the school every morning and brings home the *Gazzettino* for us to read with breakfast.'

This time it was Brunetti who nodded.

'He says it's proof that he doesn't have to rush off to work or go and see how things are being done. He can sit here with me, like a man of leisure, drink his coffee, and read his newspaper.'

She stopped speaking, as though she had run out of energy or was trying to imagine herself back in the moment when her husband had brought the newspaper home, before he'd read it.

He let her sit quietly for a while and then asked, 'What happened this morning?'

She was startled by the question, as though they'd been discussing something else. 'He came home. With the paper. I had the coffee ready, over there,' she said, pointing to a small table and two chairs, the cups still in place, one chair tucked under the table, the other thrust almost a metre away from it.

'He sat down and I poured his coffee and left it for him to put the sugar in. I poured mine and started to drink it.

'Bruno passed me the first section. He does that every morning. He says it's because he doesn't have to worry about what's happening in the world any longer now that he's a pensioner.' It looked as though she might have tried to smile, but Brunetti wasn't sure.

She paused and glanced again at Brunetti, who said nothing.

'All of a sudden, he put the cup on the table and stared at the paper.' She paused again. 'He gasped and said something under his breath. He sounded really shocked: I thought he was sick or having some sort of attack. I asked him what was wrong.'

Brunetti watched as she thought of all of the terrible things that can happen to retired men, and she said, 'He didn't answer. After a while, he handed me the paper. I saw the headline and recognized the name because Bruno knew him well.'

She put her hands on the arms of her chair and pushed herself up, as though she were preparing to stand, but she forgot what she was doing, hung suspended for a moment, then lowered herself back down.

'He started to shout, "It's all lies, all of it. I have to talk to him." He put on his coat and left. I waited a while and tried to call him, but his phone was turned off.'

She pushed on the arms of her chair again and this time got to her feet. 'I have to go and see how he is,' she said, her voice and face tightening.

'I'll go with you, Elisabetta.'

She nodded, left the room, and came back wearing her coat. When they left, she made no attempt to lock the door. Brunetti asked if she'd forgotten and had to repeat the question before she understood. She had her purse with her and rooted around until she found her keys, then the proper key, and locked the door.

They walked silently downstairs, passed in front of the office, where a light was now shining through the narrow transom window above the door, then out into the *campo* without saying a word. Sensing motion beside him, he saw that it was Elisabetta, opening her purse and pulling out a simple blue and white mask. Brunetti rifled through his pockets and found an old one he'd not used since he'd abandoned it in the pocket of this jacket, late in the spring. He slipped it on but had to make a circle with the strings to accommodate the way the elastic had given up after so much time.

While adjusting the mask, Brunetti's pace had slowed as he thought about the similarity between this disease and Elisabetta's story. Get told what seems a simple event, and soon it's expanding out of control; understand the basic facts, until a new variant appears. Believe you've found the source, only to stumble upon new information that changes everything. Conclusions vanish, explanations fail. Stop being attentive, and the next day there are new victims.

A child's shout of joy from the other side of the *campo* pierced his reflections; he looked around for Elisabetta, only to see her standing just outside the entrance to the hospital. He hurried to join her.

At the plastic divider just inside the entrance, Brunetti showed his warrant card to the guard and asked for Bruno del Balzo.

The guard typed in the name and directed them to Pronto Soccorso.

Brunetti and Elisabetta walked through the enormous hall, down the vaulted corridors, past the garden, across an open space and another corridor, and finally through the doors with the large red letters. The nurse on duty recognized Brunetti and came out of her office to greet him.

'Good afternoon, Commissario. Are you here for someone?' She glanced at Elisabetta, trying to work out why Brunetti would have arrived with a woman.

'Bruno del Balzo. He's just been brought in.'

Trying to be helpful, the nurse told him, 'The admitting doctor sent him upstairs.'

'To?'

'Surgery.'

To satisfy her curiosity, Brunetti said, 'I'm here with his wife.' Elisabetta was standing behind one of the orange plastic chairs, hands propped on the back, head lowered.

Her posture seemed to affect the nurse, who said, 'Would the two of you like somewhere to wait?'

'That would be very kind of you,' Brunetti said.

Leaning towards him so that, perhaps, no one else would hear, she said, 'Take the lift to the fourth floor and turn right when you get out. The third door on the right has a sign: "Linen Closet". In the back, there's a table and a coffee machine. Only staff go there.'

Brunetti pulled out his notebook, wrote his *telefonino* number on a sheet of paper, ripped it out and gave it to her. 'Could you call me when there's any news?' Seeing she was about to protest, he added, 'I know surgery won't call me, but they might call you.'

Not smiling, not pleased, she took the paper and put it in her pocket. 'A friend of mine works in the operating room. I'll send her a message.'

He thanked her and went back to Elisabetta, stood still for a moment, but failed to gain her attention. He put his hand lightly on her arm. She did not leap away, but she did step back, and it took a moment for her to recognize him.

'What's going on?'

'The nurse told me he's in surgery, but there's a place where we can wait until it's finished. She'll call us when it is. We have to take the lift to the fourth floor.'

She blinked. He knew that people in a state of shock were often relieved to be told what to do. Brunetti had always thought it reflected their need to know that somewhere there still existed the comfort of safety, even if it was no more than some other person who knew what to do.

The linen closet proved to be just that, with packages of plastic-sealed sheets and bedcovers shelved neatly on both sides from floor to ceiling. As the nurse had said, beyond the shelves, to the right, was a narrow space with a table and windows that provided a view down into an inner garden. There was a solo pine tree that had grown as high as the windows of the floor below and a view out over the *laguna*. Only that gave Brunetti any sense of orientation.

The coffee machine was besieged by a ragged band of paper cups, all soiled by use. They both turned away from it. Brunetti pulled out chairs on opposite sides of the table and waited for her to sit, then went around and sat facing her.

'Did they tell you what kind of surgery it was?' Elisabetta asked.

'No,' Brunetti said. When he saw that his answer sufficed, he continued, 'There are some things that are unclear.'

'Like what?' she asked dully.

'To begin with,' Brunetti answered, 'how much you know about your husband's charity.'

She slipped off her coat and let it half fall over the back of her chair, lay her purse on the desk, and folded her hands. 'I told you all I knew when we first spoke.'

'And I believed you, Elisabetta. But I don't now, not any more.'

Her face was shocked, but her words, coming later, were not. 'Why is that?' she enquired, managing to make it sound like an honest question with only the slightest suggestion of recrimination, as though she could not believe he could think of doubting her.

He decided not to waste time in sparring and to start with the big guns. 'Because someone saw you coming out of Flora's clinic that night. And recognized you.'

Her mouth fell open and she stared across the table at him; Brunetti had the distinct impression that she was trying to find the right expression with which to display both her astonishment and her disappointment in him.

'What did she tell you?' Elisabetta asked. She tried to say it as though she had every right to demand he tell her.

'Isn't it enough that she recognized you, Elisabetta?' Against his will, sadness seeped into his voice as he asked her this. It was perhaps this feeling that prevented him from asking Elisabetta how she knew it was a woman who had seen her.

'But ... but,' she stuttered; then her attention seemed to wander away from the sentence and from Brunetti. He watched her try to find a way to explain her presence there, to airbrush it into innocence, and he watched her fail to do so.

She looked across the table at Brunetti and paused for some time. At last she said, 'I didn't mean for the dog to be hurt.'

Brunetti was not prepared for this and was rendered speechless for a moment to hear Elisabetta sounding as though someone else were responsible, or perhaps the dog had hurt himself.

She ran her hand across the top of the table a few times, wiping away invisible crumbs.

'I didn't know there would be another dog there that night. When I tossed in the treats, to stop him barking when he saw me, I saw there was another dog, and they started fighting over the treats, so I had to open the cage and pull him out. The other dog was much bigger and he went for the ears. He would have hurt him badly, so I had to get him out. But I didn't do anything to hurt him. I never would.' As if to explain this, she paused and, speaking in an artificial voice, said, 'Flora loves him so much.'

Brunetti, hearing the incantatory rhythm, finished the sentence in his mind: '... instead of loving me.' His memory of the blood on Flora's jacket formed a veil between himself and Elisabetta's claim that she would never hurt the dog.

'Why did you do it, Elisabetta?' Brunetti asked, curious to learn what she believed.

She moved restlessly in her chair, crossed her legs, then got up to move the chair farther back from the table and sat down again. But she didn't like that and stood up to move the chair back to where it had been.

Like a schoolgirl caught breaking a rule, she sat up very straight, head lowered, hands in her lap. 'I thought it would make you believe me.'

'I beg your pardon.'

'You'd believe me that Enrico had reason to be afraid for himself and Flora.'

'What did you think I'd do then?'

'Take a closer look at what I told you.' She paused after she said that, as though listening to herself for the first time.

'What did you think I'd discover, Elisabetta?' Brunetti asked.

'What was going on with his charity,' she said, her voice tightening over the last word. 'Sooner or later you were going to start asking questions about Belize nel Cuore.' She, too, pronounced the name in an emphatic way, but there was no irony, only rancour.

'What *was* going on with it? Can you tell me?'

'She's deceiving him, that woman.' The last word could have emerged in a stream of fire.

'Which woman?' he asked, sounding confused.

'His publicity director or his consultant, or whatever he calls her.'

Not wanting to be scorched by the rage she was doing so little to disguise, Brunetti returned to the first thing she had said. 'What's going on?' Stony silence was his reward. 'What's happening with the money?'

Elisabetta struggled to keep herself from speaking, but she failed to resist the power of her wrath. 'She's set it up so the people who donate it get most of it back. I don't understand how it works. She does.' As her sentences shortened, her anger increased. Before Brunetti could go through the motions of pretending not to understand, she went on, heedless, reckless. 'He gets part of the money they all send. So he can spend it on her.' She seemed compelled to bring everything back to this other woman. Brunetti allowed himself to show surprise at her revelations, as though he were hearing all of this for the first time.

'How do you know this, Elisabetta?' he asked.

'Bruno's secretary warned me about her. Both of them think she's a fool because she's old. But she's not.' She paused here, and Brunetti waited for her to declare that she was not a fool either, but she did not.

'She told me all about it. All about her.' It took Brunetti only a moment to work out the pronouns.

'Can we go back to talking about this morning, Elisabetta?' he asked.

'What about it?' she demanded, clearly irritated by his lack of interest in the other woman.

'You said your husband was upset by the article.'

'Yes, he was,' she said and then added, as though it should have been obvious to Brunetti, 'Bruno's known him for a long time.' Strangely, she said this as though it were of no particular importance. 'So instead of worrying about what's going to become of us, he was worried about that old general.'

'Admiral, I believe,' Brunetti corrected her mildly.

'It doesn't matter,' she said, her anger now circling closer to Brunetti. When Brunetti did not comment, she went on. 'Bruno and Fullin's younger brother were best friends when they were boys. They were in the same class at the Morosini,' she explained, as if that put an end to the matter.

'What happened?' Brunetti enquired before she could lead the conversation astray again.

'He died.'

'Fullin's brother?'

'Yes.'

'How?'

'In an automobile accident. When he was at school.'

'Here?' Brunetti asked, thinking he would have some vague memory of an event as unusual as this, but nothing came.

'No, in Padova. He was at university.'

'I don't understand,' Brunetti exclaimed, confused by the sudden plot twist.

'I think he was hit by a car in the city,' she said vaguely, as though it was not of much importance.

Brunetti said nothing but kept an interested expression on his face. When he realized that Elisabetta seemed finished with the subject, he said, 'But how does that affect your husband?'

'The Admiral, as you call him, sort of adopted Bruno after his brother died and treated him like a younger brother,' she said, then added, with scorn, 'A replacement.' Obviously, to Elisabetta, Fullin's feelings had to be false.

Brunetti, unwilling to provoke her with questions, twisted his face in confusion, and she said, 'Don't ask about Bruno's parents. They were both dead before I met him, and he never talks about them.' After pausing in thought, she added, 'I suppose Fullin thought he could be some sort of guardian angel to Bruno.' She gave a sniff of contempt at the very idea.

Brunetti recalled the kick the Vice-Admiral had given at the sound of del Balzo's name: had it been merely a response to a familiar name or a sign of the end of a strong bond?

'He's one of the signatories for the charity, isn't he?'

Elisabetta tried to hide her surprise that Brunetti would know this. 'I think so,' she finally answered.

Brunetti believed that Fullin was honestly confused about what happened around him, but more and more Elisabetta's vagueness seemed a construct rather than a fact. He thought it was time to try to shock the same sort of instinctive kick from her and so he asked, 'Where did you get the idea of getting that article into the newspapers?'

30

Elisabetta froze. It reminded him of the way most people react to an unexpected loud noise. Stop, look around, wait to figure out where the noise is coming from and what might have caused it. Don't move until then.

Too many seconds passed before she took a breath and asked, 'What are you talking about?'

Brunetti remained calm and answered as he would an ordinary question. 'All you needed was someone who had access to a journalist or two. Scandal about people in high positions is always sure to sell.'

Impulsively, rashly, she shot back, voice sour with contempt, 'I wouldn't do something like that for money.'

'What would you do it for, then, Elisabetta?' He made it sound like a taunt.

She took another deep breath, paused in search of the right answer, and finally said, in a voice so calm and soft that Brunetti was unprepared for it: 'Justice.'

'For whom?'

'Me,' she answered fiercely, giving her heart a quick, angry slap.

'How will the article give you that?'

'Because people will know what Bruno's been doing. His friends will know. The people who worked for him will know. They'll know how much money he's keeping.' Then, after taking a deep breath, she said, almost shouted, 'And they'll know about that whore.'

'I suspect a number of people knew this already.'

It took her some time to find an answer. 'Not all of them,' she said finally. 'I'm talking about the ones who didn't know what was going on and what Bruno was doing with the money.'

'The way you did?'

'Yes,' she answered, brazen with the truth. 'But not for a long time.'

'Who else knows?'

It took her some time to find a tone sufficiently venomous to hiss, 'She does.'

'I see,' Brunetti said fell silent. It was not necessary to hear her say Signora Bagnoli's name. Far more important to Brunetti was the name of the person who had passed the information to the journalists at Il Gazzettino and La Nuova Venezia, someone who had access to the information found during their unofficial investigation.

He thought of his first glance across the entrance hall of the Questura at the woman who had come to speak to him. And not seeing Elisabetta because her body was blocked from his gaze by Lieutenant Scarpa, standing there in what appeared to be easy conversation with her. This memory caught him on Occam's razor: location, opportunity, ease of access. Scarpa had them all. Plus desire.

Pendolini might well have told the Lieutenant that the woman was waiting to see Commissario Brunetti, and the ever-helpful Scarpa had but to amble over, remove his hat – a detail Brunetti recalled only now – and ask how he might be of service to

Signora ...? The Commissario might not be there for some time, so how could he – probably saying he was the Commissario's assistant – possibly help her?

To put an end to his uncertainty, Brunetti said, 'I suppose the Lieutenant offered to help you.'

Elisabetta actually smiled. 'Yes, he was very kind. All along.'

With a matching smile, Brunetti said, 'He always thinks things through. It's one of the reasons it's so interesting to work with him.'

For the first time since they'd entered the room, Elisabetta appeared to relax. Leaning towards him across the table, she said, 'I didn't call him until two days after ...' Apparently, she didn't know how to refer to the vandalism of her daughter's clinic; Brunetti would not help her and sat, making it evident how eager he was to hear what she told him.

'... after I went to Flora's clinic.'

Brunetti nodded. 'I'm sure he was very helpful.'

She smiled again, relaxed and easy. 'Yes, he told me about the break-in, that most people at the Questura thought it was the baby gangs.'

'What a great relief that must have been,' Brunetti found himself saying.

Tone-deaf, she replied, 'Yes, it was. And then, somehow, we were talking about the woman.' Somehow, indeed, Brunetti thought.

'Did he tell you who she was?'

'Not only that,' she said, and then in a whisper, 'but all about her.' She allowed time for a dramatic pause before adding, 'And what she was up to.'

'With the money?' Brunetti asked.

'The money's not important,' she said with a dismissive wave of her hand. He had heard the same remark and seen the same gesture many times in his career; no one using them had ever been telling the truth, and he doubted that Elisabetta was either.

'It's what they spent it on,' she continued, fitting easily into the role of betrayed wife. 'Vacations, first-class flights, five-star hotels,' she recited, as though she'd memorized the list Vianello had given Brunetti. The same list, Brunetti realized with great chagrin, that he had so confidently left in the front drawer of his desk. He turned his attention back to Elisabetta and saw how anger aged her, narrowed her eyes with disgust, tightened her mouth with malice, deepened the lines on her forehead. 'I've seen the photos on his phone of where they went,' she said, voice rising. 'Bruno never treated me like that.'

At last she had said something Brunetti understood and did not doubt. It explained her coolness to the young Brunetti: she'd caught her mother being kind to him. The string of boyfriends he'd seen her with over the years, had they all failed to love her best? Until Bruno that is. Flora had loved her until she'd found a husband and a dog. And now Bruno had found another woman, so Elisabetta had the right to destroy his reputation. Jealousy made its own rules: pain had to be repaid in pain.

Elisabetta had just opened her mouth to continue when Brunetti's phone rang. He answered with his name.

'Commissario, this is Arianna, the nurse from Pronto Soccorso.'

'Thank you for calling me, Signora.'

Brunetti covered the mouthpiece with his hand, looked over at Elisabetta, then held up his hand to signal her to be patient.

'Are you there, Commissario?'

'Yes. Is it over?'

'Yes,' she said in a voice that troubled him with its neutrality.

'Can you tell me what happened?'

'All I was told was that there was a lot of bleeding in the brain, and the blood caused an increase in pressure that they tried to resolve. But,' she said and paused, as doctors and nurses have learned to do when there is bad news to give, 'it seems that they weren't entirely successful.' This was meant, it seemed to

Brunetti, to tell him something while saying little, and keeping even that vague.

'I don't mean to cause trouble, Signora, but could you make that clearer for me? Please.'

'There might be damage to the brain,' she said. Well, thought Brunetti, it can't be clearer than that.

'Thank you again for calling, Signora,' Brunetti said. 'His wife is here, and I'll tell her what you've told me.' He waited a moment and asked, 'Can she see him now?'

'I can't answer that, Commissario. You'll have to speak to the people on the ward.' She paused and asked, 'You know where it is, don't you?'

'Yes. I'll take her there now.' Before he broke the connection, he said, 'You've been very kind, Signora. Thank you for it.'

'It's my duty, Signore,' she said, and was gone.

Brunetti repeated to Elisabetta the information he had been given. In a gesture he thought melodramatic, Elisabetta put her elbows on the table and covered her face with her hands. She sat like that for what Brunetti thought was a long time, then removed her hands and stood, saying nothing.

Brunetti was familiar with the hospital and led her from the Pronto Soccorso pavilion back across the open courtyard to the building where, on the second floor, surgery was performed. The nurses' desk stood outside and in front of the surgical ward. Protected by clear plastic barriers on three sides, it effectively prevented unauthorized entrance.

Two nurses sat there, one facing the people who arrived and the other busy looking at a bank of screens, each one showing a patient lying in bed. A man Brunetti thought was del Balzo was visible in the third, his head covered with bandages. All of them seemed to be asleep.

He pulled out his warrant card, never sure whether it had any authority in a hospital, and showed it to the first nurse. 'My name is Brunetti. Commissario. And this is Signor del Balzo's wife, Signora Foscarini.'

The nurse looked at his warrant card, at his face, and handed back the card. Ignoring him, she spoke to Elisabetta. 'He's just back, Signora. He'll be asleep for at least another two hours.'

Brunetti glanced around and saw no chairs, as clear a sign as there could be that visitors were not welcome. 'Where can I wait?' Elisabetta surprised him by asking the nurse.

She had heard this question a few thousand times, Brunetti imagined; she answered in the manner of an automaton. 'Downstairs. Because of the *pandemia*.' When she saw Elisabetta's expression change, she added, 'Only patients and doctors are allowed in here.'

He saw Elisabetta's right hand turn into a fist and wondered if she would turn to violence, here, in a public place. She chose not to. Making a guttural noise of disgust, she wheeled round and walked quickly to the lift and jabbed her thumb repeatedly against the Down arrow. From below, the machine made a similarly unpleasant noise.

Brunetti followed her and stood to her right. When the doors opened, Elisabetta stepped quickly inside and poked at the flickering green button, once, twice, then turned towards the waiting Brunetti.

He found himself unable to move, incapable of committing himself to sharing that small space with this woman. He did not step back, but he felt his body arching away from her. He watched her face, frozen with surprise. 'Guido,' she said in a rough voice.

Brunetti raised his left hand in front of his chest and waved it quickly back and forth, back and forth. He was still waving it when the doors shut on her still startled face.

Five minutes later, Brunetti emerged into the light of Campo SS. Giovanni e Paolo and walked directly across to the statue of

Colleoni. He stood behind the low metal railing and studied the face of the mounted *condottiere*, the sneer of cold command, and thought about what he had been taught at school. Colleoni was a paid warrior who'd fought for the highest bidder, and fought for them until the war was over, when he, and all the other *condottieri*, were free to find new masters. During the endless wars of the fifteenth century between Venice and Milan, he'd finally opted permanently for Venice and had defended her valiantly. His loyalty, once given, was constant and true, for he was always faithful to the side for which he fought. Promised by the city a monument in San Marco, the defender had instead been granted one near the Scuola Grande di San Marco and was thus tricked into ending up here. Not a bad place to be, but, still, it was not Piazza San Marco, nor was it what he'd been promised.

Brunetti looked beyond the statue and saw the façade of the Basilica and then that of the hospital. Could these things be real? he wondered.

His thoughts returned to Colleoni. He pressed his lips together and looked up at the horse. His father had told him, when he took his small son to the *campo* for the first of many visits, that anyone lucky enough to view the statue from a very low perspective would see that he was balanced – as only magic horses could be – on only two feet. Taller people saw it all wrong and thought he needed three feet on the ground, but this was the horse of Colleoni.

Brunetti was an adult before he finally understood that his father had been joking. He'd seen the photos of the well-grounded horse, he saw him now from a much higher perspective than had his child self, but he'd continued to believe, and had taught both of his children to believe, that the magic horse of Colleoni was balanced on only two feet. Let the horse be doing something impossible, so long as his master remains faithful to the side for which he fought.

31

In mid-February, it snowed in Venice for the first time in the memory of many residents, at least those under ten, not that there were very many of those left. It started in the middle of the night between Tuesday and Wednesday, when Venice awoke to fifteen centimetres of snow.

Before dawn, the garbage men were busy shovelling, sliding what snow they could into the canals, using shovels made for digging the earth and thus of less practical use than snow shovels. A city administration that could not find money to clean the canals could hardly be expected to find money for shovels that would be used once a decade, if that, and so by nine o'clock the inmates from the prison had been dragooned – much to their delight – into shovelling, while the *spazzini* went back to their rightful job of collecting rubbish, today from atop the snow.

Because there was no plan for how to deal with snow, it took some time before footpaths had been created in the middle of the major arteries, even longer before footpaths had been created in the smaller *calli*. The sirens for *acqua alta* had sounded a little after seven, adding to the general confusion by shrieking falsely that the tide was rising. By eight-thirty, as people left for work, the schools and public offices had been ordered closed for the day, and thus a general mood of shared foolishness was let loose in the city, leading men in suits to get caught up in snowball fights and the Vigili Urbani to play tunes such as *'Bella Ciao'* on their whistles, while the liberated kids, most of whom had never seen it, rolled in the snow like puppies.

The owners of bars carried coffees out to the prisoners, and then, a little after eleven, they started taking them *tramezzini*, *cichetti*, and more than a few glasses of wine. At noon, the prisoners decided it was time to go back for lunch, so they lined their shovels in neat rows in whatever *campo* they had been taken to and walked, chatting with the ease of free men, along the *calli* they had cleared, back to prison, where they had all returned by the time lunch was served.

At two o'clock, the sun emerged from half-hearted clouds and battered the city with light. Guido Brunetti, Commissario di Polizia, had already decided that he was not going to return to work that afternoon but was, instead, going to begin his reading of Artemidorus' *On the Interpretation of Dreams*. To do so, he had invaded the study of his wife, Paola Falier, professor of English literature at the University of Ca' Foscari, and had laid claim to her sofa by arranging the pillows so that the sunlight fell on the pages of his new book. That done, he stretched himself full length, took his reading glasses from their case, and opened it.

Telling himself that it was a dream not to return to the Questura that afternoon, he consulted the writer for his interpretation of dreams featuring snow. He had just begun to read the passage when the rightful owner of the room entered and, seeing him there, went boldly to the end of the sofa, lifted his crossed feet, slipped under them, and opened the book she was carrying.

'Are you interested in what Artemidorus has to say about snow?'

Sighing, she set her own book face down on her husband's legs, and said, 'Tell me.'

'"It foretells that the dreamer's current plans and business will not progress,"' Brunetti said and set his own book down on his chest.

'It sounds like something that applies to your friend Elisabetta,' Paola said.

'She's not my friend,' said Brunetti. Then, speaking with a vehemence that surprised them both, he added, 'She never was.'

'Your former friend Elisabetta,' Paola amended.

Brunetti picked up the book and reread the sentence to himself, then set the book down again. 'It sounds like it might apply to all of them, poor devils.'

'"Poor devils"?' Paola asked.

'Most of them,' he said, 'except for the perfidious Signora Bagnoli.' After a moment's reflection, he added, 'Even Signorina Elettra can find no trace of her.' In answer to her raised eyebrows, he said, 'The Guardia di Finanza would like to speak to her.'

'Something you never managed to do,' Paola observed.

'No, I didn't. Like many villains, she's managed to disappear completely.'

'Invisible, untouchable, gone,' Paola said.

'But she left behind evidence of what she is.'

'Which is?'

'Willing to do anything and use anyone to get what she wants.'

'And that is?' Paola asked.

'Money and pleasure.'

'Usually it's money and power.'

'In her case, it's pleasure – expensive pleasure.'

'Will anything happen to her?'

Brunetti dropped his book on the floor and folded his hands on his chest. 'God knows.'

'Was she behind the scam?'

'That's open to question.'

'What?'

'That it was a scam.'

'What do you mean, "open to question"?'

'The Guardia di Finanza has blocked her bank account and the account of Belize nel Cuore, but has yet to find evidence of a crime.'

'Even though hundreds of thousands of euros were sent to Belize?'

Brunetti squirmed around on the sofa a bit, sinking lower on the pillows until his neck felt comfortable. 'For all of which the hospital has submitted very convincing receipts that provide evidence of how the money was spent. There are receipts from builders and dealers in medical equipment, as well as for the salaries of four staff members. For every euro spent.'

'And her vacations with Signor del Balzo?'

'No one gets sent to prison for taking an expensive vacation, my dear.' Then, before Paola could ask, he added, 'Even if the vacation is paid for by the hospital.'

'So nothing's going to happen to her?' Paola asked flatly.

'It's very unlikely that anything will, at least not legally. All of the documents, letters and emails that were sent to the many donors bear the signature of Signor del Balzo or, in some cases, of Vice-Admiral Fullin.' He looked beyond his feet to see Paola's face and added, 'There is no evidence that she signed anything. Besides, she was only an employee and had no executive powers.' Before Paola could speak, Brunetti said, sounding strangely agitated, 'And I mean *anything.*' Then, voice calm again, he added, 'Fenzo was right to be suspicious of her.'

'And the others?'

'You really want to know?'

'If you'll start with your fr— former friend Elisabetta.'

'She's done nothing criminal, Paola. She asked me to help her understand if her son-in-law had reason to be afraid of something.'

'What about breaking into her daughter's clinic and hurting her dog? Isn't that criminal, for heaven's sake?'

'Unfortunately, the only witness is almost eighty and was not wearing her glasses when she saw someone she thinks was a woman outside the clinic on the night of the break-in.'

Paola closed her eyes and shook her head. 'Didn't Elisabetta tell you she'd done it?'

'She didn't tell me in an interview recorded at the Questura, and she never signed anything.' As Brunetti continued to answer Paola's question, his tone moved farther and farther from the self-protective irony he had begun with.

'But she did those things,' Paola insisted.

It is difficult to shrug in a supine position, but Brunetti managed it. 'Paola, one of the first things we were taught as policemen – and I suppose your professors taught you the same – is that witnesses are unreliable, people repeat distorted versions of what they've seen or heard, and evidence is always open to question.'

Paola's response was to grasp his left ankle strongly with both hands and hold on to it for enough time to absorb what he'd said. As her hands relaxed, she said, in a softer voice, 'And the money del Balzo sent out of the country so that the supposed donors wouldn't have to pay tax on it?'

'Do you think that, in the presence of receipts showing where and how their money was spent, they'll say their real reason was to avoid paying tax?' He paused a moment and then added, in a reproving voice, 'Come now, Paola.'

'And del Balzo? He set the whole thing up.'

'He didn't set up what you call the scam, even if he did set up the charity. He was captured by the ample charms of Signora Bagnoli. Remember that the big donations from the people in Brescia didn't start coming until she started consulting for the ONLUS. Until then, it was simply a trickle of money to a small hospital in Belize: simple people trying to do some good in the world.'

'You believe that?'

'Yes. Besides, he's never going to be held responsible for anything that was done. He's going to lie in his bed in the clinic, probably for the rest of his life, and please may it be brief.' Brunetti's voice suddenly took on the hoarse tone that affected him when he struggled against his emotions. 'And Elisabetta will spend her time visiting him every day, making sure the nurses keep him clean, speaking to him in the hope that some day he'll look at her or speak a single word.' He stopped there and let silence spread away from him, then added, filled with a sense of disgust at this destructive woman, this stupid, destructive woman, 'And it's a life sentence. So, yes, "poor devil".'

Paola, knowing him, let the right amount of time pass in silence before asking softly, 'And the Vice-Admiral?'

'I spoke to his grandson a week ago. He's much the same as he was: he comes and goes.'

'Ah.'

He raised a hand to gain her attention and said, 'He's more than eighty, so he can't be sent to prison, even if he had meant to hurt del Balzo. Besides, his disease is a form of house arrest.' After a moment's reflection, he added, 'His grandson saw it happen. There was no intent to do del Balzo any harm.'

'The daughter?' Paola asked.

'Ah,' Brunetti sighed. 'At least she managed to escape. She and her husband have moved to Trento, where she's working with a friend from university.' He looked across at Paola and wiggled his toes. 'And she's taken her earless dog with her, I'm told.'

Paola smiled and said, 'Happy ending?'

'Well, for one of them at least,' Brunetti said and closed his eyes.

Paola tossed her book onto the floor beside his, lifted his legs, and stood.

'Would you like something to drink, Guido?'

He turned his head and looked outside at the snow covering the roofs, silencing the worried voices of the people in the city.

'Yes, please.'

'What would you like?'

He waved towards the window and, beyond it, the snow. 'I think hot chocolate seems in order. We could drink it on the terrace and be in the snow.'

'How clever you are, Guido,' she said and turned towards the kitchen.

To her retreating back, Brunetti said, 'I'm not sure I'm clever, my dear, but I am always faithful to the side I fight for.'

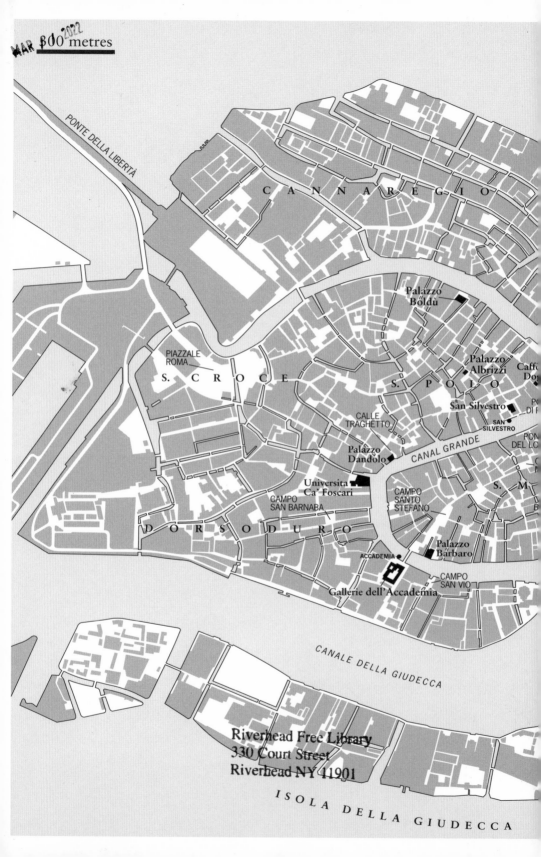